Just
Another
Hero

ALSO BY SHARON M. DRAPER

Copper Sun
Double Dutch
Out of My Mind
Panic
Romiette & Julio
Stella by Starlight

The Jericho Trilogy:
The Battle of Jericho
November Blues
Just Another Hero

The Hazelwood High Trilogy:
Tears of a Tiger
Forged by Fire
Darkness Before Dawn

Clubhouse Mysteries
The Buried Bones Mystery
Lost in the Tunnel of Time
Shadows of Caesar's Creek
The Space Mission Adventure
The Backyard Animal Show
Stars and Sparks on Stage

THE JERICHO TRILOGY #3

Just Another Hero

SHARON M. DRAPER

A Caitlyn Dlouhy Book

NEW YORK LONDON TORONTO SYDNEY NEW DELHI

atheneum

An imprint of Simon & Schuster Children's Publishing Division | 1230 Avenue of the Americas, New York, New York 10020 | This book is a work of fiction. Any references to historical events, real people, or real places are used fictitiously. Other names, characters, places, and events are products of the author's imagination, and any resemblance to actual events or places or persons, living or dead, is entirely coincidental. | Text copyright © 2009 by Sharon M. Draper | Cover illustration copyright © 2017 by Edel Rodriguez | Passages on pages 50, 99, 100, 101 are taken from *Beowulf*, translated by Burton Raffel, copyright © 1963 renewed © 1991 by Burton Raffel. Used by permission of Dutton Signet, a division of Penguin Group (USA) Inc. | All rights reserved, including the right of reproduction in whole or in part in any form. | Atheneum logo is a trademark of Simon & Schuster, Inc. | For information about special discounts for bulk purchases, please contact Simon & Schuster Special Sales at 1-866-506-1949 or business@simonandschuster.com. | The Simon & Schuster Speakers Bureau can bring authors to your live event. For more information or to book an event, contact the Simon & Schuster Speakers Bureau at 1-866-248-3049 or visit our website at www.simonspeakers.com. | Also available in an Atheneum hardcover edition | Book design by Debra Sfetsios-Conover | The text for this book was set in Trade Gothic. | Manufactured in the United States of America | First Atheneum paperback edition July 2017 | 10 9 8 7 6 5 4 3 2 1 | The Library of Congress has cataloged the hardcover edition as follows: | Draper, Sharon M. (Sharon Mills) | Just another hero / Sharon M. Draper. | p. cm. | Sequel to: November Blues. | Summary: As Kofi, Arielle, Dana, November, and Jericho face personal challenges during their last year of high school, a misunderstood student brings a gun to class and demands to be taken seriously. | ISBN 978-1-4169-0700-8 (hc) | ISBN 978-1-4814-9030-6 (pbk) | ISBN 978-1-4169-9521-0 (eBook) | [1. High schools—Fiction. 2. Schools—Fiction. 3. African Americans—Fiction.] I. Title. | PZ7.D78325Ju 2009 | [Fic]—dc22 | 2008030961

This book is dedicated to *my* hero,
Larry Draper

"GRAB HIS ARMS!"

"Now pick up his legs!"

"Hey, quit! Stop! Leave me alone!"

"This is gonna be *too* funny!"

"Hurry up, before a teacher shows up."

"He's slippery like a little worm, man."

"Quit wigglin', little punk! You gonna make me throw *you* in the pool!"

"Let me GO!"

Arielle Gresham, who had come to school early to get some homework done, was sitting alone in a side hall near the boys' gym, lost in her own thoughts. Startled by the noise, she turned her head to see two big guys carrying a kicking, flailing smaller boy into the hall that led to the swimming pool.

"Put me down!"

"Make me!"

"PLEASE just leave me alone!"

"This is gonna be the best YouTube video ever!"

"Make sure you film just him and not our faces, dude."

"I'm not *stupid*!"

Arielle heard screeches of complaint, more laughter, then silence. By this time she was already on her feet and marching toward the locker room that led to the boys' entrance to the pool. She'd never actually *been* in a boys' locker room before, or any male bathroom for that matter, but she figured she could handle it.

The smell hit her first. *How could a room that had to have been cleaned last night still reek so bad?* The room was brightly lit with fluorescent bulbs that illuminated everything with a purplish glare. The row of urinals lined up against one pee-spattered wall helped explain the smell. Battered green lockers and benches lined the far wall.

She hurried out of there and down the hall to the pool. The voices, louder and clearer, made her break into a run.

"Throw his jeans into the pool!" A soft splash.

"He's wearin' tightie-whities, man!" Lots of deep laughter echoed.

"Throw those in too."

Arielle opened the door to the pool area. Damp, moist air, sharpened by the pungent tang of chlorine, hit her face.

The scene in front of her made her gasp. Two guys, students she'd seen around but did not know, were holding a squirming, crying student facedown on the tiled floor. He wore only a navy blue hoodie and his socks. His shoes lay a few feet away, but his jeans and underpants floated nearby in seven feet of water. A third boy was holding a cell phone, obviously filming the scene.

"What is *wrong* with you?" she screamed. Her voice echoed against the damp walls. "Let him go!"

"Busted!" the largest of the three said. "By a girl! Too cool!"

"No sweat. We got enough to post," the filmer crowed gleefully, flipping his cell phone shut. "Hey, Wardley! Your butt's gonna be famous!"

And with that, all three bigger guys hooted with laughter and ran out of the pool area.

The kid who'd been released lay there, his hands clasped over his head, trembling.

Arielle, unsure of what to do, knew he had to be mortified.

"Get out," the boy mumbled.

"Do you want me to try and fish your clothes out of the pool?" she offered.

"I said get out!" the boy said louder.

She was pretty sure she recognized that voice. "Osrick?" she asked.

Osrick Wardley was in her chemistry and English classes, but Arielle barely knew him. He was seventeen—a senior like the rest of them—but he was only about five feet tall and couldn't have weighed more than a hundred pounds. With dirty blond hair, a mouth full of braces, and a narrow, sunken chest, the kid was a magnet for guys who liked to act tough. Members of the football team sucker punched him and tossed him into wastebaskets with regularity. And now, it seemed, the swimmers were taking their turn.

Of course, everybody called him Weird Osrick. *Who would name a kid Osrick?* Arielle thought. His parents might as well have pinned a sign on him that said, PLEASE MAKE FUN OF ME!

Osrick had never scored anything lower than an A in any class Arielle had shared with him. Except for gym, which had to be rough for a guy who could be knocked over by a wildly tossed basketball.

"Osrick, are you okay?" Arielle asked. She touched her carefully curled hair, which was beginning to droop in the humid air.

"Please, promise you won't tell *anybody*!" Osrick pleaded. "Please!"

"Okay, okay! I promise." Arielle frowned, pondering whether that was the right thing to say. Surely she should tell a teacher?

"Now please just leave," Osrick begged.

"Suit yourself," Arielle said with a shrug. "I was just trying to help." She picked up a towel, tossed it toward him, then hurried out of the pool area, leaving Osrick to the privacy of his humiliation.

AN HOUR LATER ARIELLE WONDERED IF she'd handled the situation correctly. *Maybe I should have reported it to the principal,* she thought. *But that would have embarrassed the kid even more. And who am I to narc on somebody?*

But she knew she wasn't any better than the haters who'd picked on Osrick. It was why she was sitting alone right now. She thought back to the beginning of the school year, when she'd had a boyfriend to show off and girlfriends to hang out with. But she'd treated them all like dirt. In just a few months, she'd managed to alienate them all. *How could this have happened so quickly?* Arielle mused.

She thought about her friend November, who'd gotten pregnant last year. *I laughed at her fat gut and her swollen feet. I called her stupid for being dumb enough to get caught in the baby trap. I never even told her how sorry I was about Josh's death.*

Then Arielle's thoughts turned to Olivia Thigpen—a girl with legs like tree trunks and a body to match. Arielle had treated her like a meaningless toy to laugh at and humiliate. *I can't believe I threw food on her and made jokes about her size! How could I have been so cold?* Arielle shook her head. *And who woulda thought she'd end up with my dude? She slid the rollers right up under me! And I never even saw it coming.*

Arielle had always assumed the world revolved around her size-two waistline. But by the time she figured out that the universe didn't even know her name, she'd lost just about everyone who'd once mattered to her.

She finished her chemistry homework and closed her laptop. She unplugged her earphones, put her brand-new iPhone carefully back into its case, and tucked both items into her backpack. Then she headed toward her second-bell class—chemistry, room 317, smoothing on a touch of MAC lip gloss as she hurried down the hall.

"Lookin' good, sista-girl," a boy named Ram yelled from across the hall. "I'd like to taste a little of that sugar you got in your coffee!" He then whispered something to his friends, who burst out in loud, rowdy laughter.

Arielle ignored them and dashed up the steps to the third floor. She hated that her cheeks burned red so easily.

With a few minutes to spare, she eased into her seat, pretending she didn't care that although lots of kids sat together in small groups and talked quietly, not a one spoke to her. Osrick, she noticed with surprise, was already in his usual place in the back of the room. Wearing a pair of worn sweatpants instead of jeans, he sat quietly with his head down and his hoodie covering his face. He looked just as alone as she felt.

She glanced away, not wanting to embarrass him, and saw Jericho Prescott, sitting two rows away from her. He was laughing and chattering with Olivia, who was *not* a size two. Olivia played the tuba, of all things, and Jericho looked at her like she was a whole cheese pizza. Actually, she looked like she'd eaten her share of pizzas and burgers and fries as well—nothing about her was petite. She had a round face and an even rounder middle, and Jericho seemed to love every inch of her. Arielle didn't get it. How could someone like that take someone as cool and popular as Jericho away from her? It was *so* not fair.

She ran her fingers through her hair almost unconsciously.

"Your hair looks perfect," Kofi Freeman said quietly, leaning forward in his seat behind her. "It always does."

"You better not let Dana hear you say that," Arielle replied, turning halfway around. "I got enough trouble without the claws of Dana the Wolfe in my back." But she smiled at the compliment anyway.

"Aw, Dana's my girl—everybody knows that. But I ain't blind!" Kofi chuckled and got out his book. "Besides, she's absent today—she went on another college visit."

Arielle sighed. She envied what Dana and Kofi had going on. They reminded her of silk and satin—flowing smoothly and softly. They'd been together for a couple of years—a lifetime in the world of "let's hook up for a night" relationships that most kids seemed to find.

Miss Pringle, the new science teacher, a slender woman

with short, spiked hair, sat at her desk, sipping her coffee and grading papers.

Arielle wasn't sure whether it was for negligence or carelessness, but cool Mr. Culligan, their former science instructor, had been fired last year after the investigation into the death of a student. Somebody had to be blamed, and Culligan got it all.

Josh Prescott—good-looking, fun loving, and lighthearted—had died when a group of boys decided to jump from a second-story window as part of pledging a club called the Warriors of Distinction. Josh had left behind dozens of grieving friends, including his girlfriend, November Nelson, and his cousin Jericho. Arielle winced just thinking about it.

Arielle looked up with a start and almost did a double take. November Nelson breezed into the classroom at just that moment. November was back to thin already! She'd lost all that baby weight! Arielle nodded in approval at the orange print tank top and short denim skirt November was wearing, which hugged her curves in all the right ways. *I would have bought that outfit.*

November tossed an enrollment form onto the teacher's desk. "Hi! I'm back!" she said cheerfully, as if she had gone out for pizza.

"And you are . . . ?" said Miss Pringle, looking over thin-rimmed, red-trimmed glasses.

"November Nelson. I was out for a few months, and this is my first day back." She grinned at the class and waved at Jericho and Olivia, at Kofi, and at Eric Bell, who sat in a wheelchair at the front table. Everybody seemed glad to see her.

"Back from what? Vacation in Europe?" Miss Pringle asked. Her voice sounded like bullets when she talked—fast and sharp. Nobody ever laughed at her lame jokes.

"Not exactly," November replied. "I had a baby—but I tried to keep up with all my classes through the home-school instructor. She said she'd turn in my grades to all my teachers."

"I see." Miss Pringle gave November a chemistry book and a pair of lab goggles. "Take a lab sheet and find a seat. I'll have to check later to see if your makeup work is sufficient," she said curtly.

"Okay," November told her pleasantly. She found an empty seat near Jericho and Olivia and flopped down. "Wow! Feels great to be back in chemistry! Did I just say that?" she said, a little louder than necessary, Arielle thought.

Arielle and November had been close friends up until their junior year. But she hadn't seen November since she'd had the baby, and she wondered if November would even give her the time of day now. She watched November slip right back in with their old crowd.

"Welcome back, little mama," Olivia said.

"What's up with the new chem teacher?" November asked in a low voice, tilting her head toward the teacher.

"Oh, she's just one of several we've had since Culligan got canned," Jericho told her.

"What happened to the last one?" November asked.

"Somebody set her wig on fire!" Olivia stifled a giggle.

"Shut up! Who did it?"

Olivia shrugged.

"Nobody ever told," said Kofi, who had walked over to join the conversation. "Hey, kid."

"Hey, Kofi," November said, smacking palms with him. "Where's Dana?"

"At Ohio State checking out scholarships and stuff. She'll be back by lunch."

"You still pullin' down the straight As?"

"Every day," he told her with a bit of pride.

Arielle knew lots of kids thought getting good grades was stupid, and they even made fun of those who put in the effort to hang with the best. But Kofi quietly took lots of AP classes, racked up a high GPA, and sailed though the SATs.

"So is Pringle okay?" November asked.

"She's got issues," said Olivia. "But they all do, I guess."

"She seems to be surgically attached to that coffee mug," Kofi observed.

"And those keys around her neck," Olivia added. "Twenty-four/seven."

"Don't forget the hokey-pokey dance she taught us to memorize the periodic table of elements!" Jericho said with a laugh. He stood up and did a bit of the dance.

"Funny thing is—it worked!" said Olivia.

"What is the woman *wearing*?" November whispered. "She looks like she's ready to clean out her garage, not teach a class!"

Arielle had wondered the same thing. Miss Pringle wore an oversize sweatshirt with pockets, baggy slacks, and a hideous pair of earth shoes.

Arielle quickly sketched a pencil drawing of her on a blank notebook page, with arms like those bendy straws that little kids use and stick-straight hair. The woman's body was lean and taut—no flab anywhere. Everyone knew she worked out all the time. Before school every morning, and in the afternoon after most folks had gone home, her raggedy green Volkswagen could be seen parked outside the gym and her skinny legs pumping around the track— even in snow. *Get a life!* Arielle thought. She drew the woman with sticks for legs, bent and ready to run.

"How's the baby?" Olivia asked November just as the bell finally rang for class. "I haven't seen her in a couple of weeks."

"Miss Sunshine?" November grinned and pulled a small photo album from her purse. She handed it to Jericho, who passed it to Olivia and Kofi. "She's getting stronger and better every day. The doctors are really pleased with her progress."

"I think Sunshine is startin' to look like Josh!" Jericho said as he peered at one of the photos.

November pulled the photo book back gently and touched the picture lovingly.

"I feel sorry for the kid, then," Kofi said with a laugh. He ambled back to his seat, smacking hands with Luis Morales, Roscoe Robinson, and Cleveland Wilson, all survivors of the Warriors of Distinction tragedy.

Arielle turned to a clean page of her notebook, sighed, and began to copy the homework assignment off the whiteboard at the front of the class. It seemed so long ago: Jericho—cool, laid-back, and completely hers; Josh—his

11

lighthearted cousin, always at his side; and the Warriors of Distinction—best club in the school, best parties on the weekend, and best chance to be somebody around here. But all that had vanished in an instant. Josh died. The Warriors disbanded. She'd lost Jericho for good. And everybody seemed to hate her now.

Miss Pringle cleared her throat. "Miss Nelson, do you think it would interrupt your social calendar if you let us have class today?" she asked. "Or should we just look at baby pictures?"

Arielle had to stifle a giggle. She was sure November wanted to reply with a smart remark, but it probably wouldn't be a good idea, considering it was her first day back. November wisely replied, "I'm sorry. Let's do some chemistry!"

Miss Pringle gave a faint smile. "Good choice."

While the teacher began the class in her rat-a-tat voice, Arielle glanced over to the windows, wishing she could open one to get the smell of chlorine out of her nose. One whole wall was filled with windows, which was why she liked this room better than those interior ones. But the windows, Arielle remembered, did not open at all. Sealed by paint or an ancient school board decision to prevent lawsuits in case some kid fell out—she wasn't sure which—none of the third-floor classrooms allowed for any fresh air to get in. Last spring, when the building's air-conditioning system broke down, it was brutal.

An odd, fading assortment of blinds and shades—some with holes from dry rot, some just torn and tired—covered most of the windows, keeping out the hot afternoon sun on summer days, but opened wide to celebrate the first snowfall of the winter.

"We will be using the computers today," Miss Pringle was saying, "for recording your lab reports."

Roscoe Robinson, a football player with a history of stunning touchdowns and a smart mouth, raised his hand. "You talkin' about those prehistoric green-screen antiques on the side table?"

The far wall of the classroom contained a long row of tables on which sat twelve ancient IBM computers. Arielle knew that the science teachers constantly begged for new equipment, but in the four years she'd been at the school, nothing had been upgraded.

"You know how hard it is for schools to come up with money for new technology, Roscoe," the teacher replied.

Roscoe cracked up. "If you tried to connect one of those computers to the Internet, it would explode!"

"We do the best we can," Miss Pringle said with a sigh. "Kofi, can you take a look at a couple of them after school this week? You're the computer genius around here."

"Yeah, sure, Miss P," replied Kofi.

Arielle noticed that neither Miss Pringle nor Kofi seemed to give a thought to Osrick, who could probably handle all that electronic tech repair stuff with ease and skill.

"Mrs. Witherspoon's got lots of electronics and computer toys in her room," Luis commented. "But all we got here is that beat-up TV on the wall."

"She won some kind of teacher award, and she used all the money for her classroom, I hear," Miss Pringle replied.

"If you won a prize like that, would you do that, or spend it on yourself?" Cleveland asked, leaning forward on his desk.

Miss Pringle responded by saying, "I'll get the lab equipment out now." She removed her keys from around her neck.

"Can I help?" Roscoe asked.

"You know my procedures, Roscoe. Are you just trying to get on my nerves?"

"Yep!"

"It's working," replied the teacher, but with a smile.

"Maybe we should use the stuff in the cabinet behind you," Roscoe suggested. "At least that would match the computers they stick us with!"

"I think that stuff came from the ancient history museum!" Jericho agreed. "Cavemen used it to measure mammoth stew!"

A cabinet made of wood and glass stood behind the teacher's desk. Many of the glass panes had been cracked or broken over the years, and the equipment hadn't been used in ages. Full of dust-covered, old-fashioned test tubes and beakers and dozens of pieces of ancient glass paraphernalia, the cupboard was truly a remnant of classrooms of long ago.

"No, we'll use the good stuff—at least the best we have. That's why I keep it locked up," the teacher explained as she began what had become a daily pattern of locking and unlocking that back door a dozen times in five minutes. Get out test tubes. Lock. Unlock. Bring out nitric acid. Lock. Unlock. Carry out five beakers. Lock. Unlock. All the while yap, yap, yapping about measurement and chemicals and formulas. It was hard to keep up with her as she walked and talked at the same time.

As Arielle watched the teacher yo-yo back and forth, she again noticed Osrick sitting by the storeroom. Arielle tried to make eye contact with him, but he had a habit of pulling his hood over his head so his face could not be seen.

As she turned back around she saw Jack Krasinski on the other side of the room and instantly grinned. Kids called him Crazy Jack, and he loved it, even encouraged it. Tall and skinny and generally liked by everybody, Jack always wore bright, showy colors—like green neon shirts and red plaid pants.

When Osrick dressed in wacky clothes, students laughed and made fun of him, but if Jack decided to wear pajamas to school, Arielle noticed, everybody thought it was really cool. She wondered why Jack could get away with it, but Osrick couldn't.

Jack played in the school band—cymbals and drums, instruments that made maximum noise. The louder the better. Jack had once told her the racket made the voices in his head get quiet. She had no idea what he'd been talking about.

As Miss Pringle was bringing out the last of the test tubes, Jack raised his hand.

"Miss P, I forgot to take my meds this morning. Can I go do that and pee? I'll be right back!"

"Jack, you know you're supposed to take care of those things before class," she said, but she grudgingly handed him the hall pass. Lots of kids took meds at school for one condition or another, but everything had to be distributed by the school nurse. Anyone caught medicating themselves could get suspended from school.

Jack, his long legs protruding from the purple gym shorts he'd worn that day even though the temperature was in the thirties, jumped up and left the room.

Miss Pringle continued with the lesson, trying to explain the chemical equations necessary to work the lab problems. She really wasn't a bad teacher, Arielle thought—just a little strange. She shifted in her seat and tried to get comfortable. It would be a long fifty minutes.

Just as Miss Pringle was telling them how to measure the liquids in the test tubes, the fire alarm rang out shrilly. *Clang-clong! Clang-clong! Clang-clong!*

"Grab your personal effects, students, and line up quickly!" Miss Pringle ordered. She looked really annoyed with the interruption.

"Should we take our books or leave them to burn up in the fire?" asked Roscoe.

"Leave your books and papers; you know this is just a drill, Mr. Robinson," Miss Pringle replied as she gathered up her materials. "Now, no more talking. Let's go, class. Down the steps and out the side door. You know the procedures."

Students started pulling on coats, grabbing purses, and heading to the door. The alarm kept ringing, piercing the air.

As Arielle reached for her purse, she heard November tell Jericho, "Good chance to check with the babysitter.

This is the first time I've left the baby all day, and I'm a little worried."

"Aw, man, it's freezin' out there!" Cleveland complained. "Who'd be dumb enough to plan a fire drill in February?" Six feet tall and weighing well over two hundred fifty pounds, the linebacker was unlikely to freeze, Arielle thought, but he was known to complain good-naturedly over just about everything.

"I got *my* coat," Luis said as he zipped his down jacket over his slim frame. "A man's gotta be prepared!" Luis, who ran track, had been offered both academic and athletic scholarships to several schools. His entire family always showed up for his meets. Arielle wondered wistfully what that must be like. Her family sure wasn't like that.

"So you gonna let your main squeeze freeze?" Rosa asked Luis, her voice sounding pitiful. "I left my coat in my locker." She rubbed the arm of his jacket.

"Girl, it's a good thing you look so good!" Luis said with a laugh. "Here, my sweet señorita Gonzales, take the coat—my gloves, too. I'll let you warm me up—later."

Rosa took the coat, and they hurried out the door with the others.

Osrick darted out ahead of most of the students. He was no fool. Fire drills were a great chance for teachers to be looking elsewhere while a kid like Osrick got punched or kicked down the stairs. Jack got back from the bathroom just in time to leave again.

Clang-clong! Clang-clong! Clang-clong! Clang-clong!

"Why do they have to make that alarm so loud and so ugly?" Roscoe asked.

"To make sure people in gym and music and choir classes all can hear it," Miss Pringle told him.

"People in *China* can hear that thing!" Jericho said, shaking his head, tugging Olivia by the hand out the door.

Arielle was one of the last ones to leave the room. It was just another false alarm, so what was the hurry?

When nearly everyone had moved into the hallway, Kofi tapped the teacher on the shoulder. He was at least six inches taller than she was. She turned, jerking away from his touch. "What is your problem, Mr. Freeman?" she asked, annoyance in her voice. "They time us on how quickly we clear the building, you know."

"You forgot Eric, Miss Pringle," Kofi reminded her.

The teacher gasped. "Oh my Lord! How could I?" She rushed back into the room, where Eric Bell, sitting quietly, his hands on the controls of his electric wheelchair, sat waiting. He looked embarrassed.

"Fire drill procedure 101," Eric said with a sad smile. "Elevators are shut down. Crippled kid has to be carried."

"I was informed of the procedures," Miss Pringle tried to explain, "but I'd never really thought about exactly how we'd accomplish it. Aren't there supposed to be two male teachers assigned to do this?" She looked around helplessly.

Who's she waiting for—Superman to come flying around the corner? Arielle thought.

"I guess they forgot. I hate this, you know," Eric said through clenched teeth.

Kofi ran out into the hall and returned with Jericho and Cleveland, both football players. "We got this, Miss P."

"You can leave me up here, you know. No one will ever find out. Like you said, it's just a drill," Eric said.

"Oh, no, I couldn't do that!" replied Miss Pringle. "I'd lose my job. The law says everybody must leave. Plus, I'd never forgive myself if it were a real fire and you got hurt. On top of that, you're the only kid in my class who hasn't yet mastered the periodic chart dance, so we've got work to do!"

"I got an A on the chart test, you know," Eric replied, laughing.

"Without my dance? Unheard of!"

Looking at Eric grinning at the teacher, it dawned on Arielle that he probably preferred being teased like a real person rather than treated like a special case. She'd never thought about that before.

Jericho and Cleveland made a chair of their arms while Kofi pivoted Eric up from his wheelchair, his legs swinging limply.

"Okay, let's get this dude to a dance hall! Honeys are waiting below!" Jericho shouted, trying to lighten the mood. Together he and Cleveland carried Eric out the door and down the steps. Arielle walked behind them, while Miss Pringle locked the classroom door.

WHEN THEY REACHED THE GROUND FLOOR, Kofi darted into a classroom and grabbed a straight-back chair. Once outside, the three of them gently set Eric onto the chair and stood close to him so he wouldn't tilt and fall. Eric had broken his back the summer before seventh grade playing Daredevil by jumping from a tree to a swimming pool. He'd missed the pool and landed on concrete. Kofi winced just thinking about it.

"Thanks, dudes," said Eric. "And props on the chair, Kofi. This is a whole lot better than coolin' my butt in the snow."

"Like Weird Osrick over there?" Kofi asked. "The kid is sitting in a snowbank!"

"Did somebody toss him over there?" Cleveland asked, frowning.

"No, I think he did it on purpose to beat them to it!"

"Definitely weird," said Cleveland, turning back to Eric.

"You know, if we had tried to move your electric car, we'd still be up there!"

"Yeah, that thing weighs, like, a million pounds," Jericho added. "What do they do in your other classes when Crazy Jack pulls the alarm?"

"You think it was Jack?"

"Well, he did have to go to the bathroom just as the alarm went off."

"He got *shorts* on, man," Cleveland said. "Even Jack ain't that crazy."

Jack, his legs bright red in the cold air, was doing a series of jumping jacks to keep himself warm. A few other kids had joined him, laughing as they jumped on the snowy sidewalk. Kofi noticed Susan Richards, the girl who had won a free ride to Juilliard for dance, quietly doing stretches instead of leaps.

"We ought to change your name to Jumping Jack!" a senior named Rudy called out breathlessly.

Eric shivered in the cold morning air. "Well, most of my classes are on the first floor, so getting me out of the building is not usually a problem. I just roll out down the ramp. It's just math and chemistry that are upstairs."

"Man, it is cold!" Cleveland moaned, shifting his weight from one foot to the other. "A fire drill in February is just plain stupid!"

Other kids from the chemistry class huddled close to them, shielding Eric and using one another for warmth. Jericho had his arm around Olivia. November was on her cell phone, as were many other kids.

"For a school that doesn't allow cell phones, this place

looks like a TV ad for a cell phone company!" said Kofi.

He was standing close enough to November to overhear her side of the phone call.

"So she's asleep? . . . How much formula did she take? . . . She likes that yellow blanket, you know. Just put it close to her. . . . Rub her tummy if she gets fussy. . . . And don't forget the music. She loves classical! . . . I'll see you at three. Thanks, Laura."

She clicked her phone closed, and her shoulders slumped.

"It's hard being a mom, right?" Kofi asked her gently.

"Yeah. I never thought how hard it would be to leave her."

"Who watches the baby?" asked Rosa.

"A woman who lives two blocks away has a home day care. She's like a mama-grandmama rolled into one. A cute little old lady. She's really sweet with the kids and experienced—but most important, I can afford her! I filled out some paperwork and got some help from the state, but I gotta find a job when school gets out," November explained.

"And all I got to worry about is what color to do my nails this week!" Rosa said. "Better you than me!"

Kofi told November, "You know, it is what it is until you make it better."

"That's deep. Where'd you get that? I'm gonna put it on my wall at home."

"Kofi's Book of Quotations. Chapter Three: Deep Thoughts."

"You're silly," November replied.

Olivia joined them then, clapping her hands together to keep them warm. "What's up, little mama?" she asked. "How's my favorite baby girl doing at the babysitter?"

"I just talked to Laura, who said Sunshine is eating and burping and not crying for me! Ungrateful kid. The least she could do is scream and holler and miss her mother," November joked.

"I'm sure she misses you, November. You've been there for her twenty-four/seven ever since she was born. It's gotta be hard for both of you."

November sighed. "Yeah, it is. I know by the sound of her breathing what she needs or wants. Every cry she has is different—every noise she makes I understand. I can't wait to get home this afternoon."

Olivia touched November's shoulder. "She'll give you the biggest smile when she sees you!"

November grinned. "She might punch me in the nose instead!"

"Or poop all over you," added Kofi. "Kids do that sometimes, you know." Both girls laughed.

Olivia paused for a moment, her brown eyes growing serious. "So, what's the latest from her doctors?"

November shivered, perhaps from the cold and perhaps from the thoughts of her daughter, born three months early, whose future might include some disabilities. Kofi wasn't in on all that girl stuff, but he knew from Dana that the baby might have mental or physical developmental delays.

"She's five months old now, and well, I guess she's still behind on those baby charts they use to measure growth, but she's catching up slowly. It's like that old story of the tortoise and the hare. She's my little turtle—slow and steady. She may not be the first kid to the finish line, but she'll get there."

"Doesn't the tortoise win the race in that tale?" Olivia asked, scratching her head.

November brightened. "You know, you're right!"

Cleveland yelled loudly then, "Hey! Somebody! Anybody! I'm freezin' my buns off here! Somebody let us back in the building!"

Other kids started to grumble then as well. "Do you see any fire?"

"Or fire engines?"

"Anybody smell smoke?"

"It's another false alarm."

"Maybe they're keepin' us outside to punish us for pullin' the fire alarm."

"Did somebody have a test this period and just wanted to get out of it?"

"Who knows?"

"Where's Jack?"

"Didn't he go to the bathroom?"

"Jack only pulls the alarm when he has a test, man. Jack's wack, but he's got rules!"

"Oughta be a rule that no fire drills can be called when it's cold like this! I'm gonna sue if I die of pneumonia!" Cleveland complained.

The all-clear bell finally sounded, and everyone hurried back into the warmth of the building. Jericho and Cleveland once again chair-lifted Eric with their arms and deposited him safely back into his own wheelchair upstairs.

"I can't believe I'm glad to be back in this thing," Eric remarked. "It's like my second skin."

But before Miss Pringle could get the class back in order, the imposing, powerful image of Mrs. Sherman, the principal, also new this year, appeared on the TV screen in the corner of the room. Each classroom had a closed-circuit television available so that morning announcements, special presentations, and video events could be seen by everyone.

A thick woman with arms and legs that looked like clay, Mrs. Sherman boomed, "Good morning, students of Douglass High School. Thank you for your orderly evacuation of the building, and we apologize if any of you were chilled by the inclement weather."

"You think it's a law or something that principals have to use big fat words like that?" Jericho whispered to Cleveland.

"Too much alphabet soup!" Cleveland agreed.

Kofi wiggled his toes to get them warm again as Mrs. Sherman continued.

"The fire alarm was not triggered by anyone in the administration or the fire department. Nor have we been able to locate any smoke or fire. The alarm this morning was set off by a student—one of you." She paused for effect.

"Like we didn't already know that!" Luis said with a smirk.

The principal droned on. "One of your peers deliberately

chose to interrupt your studies and endanger your health by forcing you to stand in the cold while we evaluated the situation. This is the fourth such false alarm this semester. We want them to stop. Setting off a fire alarm when there isn't a fire is illegal, dangerous, and punishable by suspension."

Kofi hadn't actually seen Crazy Jack pull the alarm, but he was pretty sure he was the one who had done it. Jack was just plain wack. He kept his band cymbals with him all day long and would crash them for no reason at all—in the halls, at lunch—wherever he felt like it. Teachers would frown and write him disciplinary reprimands, but the next week he'd be at it again.

If anybody had the nerve to pull the alarm to get out of class, it would be Jack. He made no secret of how much he hated chemistry and history. So far they'd had three tests in Jack's history class, and there had been a fire drill during every single one. Nobody in the administration had made the connection yet, but principals, Kofi had noticed, were sometimes slow to catch the obvious.

Mrs. Sherman continued, "You know the identity of this person. He or she is endangering us all. You may send an anonymous e-mail or text message to my office with the name of the perpetrator. Or you may just write the name on a piece of paper and place it in my mailbox. I appreciate, and expect, your cooperation. Let us continue the school day with no further interruptions." The television screen went blank.

"Yeah, right," Kofi whispered to Arielle in front of him. "Like who's gonna tell?" She just shrugged and bent over her work. There were only about ten minutes left before the next bell.

Kofi felt restless and had no desire to finish the chemistry lab. The left side of his forehead was throbbing. It had been almost a year since he had broken his arm in the same pledge stunt that had gotten Josh killed, and although his arm no longer ached like it used to, he found his headaches had increased. He also found that his doctor seemed to have no problem refilling his pain-med script for him.

Kofi reached down into his book bag with both hands, felt around until he found the small plastic medicine bottle, uncapped it, and removed one small round pill from it. On the street his meds were called Killers or Kickers or the Ox. *But this is a legal prescription for OxyContin,* he thought. *I'm not like those kids who are using.* He glanced around to make sure no one was looking, then popped it into his mouth and swallowed it dry. He then took a deep breath. By the time the bell rang, he was feeling much better.

IT WAS A DREARY FRIDAY AFTERNOON.
Arielle picked at the polish of one of her
fingernails nervously as she sat on a stool
in the elaborate, custom-designed kitchen
of her stepfather's house and waited, shivering. Chadwick Kensington O'Neil kept the
thermostat at fifty-five degrees in the winter,
eighty-five in the summer. He seldom ran the
heat or the air-conditioning.

She gazed at the gleaming stainless-steel
refrigerator and stove, the sleek, built-in dish-
washer, the marble counters, and the shiny copper
pots and pans hanging from hooks in the ceiling,
but she felt no pride. Her stepfather made it clear
that all of that, as well as the lush white carpets and
the original oil paintings on the wall, and she and her
mom—belonged to him.

The lush white carpet was what had her worried at
the moment. She'd spilled cola on it last night, and she'd

spent more than an hour on her hands and knees, scrubbing and scrubbing, trying to erase the brown circle. Chad had not said anything—yet.

She knew she shouldn't have taken that Coke into the living room. White carpet? How stupid!

Her mother, Michelle, was in Chad's home office with him, completing one of Chad's required rituals—going over the expenses of the day. She'd gone in there twenty minutes ago with receipts in hand, looking pale.

Arielle wondered how long it would take this time. Chad sometimes spent two hours going over every item her mother bought. Even ice cream cones and cookies bought at a school bake sale had to have a receipt. Chad was very generous with what he gave them to spend, but every penny had to be accounted for at the end of each day.

Arielle could hear them from where she sat. In fact, she was sure that Chad had left the door ajar to make sure she would overhear what was being said.

"Now, what about your dry-cleaning bill?" Chad's voice was deep and modulated, like a newscaster's.

"It came to seventy-six dollars and twenty cents, which included Arielle's winter coat," her mother explained.

"Why is the stamp receipt higher than normal?"

"They just increased postal rates by two cents," her mother answered hurriedly.

"I'm aware of that. What did you have done at the hairdressers?"

"Well, I got a cut and a shampoo and a new style. Do you like it?" Arielle knew her mom was shaking her curly hair and pasting a smile on her face.

"It looks very nice," Arielle heard him say. "Where is the receipt?"

"Here it is, and it even shows the tip I gave her," Arielle's mother added.

"You tip too generously, Michelle," Chad said. "Ten percent is more than enough."

"Well, she does such a good job. . . ."

"Ten percent is plenty," he repeated.

"Okay, if you say so."

"And your grocery receipt, please."

"I went to Kroger's today," her mother offered hopefully.

"Did you use your discount card?"

"Of course. That gave me a ten percent discount on all fresh produce this week. See, it's recorded on the bottom here."

"Good. Okay, that came to one hundred thirty-two dollars and seventy-seven cents." There was a slight pause, then Chad said in a tone one usually uses with a child, "I gave you exactly four hundred dollars this morning, and you've spent three hundred ninety-seven dollars and seventy-seven cents. That means you should have two dollars and twenty-three cents in change."

"I, uh, let me see." Arielle could hear her mother digging in her purse. She heard coins jingle onto Chad's desktop—imported mahogany, polished and gleaming.

"Here's two dimes, and three pennies, and let's see . . . Ah! Here are the two dollars!" Her mother sounded jubilant.

"Very good," said Chad. Arielle rolled her eyes. He sounded as if he were praising a dog.

Chad sounded pleased. "You came out even today,

Michelle," he said. "As a reward, I'm giving you a thousand dollars for the weekend. I'll check your receipts on Monday."

"Oh, thanks, Chad. I love you, sweetie!" Arielle rolled her eyes again, this time in disgust.

"I love you, too, Michelle."

What an ass, Arielle thought. Hallmark cards had more emotion.

Then she stiffened as she heard Chad order, "Send Arielle in here."

Her mother came into the kitchen, looking drained but triumphant. She ran her fingers through her golden bronze curls exactly the way Arielle did. "Chad's ready for you, honey."

Arielle's mother, who never left the house without makeup and the perfect outfit, was slim and fit. She looked almost young enough to be Arielle's sister. She worked out every day, had a facial once a week, and had recently looked into cosmetic surgery.

Arielle couldn't understand why, however. The woman was gorgeous. She had skin the color of café latte, and silken, curly hair. She was often mistaken for a white woman, which Arielle knew she secretly liked. Only her lips and her nose made it clear she was African-American.

"I hate this, Mom," Arielle groaned, sliding off the stool.

"I know it's a pain, sweetie, but he takes such good care of us," her mother said in a low voice.

"It's so . . . demeaning. Like he owns us or something."

"Oh, stop, now. We live in a lovely home, we have all

the things we could ever ask for, and—well . . . Chad loves me—loves us," Michelle whispered, glancing back at Chad's door.

"If you say so." Arielle shrugged. "And what about you? Do you love *him*, Mom?"

Her mother tucked a stack of hundred-dollar bills into her purse, then scrunched up her nose to think. "Yes, I suppose I do. It's different when you're an adult. You marry for lots of other reasons than romantic love. But . . . I'll never love anyone like I loved your father, of course."

"Well, I guess Chad is the best stepfather so far," Arielle conceded. Chadwick Kensington O'Neil—good Lord, what a mouthful. He was a real piece of work. Her mother had met him on an airline flight about three years ago, and they'd gotten married a few months after that. Chad was her third stepfather.

"I'm waiting!" Chad bellowed from his office.

"You'd better get in there, Arielle. And don't give him the attitude this time. Just tally up and get your allowance, okay?"

"Whatever!" Arielle wanted to flounce into the room and throw the receipts at him, but instead she placed them neatly onto Chad's desk. Her only defiant act was to flop onto the sofa. She knew full well that Chad preferred she sit in the straight-back chair in front of him.

"Are there any others?" he asked, glancing through the messy pile in front of him.

She double-checked her purse. "I have a McDonald's receipt from two days ago." She handed that to him. "Oh, and here's one for a bottle of Tylenol and a pack of cough drops, and one for some deodorant I bought at the drugstore." She hated herself for trying to smooth out the wrinkles on the thin pieces of paper. He took each one and stacked it with the others.

She felt like dirt under his fingernails.

Then he picked up a small calculator, entered the amounts on the bottom of Arielle's receipts, and proceeded to do his calculations. His upper lip always seemed to sweat when he figured the accounts for the day.

"You and your mother are on the ball today," he said, looking up at Arielle. "Proof of payment down to the penny. I like that."

"Just tryin' to keep you happy, Chad," Arielle told him, though she couldn't resist adding, "But getting a receipt for a Coke and chips is a pain."

"Speaking of Coke . . ." Chad spoke slowly and evenly.

Arielle felt herself break out into a sweat. She didn't know what to say—which road she could travel without running into a landmine. She looked toward the door longingly.

"I noticed the stain on my carpet, of course," Chad said.

"I, uh, I cleaned it up. I used carpet cleaner and everything," Arielle told him.

"Obviously not well enough," Chad countered.

"I'm sorry." Arielle's voice dropped to a whisper. "I'll clean it again and make it right. I promise."

"Are you aware that that carpet is imported Persian wool and worth thousands of dollars?"

"Yes, sir."

"And you've been told time and again, no drinks in my great room?"

"I was on my way to my bedroom. I just tripped. It was an accident."

"Don't you understand the rules of this house?"

"Yes, sir."

"You know there are consequences when rules are broken." His voice threatened like an oncoming storm.

"I said I was sorry," Arielle said, getting angry.

"'Sorry' doesn't clean the carpet, Arielle," said Chad, restacking the receipts.

"I don't know what else to tell you," Arielle said helplessly.

"I've hired a professional cleaning crew to come in and remove the damage you caused through your carelessness."

Arielle relaxed a little. "Thank you."

"Oh, don't thank me. *You* are going to pay for it!"

"Me?"

"The cleaning company has given me an estimate of six hundred and fifty dollars to have the stain removed and the carpet returned to its full beauty."

"Six hundred dollars to clean one little spot?" Arielle said incredulously.

"Six hundred and fifty. They have to clean the whole carpet, of course," Chad replied.

"Of course," Arielle replied sarcastically.

"That amount will be taken from your allowance, starting today."

She looked up in alarm. "But I don't have any money left from last week," she said in protest.

"That is not my problem," said Chad.

"What am I supposed to do for lunch money and lipstick?"

"That is of no concern to me."

"You are *so* not fair!" Arielle cried out.

"And *you* are quite irresponsible, Arielle."

Arielle didn't know how to answer him. She slumped in the chair and focused on her toenails.

Chad continued, "I, however, think I'm extremely generous to both you and your mother. I give you one hundred dollars every week—sometimes more—and I allow you to spend it as you wish."

Arielle looked at the polished hardwood floor. "I know," she muttered. "Kids at school are totally jealous."

"The carpet-cleaning fee will be repaid in six and a half weeks, and you will have learned your lesson," Chad said.

"But that's, like, *forever*!" she wailed.

"One day you'll thank me for this."

"I doubt that," Arielle mumbled. She watched Chad make a notation in his ledger, then left his office.

She went to take another look at the cola stain. It was just the faintest of shadows, but is seemed to scream out at Arielle.

Her mother sat by the bay window, looking relaxed in the leather recliner. Ear buds hidden under her curls, eyes closed, she smiled as she listened to the music on her iPod. Arielle tapped her on the shoulder.

"What's wrong?" her mother asked, turning off the music. "Your receipts didn't tally?"

"No, everything balanced out."

"So what took so long?" her mother asked.

"He's trippin' over that spot on the rug."

"Oh, honey, he's just particular. He appreciates what

he has. Lots of men are slobs and toss their dirty socks all over the floor. So Chad is a really refreshing change," her mother said soothingly.

"You gotta be kidding, Mom! He's crazy!" said Arielle frantically. "He's making me pay to clean the carpet. Six hundred dollars!"

"Look at it this way, dear. You're really paying with his money. He gives us so much every week!"

Arielle gave her mother a look of disgust and said, "Some of that money is *yours*, Mom. You ever think of getting your own checking account? You have a *job*! Don't you even get to keep what you make?"

"I don't really need a separate account, Arielle. My little check is direct-deposited into our joint account. I only work because I enjoy it, not because I have to."

"You mean you give him all your money? I don't believe it!" Arielle shouted. She didn't care if Chad overheard or not.

"We're family, Arielle. Families share," her mother said simply. "He gives me much, much more than I put into that account. You know that."

"If we're so tight as a family, how come he comes off as king of all that, and I feel like I have to account for every breath I take?" Arielle asked angrily.

"He deprives us of *nothing*, Arielle. Not to mention that he donates thousands to charity every year," her mother reminded her.

"He measures the *toothpaste* I use, Mom. He counts the sheets of notebook paper I take to school."

"He's efficient."

"He's a control freak!" Arielle fumed. "Slaves back in the day were no better than us, Mom! A master provided everything as long as the slave obeyed. And he was punished if he made the master mad. What's the difference with us? Why do you let him do this to us?" But she already knew the answer.

"It's a minor inconvenience, Arielle. Look, I know you're upset. Why don't we go to that new boutique that just opened and I'll buy you a new outfit? I saw a pale yellow cashmere sweater that will look gorgeous on you."

"I've got homework," Arielle replied with a shrug. "You go on without me."

"Are you sure?"

"Yeah."

"Well, I'll be back in a couple of hours." Her mother freshened her lipstick. "Call me on your cell if you change your mind."

"Yeah, sure." Arielle trudged up the steps to her bedroom and locked the door. Her room was any girl's dream—thick, rose-colored carpet, and a lighter pink paper on the walls. Her queen-size bed was covered with soft down pillows and a comforter, and on the table next to her desk sat a television, a computer, a video game player, and dozens of CDs and DVDs.

She glanced out through the pink dotted swiss curtains to see her mother drive away in the Mercedes that Chad had given her for Christmas, and wondered how long it would take Chad to decide her mom needed to account for every mile she drove.

EVERY MORNING BEFORE HE WENT TO school, Kofi swallowed a pain pill. As he tapped an Oxy out of its bottle, he noticed it was almost empty.

"Gotta call Doc Stinson," he muttered. Of course, he wasn't even sure anymore if the pain he was taking the pills for was real or just imagined. *I just know they make me feel smooth when everything else is lumpy.*

He'd told his parents about the recurring pain from when he'd broken his arm last year, but he might as well have reported the problem to the players on his Elite Force video game, he thought as he headed toward the kitchen. After his accident with the Warriors of Distinction, his parents had really tried to change their lifestyle and devote more attention to him. But old habits die hard, and Kofi wasn't surprised when after a few months, his life and theirs sank back to the old reality.

"Dad, the man called about the rent yesterday," Kofi said, seeing his father at the kitchen table. "I thought you paid it last week."

People said he looked just like his father—tall and thin, with reddish, fuzzy hair and glasses. His dad poured frosted flakes into a plastic bowl.

Kofi picked up the carton of milk and sniffed it. Although it was past the expiration date, the milk didn't smell sour yet. He poured himself a little in a plastic McDonald's cup. He held the pill in his hand.

"Yeah, I meant to," said his dad. "I gave him four hundred dollars and told him I'm good for the rest real soon."

"So what happened to the rest of the rent money?" Kofi asked with a sigh. He rolled the pill between his fingertips.

"I figured I could double it over at the Argosy Casino. I was hot on the slots Saturday night."

"How much did you lose, Dad?" Kofi asked, knowing the answer.

"Actually, I won, Kofi! Three thousand dollars! It's the biggest hit I've ever made."

"But then . . ." Kofi tried to be patient.

"Yeah, well, I lost it. It wasn't my fault—that machine was bogus, man."

"Why couldn't you leave when you were ahead, Dad?"

"I figured I could come home with six thousand and you and your mother would be so proud of me," his father told him. "We woulda been set for several months."

Kofi looked at the tiny white pill and wished he had a fistful of them. "But now we're gonna get evicted. Again."

"Don't you have any money, Kofi?" his father asked

hopefully. "You've been putting in those extra hours at McDonald's for a while now."

"Dad, it's still just a part-time job. It can't cover rent," said Kofi. He didn't really say what he was thinking: *Paying rent is what you are supposed to do.*

"Every little bit helps," his father said cheerfully, "and then one day that big ship comes in and we sail away to glory."

"There are no oceans around here, Dad."

"Why are you always so negative, Kofi? You gotta reach for dreams, boy, not stomp on 'em," his father said, hurt in his voice.

Kofi just shook his head. He popped the pill into his mouth and washed it down with a gulp of the slightly sour milk. He exhaled slowly.

"Dad, I just want to pay the rent."

"Can't you help your old man out this month?"

"I don't have much," Kofi told him. "Don't you get paid on Monday?"

"Yep."

"Can you bring your check home before you cash it?"

"Sure, son. I promise. But now I gotta get some shut-eye." He pushed back from the table and headed to his bedroom.

"Aren't you due at work at nine, Dad?"

"I called in sick. Don't worry—I'll do overtime tomorrow."

More and more, Kofi felt like he was the father raising two adult kids. His dad worked at a branch of the local post office—sorting mail and tossing packages—but it was Kofi's job to take his dad's paycheck and stretch it as far as it would go. His mother did temp work as a secretary when she could, or would.

Kofi spent nearly every dime he made at his after-school job on paying the utility bills and buying a few groceries. He also made a little money from fixing the malfunctioning tech toys of a few friends at school. He had a knack for it, and students paid good cash to get their laptops or cell phones up and running. That kid Osrick was better than he was on computer tech projects, but everybody thought Osrick was way weird and came to Kofi for help instead.

He'd probably be able to help pay the rent this month, but what about next month, or the next? He'd had his eye on a new pair of Timberlands, and he hadn't taken his girl Dana out to the movies in weeks. She usually made lunch for both of them, and sometimes that was the only meal he had in a day.

Kofi heard a car door slam outside. His mother. She'd be still glowing with the fire and excitement of the party she'd just left. She was really pretty, and boy, did she love to have a good time. He'd seen pictures of when she was a teenager, and she could have had any guy at her school. But she'd ended up with his goofy-looking dad, and then him—their great mistake, as his ma had once called him.

By the time she breezed in the door a few minutes later, Kofi was feeling the Oxy. He felt mellow and relaxed—like he was floating on that ocean his dad dreamed of. His mother's nightly partying usually made him feel angry and helpless. Why couldn't she just be a regular mom? But the Oxy made it sort of okay.

Her presence in the kitchen was almost electric.

"Hey, Ma," Kofi said. "Another great party?"

"It was the best! Music so loud my eardrums almost exploded." She was dressed in a gold silk dress that hugged her slim body. She slid into a chair and kicked off her matching spiked heels.

"That's great," he told her, but he didn't mean it.

"Where's your dad?" she asked, slurring her words.

"'Sleep."

"He didn't go to work?" Her eyelids had noticeably drooped—the magic of the night had already started to wilt.

Kofi shook his head.

"Good—he and I can snuggle all day." She stood up unsteadily, but flopped back down in the chair.

"I made some oatmeal. Want some?" Kofi offered, scooping a bit of the bland-looking stuff into a bowl for her.

"Maybe just a spoonful," she mumbled.

"Hey, Ma—guess what? I got my first college acceptance letter yesterday," he said with pride as he nudged the sugar bowl closer to her.

"No sugar for me, kid. I've gotta keep my girlish figure." She pushed it away.

"Ma!" Kofi yelled in exasperation. "You're not a girl anymore! You're thirty-five years old!"

"Who peed in your cornflakes?" his mother asked, looking at her son in surprise.

"I just told you, Ma. I got accepted to a college. MIT! That's Massachusetts Institute of Technology. Do you know how hard it is to get into that school? I'm gonna major in aeronautics and astronautics, Mom. I'm going to design the computer systems that take humans into space. It's one of the best colleges in the country!"

His mother blinked. "I'm not even sure I know what astronautics is, but I'm proud of you, Kofi. I really am. I don't know how me and your father produced such a smart kid. I'm gonna take a nap, then we'll talk about this college stuff, okay?" She stood up shakily and patted his cheek. "Really proud."

"But how will I pay for it, Ma?" Kofi asked before she'd left the room. "It's very expensive."

She turned and looked at her son with bleary, red-rimmed eyes. "Maybe your dad will get lucky at the track. We'll figure it out." She disappeared into the bedroom and shut the door.

Kofi sat at the kitchen table, stirring his oatmeal until it was cold and lumpy. Disgusted, he dumped it in the trash and headed for the shower. As the Oxy kicked in full force, he felt warm and surrounded by the caresses of the water. He felt like he could float.

When he got out of the shower, however, the towel was still dingy, the bathroom tiles were still broken, and he shivered from the chill morning air.

In the bathroom he picked up his bottle of OxyContin. *Another?* He looked at himself in the mirror, then put the bottle down again. *Naw, I'm straight.*

He waited until lunch before he took another pill.

He could feel the medication kicking in once more as he hurried into his English classroom after lunch. Best class of the day, as far as Kofi was concerned. Music boomed from one of the three CD players Mrs. Witherspoon had hooked up around the room. The woman was into Sting today, Kofi noticed. Well, not everybody shared his taste in music, and teachers were into stuff nobody else liked.

Mrs. Witherspoon, a petite woman with curly blond hair, boundless energy, and really cool tech toys in her class-room, greeted everybody as they came in. She seemed to know something about the lives of every single student.

"What's up, Kofi? Did you get that letter from MIT yet?"

"Yep," Kofi said, checking in on her attendance computer by the front door.

"So, you gonna keep me in suspense, or do I have to bop you on the head for information today?" Mrs. Wither-spoon asked, excitement in her voice.

Kofi broke into a grin and looked at her. "I got accepted, Spoon. They let me in." All the kids called the teacher Spoon. She even encouraged it.

Mrs. Witherspoon jumped up from her desk, grabbed Kofi's hands, and danced with him around the room to the beat of Sting, shouting, "Whoo-hoo" the whole time. When they slowed down, she announced to the class, "Kofi is going to MIT! You hear that? One of my puppies is going off to one of the best schools in the world! I am SOOO proud!" Then she did a little dance of her own all the way back to her desk.

As he watched his teacher, he couldn't help but think back to how his own mother had reacted. If she could have shown just a teeny tiny portion of Mrs. Witherspoon's excitement, it would have felt so much more right.

SLIGHTLY OUT OF BREATH, MRS. WITHER-
spoon went back to greeting the rest of
her class as they entered the room.

Eric rolled in, his wheelchair whirring
softly. "Hey, Eric!" the teacher called out.
"Do a wheelie for me, and check into my
world of literary lunacy for an hour."

Eric grinned, checked in, and spun his chair
around in a circle. "Do I get extra credit for that?"
he asked. He wore his dark brown hair tightly
braided in straight, neat lines. Freckles dotted his
ruddy cheeks.

"Not a chance," Mrs. Witherspoon replied, "but
I might let you take me to the prom with all those
moves you've got!"

Kofi secretly marveled that Eric's puppy-dog grin
managed to charm all the girls, in spite of the kid's dis-
ability. Although his legs dangled helplessly, his upper
body was muscular and taut. Eric laughed. "I'm taking

applications for prom dates. I might let you apply."

The teacher cracked up, and as Jericho walked into the room she called out, "Jericho, sign in, my splendid sportsman and brilliant musical genius. So, have you decided on Ohio State for football, or Juilliard for music?"

"Aw, Spoon, you ask me that every day," Jericho replied, bending over the computer. "I can't help it if I'm supertalented in a multiplicity of fields."

"All right, now! Ten extra points for using a big, long vocabulary word in regular context. Make it twenty!" Mrs. Witherspoon said with glee as she recorded Jericho's points on her personal laptop.

"Hey, Spoon. I had vegetarian vegetable soup for lunch. Two big words. Does that count for points?" Roscoe asked as he checked in behind Jericho.

"If you insist, Roscoe. But I think those do more for your digestive system than your SAT scores." She typed in the points for him.

As Brandon Merriweather walked in, Kofi smirked as the girls suddenly started fixing their hair and glopping on lip gloss. Arielle was the only one who kept her head down. She and Brandon had been tight for a hot minute last year, but it hadn't worked out.

"When are you going to let me ride in that sweet little BMW of yours?" Mrs. Witherspoon asked the school's track star.

"Any time, Spoon." Brandon nodded, tucking his lanky frame into his seat. "You let me pass this class and I'll let you keep it as my graduation present!"

"It's going to take more than that for you to pass my

class, big man. Doing homework every once in a while might help!" Brandon laughed and stretched his long legs into the aisle.

More students meandered in. Mrs. Witherspoon complimented Rosa on the great job she did on her book report and Lisa on her new earrings. She thanked Ram for shoveling the snow from around her car earlier, and tossed a fresh red apple to Susan Richards, the dancer.

Osrick Wardley came in next. He had the hood of his heavy winter coat up so it covered most of his face.

"Good afternoon, Sir Osrick the Great," Mrs. Witherspoon said gently. "The room is warm, so take off your jacket and stay awhile."

"Hi," Osrick said shyly. He, too, seemed to like the outgoing teacher, although Kofi noticed Osrick never seemed to have nerve enough to call her Spoon. Hers was the only class he'd put his hood down in, however. He sat at a table near the back of the room with Susan and Ram.

"My loaner laptop for you all is acting up again, Osrick," said Mrs. Witherspoon. "Take a look at it if you have time, and see if you can get the peanut butter and jelly out of the motherboard. There's no telling what these folks do to my stuff when they get it home. I couldn't survive without you, kid."

"Okay," Osrick agreed with a hint of a smile.

"And Kofi," the teacher continued, "if you can unwrap those arms from around Dana for a couple of hours, I'd like for you to take a look at my DVD projector—I think it might need a heart and lung transplant. Or maybe just a chip."

Feeling mellow from the Oxy, Kofi was about to make

a smart remark, but he just nodded instead. Spoon often paid her "tech geniuses" (as she called them) out of her own money, and he needed the cash.

Dana bounded into the classroom then, dressed in a red and gray Ohio State sweatshirt.

"How was the tour of Ohio State yesterday?" Mrs. Witherspoon asked her.

"Cool. But I think I want to go to Florida instead. I love warm weather, you know what I'm sayin'?"

"You need to stick around here and keep *me* warm!" Kofi yelled out. She blew him a kiss and signed in just ahead of Olivia and November.

"Hey, Spoon, November's back. Remember her?" said Dana as November gave Mrs. Witherspoon her enrollment papers.

"Of course I remember Miss November who took the helicopter adventure ride of the century! Almost gave us old folks heart attacks after that football game."

"Yeah, that was a night to remember," November said. "Plus, we almost beat Excelsior that day!"

"Don't be bringin' up that 'Pink Panther' game, November," said Jericho. "You be embarrassing me."

"You all embarrassed yourselves," she teased. "Running onto the football field in pink uniforms! That was just crazy!"

"Cheap uniforms. Not our fault," Jericho reminded her.

"So, how's the baby?" asked the teacher.

"Well, she's got a few problems," November admitted. "It's sure not as easy as it looks like in the movies."

"And how's the baby's mama? Are you getting enough sleep?"

"Not really," November told her, "but I'm managing."

"Are you going to be able to handle this, November? School? Doctors? Baby emergencies?"

"I'm gonna try."

"Well, let me enter you in my computer system," the teacher said. "And here is everything we've done thus far, as well as all your assignments for the rest of the semester." She handed November a green zip drive.

"Everything's in here? You're amazing," said November.

"No, just technologically magnificent!" Mrs. Witherspoon said with a smirk.

"Hey, Spoon, give yourself a couple of points for those big words," Jericho called from his desk.

"I shall do that!" the teacher replied, laughing. She turned on the whiteboard that was connected to a third computer—the one with Internet access.

The class were reading *Beowulf*, so Mrs. Witherspoon showed two video clips—one from the preview of the movie, and one from a cartoon about the monster named Grendel. Then she popped up a chart that talked about heroes and monsters and good versus evil, and brought up a website that told about Anglo-Saxon history—all in a twenty-minute span. Nobody ever went to sleep in Spoon's class. In addition, everything she did in class was saved on a zip drive that students could take home. She talked, she teased, she questioned, she sang, she twirled.

Finally, standing on a table in the front of the room, Mrs. Witherspoon put an old plastic crown over her curly blond hair and a purple cape over her shoulders.

Kofi figured they were probably left over from a million Halloweens back—they looked awful.

Spoon dimmed the lights and proceeded to recite the words from the ancient story as it might have been told hundreds of years ago beside a crackling fire. Her voice was strong and powerful as she quoted the words from memory:

> *Then, when darkness had dropped, Grendel*
> *Went up . . . .*
> *. . . . . The monster's*
> *Thoughts were as quick as his greed or his*
> *   claws:*
> *He slipped through the door and there in the*
> *   silence*
> *Snatched up thirty men, smashed them*
> *Unknowing in their beds and ran out with their*
> *   bodies,*
> *The blood dripping behind him, back*
> *To his lair, delighted with his night's slaughter.*

In the middle of her presentation, the classroom door burst open and a cold wind whooshed through the room. A few kids jumped, half-expecting, perhaps, the fiend Grendel to appear.

Standing in the doorway, a toothpick hanging from the side of his lips, a sneer on his face, was not a monster, however. It was Eddie Mahoney, who had spent most of last year at a juvenile detention center. Dana stifled a scream.

Wearing an oversize black T-shirt and baggy jeans,

Eddie looked around the room as if daring someone to say something. But even Mrs. Witherspoon was speechless.

"It's been a while, Eddie," she finally said, jumping off the table and removing the crown. To the rest of the class, she said, "You guys go ahead and work on your PowerPoint presentations on *Beowulf*. You know what to do."

Kofi had no intention of doing any classwork. He slid over to Dana's table and sat down next to her. He took her right hand in his—it was shaking. He bent close. "Don't you worry, Dana. If Eddie Mahoney so much as looks at you the wrong way, I swear I'll kill him."

"Don't talk like that, Kofi!" Dana whispered anxiously.

"I'll hurt him bad. I'm not gonna let him touch you. I promise," Kofi swore.

"I got your back, too," added Jericho, leaning across the table. "Big-time."

"You think he blames me that he got sent away?" she whispered. "It was my testimony that convicted him."

"He deserved all he got and more!" Kofi whispered fiercely. "He hurt you!"

November sat on the other side of Dana, squeezing her left hand.

Kofi leaned forward to hear what Eddie and the teacher were saying.

"So, Eddie," Mrs. Witherspoon began, looking at the papers he had handed her. "It seems you had some good teachers up there at the center. I'm surprised they sent you back to this school, however. Usually a new school is preferable." She typed some information into her computer. Kofi thought she looked nervous.

"I asked to come back here. I told them all my *friends* were here." He laughed his gravelly laugh, but there was no humor in it.

"Well, as you can see, we're in the middle of *Beowulf*," Mrs. Witherspoon told him, "and I—"

"I already read it while I was in lockup. *Macbeth* and *Hamlet*, too. I like those old stories. Everybody dies at the end." His eyes never left the teacher's face.

"Well, I absolutely refuse to allow any trouble in my classroom, Eddie. Do you understand me?" Mrs. Witherspoon was short, and Eddie towered over her, but it was clear she meant business.

He nodded as if she amused him. "No sweat, Spoon. I just wanna get my credits so I can graduate."

Kofi noticed that when most kids called her "Spoon," it was a term of endearment for the teacher who would loan a kid lunch money or help a girl buy that prom dress she couldn't quite afford. But in Eddie's mouth the nickname sounded somehow disrespectful . . . dirty.

Eddie took a seat near Osrick, who looked like he was about to throw up. His coat was back on.

Eddie ignored him, took out two pencils from his book bag, and began to beat the erasers on the desk top in a soft, steady rhythm. *Bop-boppa-bop-bop. Rop-doppa-dop-dop. Bop-boppa-bop-bop. Rop-doppa-dop-dop.*

He did it quietly, yet it was maddeningly annoying. Kofi felt like grabbing the pencils and shoving them down Eddie's throat.

As if he could sense Kofi's thoughts, Eddie turned and looked at him. Then he set his gaze on Dana.

ARIELLE HATED THE SCHOOL LUNCHROOM.
It was always hot and sweaty and smelled
of vegetable soup and old french fry grease,
regardless of what had been cooked that day.
Last year, when Jericho had been pledging to
get into the Warriors of Distinction, she'd hung
with November and Dana at lunch. November
had been dating Josh, Dana and Kofi had been
tight since birth, it seemed, and she had Jericho.
They'd giggled together and swapped clothes and
shoes and stories about the guys.

But this year was all different. Jericho was hooked
up with his honey bear Olivia, Josh was gone, and the
girls avoided her. She didn't blame them. It took her
a while, but in the end she realized she'd been a real
bitch—there was no nicer word to describe it. She knew
she deserved the cold shoulders they gave her.

She'd broken up with several boyfriends since then, and,
even though she figured she had to be one of the cutest girls

in the school, nobody was clogging up her cell phone to ask her out.

It's senior year, and I'm going to be home playing Scrabble with my mother instead of going to the prom, she thought miserably, grabbing a salad and juice box and heading to the empty table where she usually sat.

"Hey, Arielle!"

She turned to see who was calling her.

"Over here!" November waved from two tables over. "You gonna eat, or what?"

Is she serious? Arielle couldn't believe her ears. Still, she walked over to where November sat with Dana and Olivia, trying to look casual, daring to feel hopeful. She stood there, hesitating, holding her tray in front of her.

"Well, sit down. Don't just stand there lookin' all ghetto-fabulous," Dana said with a smile. "I really like your outfit," she added.

"Thanks," said Arielle quietly, sliding onto the cafeteria bench. "I got it on sale at T.J. Maxx."

"My favorite place to shop!" November said. "I need new clothes like a madman! Nothing fits me anymore!"

"Aren't you tired of sitting by yourself at lunch every day?" Dana asked Arielle.

"Yes, but I just figured . . ." Her voice trailed off, and she looked away.

"Get over it, and get over yourself," Olivia said. "I ain't mad at you—or anybody else these days."

"I'm really sorry, Olivia," Arielle began.

"I said, get over yourself," Olivia repeated emphatically. "If I had wanted to hurt you, I woulda sat on your skinny little behind a long time ago." She laughed, then stopped when she saw the look on Arielle's face. "Relax, girlfriend. Life goes on. So, anybody seen Crazy Jack today?"

"He came to art class," said Dana. "He wasn't acting any goofier than usual."

"Maybe we ought to get him a chemistry tutor—at least until the weather gets warmer," November said. "My first day back and I spent it outside in the cold. I coulda done that at home!"

"Uh, how's the baby, November?" Arielle asked. She nibbled uneasily at her food. She kept waiting for them to try to pay her back for all the horrible things she'd done to them last year—like throwing spaghetti on Olivia or talking bad about the pregnant November, or just for thinking she was all that. The list went on and on in Arielle's mind.

"Sunshine is doing really great. Of course, sometimes she decides that three a.m. is playtime, so I'm always sleepy." November rubbed her eyes.

"Can I see a picture?" Arielle asked shyly. She realized she was probably one of the only kids in their class who hadn't even had a glimpse of the baby yet. She'd almost thrown five years of friendship down the drain.

But November happily whipped out her photo album. Arielle was stunned at how pretty the baby was. Even though she was tiny, shades of Josh could be seen in her face and smile.

"She's so beautiful," said Arielle in a reverential whisper.

"Yeah, I'm pretty proud," November said, beaming. "And she's a really good baby, which is great since my mother says the baby is my responsibility, so I'm the one who has to get up at night to feed her and change her. I'm the one who has to buy her formula and clothes and diapers."

"Your mom doesn't help you?" Arielle asked in disbelief.

"Tough love, she calls it," November explained. "It was *my* choice to come back to school to try to graduate, and my job to find a place for the baby to stay and the money to pay for it."

"Deep," said Arielle.

"That reminds me," Dana said. "You heard from Josh's parents lately? I know they gave up trying to adopt the baby, but do they see her or help you at all?"

November made a face. "Not much. They only wanted her if she was healthy, and when she wasn't, they disappeared."

"That's so crazy. They were breakin' down your door with lawyers and money when you were pregnant, and now . . ."

"They've only been to see her once. They didn't stay long, and neither of them would pick her up. It was so weird. Mr. Prescott tried to give me some money, but I wouldn't take it. I mean, c'mon. How lame is that?"

"Good for you!" Arielle said, hoping she sounded positive and encouraging. She felt like a foreigner at the table.

"So, who's your latest honey, Arielle?" November asked. "I've been out of the loop for a few months. I have no idea who's hooked up with who."

"Nobody, actually," Arielle admitted. "I think the boys around here put my name on a 'Do Not Call' list." She shrugged. "But that's fine with me. I guess I've got a lot of bridges to rebuild."

Arielle glanced at Olivia, then looked away.

After a moment Olivia said, changing the subject, "Everybody's getting college letters, seems like. You decided where you're going?"

Arielle breathed out slowly, thankful the conversation had turned. "I applied to Stanford and Cornell and a couple of schools here in Ohio, but I haven't heard anything yet. What about you?"

"I've applied to a few places with rockin' marching bands and great pre-med programs. I should know something real soon," Olivia replied.

"I'm going to Florida A&M," Dana said with attitude. "I'm gonna love that Florida sun. They got a dynamite political science program. Dana the Wolfe for the defense, Your Honor. My client is innocent!"

"I'd be scared to be the lawyer for the other side," Olivia joked. "You can be fierce, girlfriend."

Dana sat taller on the lunch bench. Arielle noticed a glint of pride in her eyes. "You're already accepted?" she asked, a little surprised.

"Yep. Early decision. Grants and loans in place. Feels great to have that worry off me. All I gotta do is pack."

"What about Kofi?" asked November.

"He's gotta find a way to pay for MIT, but he's filled out lots of scholarship applications. Something will come through for him. It's just got to."

"Does it worry you that you won't be at the same school?" Arielle asked her.

"It looks like we're gonna need good cell phone plans," Dana replied with a shrug.

"What about you, November?" asked Arielle.

November sighed. "Maybe you'll get my spot at Cornell. That's where I was headed until I got pregnant. For now, I hope I can enroll in a couple of evening classes at Cincinnati State, but lots will depend on Sunshine's health and my job. Right now I'd just love to have some clothes that fit!" Her laugh fell flat.

"Well, maybe we can all take November shopping this weekend," Dana suggested. "You want to come, Arielle?"

"That'd be cool," Arielle said, trying really hard to hide how happy she was to be included once more.

"So what's up with Eddie?" November asked Dana. "How'd they let him back here?"

Dana stiffened. "After he burned me with that wire hanger and dipped my head in pee, I hoped I'd never have to see him again."

"I guess you don't get life in prison for hazing a kid during pledge stunts," Olivia reasoned.

"Too bad," said Dana, her eyes hard.

"What happens now?" Arielle wondered.

Dana thought for a moment. "I'm not sure. I thought being the only girl to pledge the Warriors of Distinction would be the straight-up highlight of my high school career. But it turned into a total disaster."

"Are you scared now that he's back in school?" Olivia asked.

"No. Angry." She drummed her fingers on the table.

"You'll be a great lawyer," November told Dana.

"I know."

Trying to fill the uncomfortable silence that followed,

Arielle spoke up. "Hey, I want to show you all something. I got that new iPhone for my birthday last week. My stepfather got it for me." She dug down into her book bag.

"I *so* want one of those!" Olivia said. "They are, like, way cool. They do everything—Internet and e-mail and all the music in the world as well. But it will be ancient and obsolete by the time I ever get one."

Arielle continued to dig in her bag.

"Yeah, like those old-time ugly black phones with cords and dials," November added with a laugh.

"Or those old typewriters that you had to put paper into, then roll the paper down each time you wanted to start a new line," Dana said. "My mom still has one of those in the basement."

"Or record players that required a needle that scratched in the grooves of a giant big black record that turned around and around," said Olivia.

The three girls laughed, but Arielle looked worried as she dumped the entire contents of both her book bag and her purse onto the lunch table.

She sorted through lip gloss and makeup and nail polish and pens and hair ribbons. She tossed her wallet, her keys, a calculator, a small bottle of cologne spray, and an apple out of the way. She stacked four notebooks, three textbooks, an assignment pad, and her laptop in front of them. Both bags were empty, with only crumbs from an old cookie wrapper left inside one of them. There was no iPhone.

"It's not here!" Arielle cried out when everything was spread out on the table.

"Maybe you left it at home," Olivia suggested.

Arielle was near tears. "No, I listened to it this morning during study hall while I was writing some stuff on my laptop. The earphones are here, but the iPhone is gone! My stepfather is gonna kill me! He told me not to bring it to school!"

November, in a calming voice, said, "Let's think backward. When did you last see it?"

Arielle's face had turned a hot pink. "First bell."

"You've had four classes since then—which ones?" Olivia asked.

"Uh, math, art, chemistry, and world history," she said, her hands shaking. "Do you know how much he paid for that thing? My life is over!" She picked up a notebook and shook it, just in case the iPhone had wedged itself between the pages.

"Do you put your book bag on the back of your desk, or under it?" asked Dana.

"Usually behind me." She paused. "Do you think someone took it?"

"Well, let's figure out who sits behind you in each class," November reasoned.

"I don't know! I can't think!" Arielle cried out. "Wait. In math, it's Roscoe Robinson. He's actually in my chemistry class too, but he sits on the other side of the room in there. He's cool, even though I think he copies my math papers. But he wouldn't have taken it—he told me he got one for Christmas."

"Lucky dude," Olivia said. "What about art class?"

"We put our bags on a shelf on one side of the room. They're in full view of everybody all the time."

"Okay, what about chemistry—you got Pringle, right?" Dana asked. "Who sits behind you in there?"

"Kofi," she said, looking away.

Dana inhaled. "Hey, look, my Kofi is scrapin' quarters together right now, but he's no thief," she snapped.

"Oh, I know that, Dana! I wasn't implying . . ." Her heart sank even further—she didn't want to make Dana mad at her on the day she decided to reach out and make up.

Dana looked at her sharply. "Just so we're straight."

Arielle nodded vigorously. "Let's see—today Miss Pringle had us doing labs, trying to make up the time we lost during the fire drill. Everybody was out of their seats, walking around most of the period."

"That's not good. It could have been anybody."

"So that just leaves world history. Who sits behind you in there?" asked Olivia.

"Osrick Wardley." Arielle's thoughts flashed to Osrick lying stripped and humiliated, Osrick huddled in his coat. She really hoped the poor guy wasn't the thief.

ARIELLE STUFFED EVERYTHING BACK INTO her book bag. "I'm going to report this to the principal." She hesitated, and then looked at the girls who had extended that thin thread of friendship. She wasn't sure how far to test it. "Will you come with me? Please?" she added.

"We're here for you, girlfriend," Dana said, as if speaking for the group. "Let's go."

"Thank you. You don't know how much this means to me." She was near tears. She hoped they didn't notice.

"You think it was Weird Osrick?" November asked as they stood to leave. "I've known him since sixth grade. He's a little different, but I've never known him to steal anything."

"He likes electronic stuff—maybe it was too much of a temptation," Arielle said slowly, thinking it through.

"Osrick could probably build an iPhone from bubble

gum and batteries if he wanted to," said Olivia. "The kid is a genius. I heard his IQ is pushin' something like two hundred."

"All I know is he was probably the last to see it, and now it's gone," Arielle said as they got to the principal's office. The thought made her increasingly uncomfortable.

"You're not a hundred percent sure of that, Arielle," Olivia said, voicing Arielle's very thoughts.

Rosa Gonzalez, who worked as a student aide for Mrs. Sherman, sat at the desk outside her door. "How can I help you?" she asked officiously, picking up a pencil and a notepad.

"We need to see Mrs. Sherman right away," Arielle explained.

"And this is in regards to . . ." Rosa put the pencil behind her ear.

"Oh, come on, Rosa," said Dana impatiently.

Mrs. Sherman opened her office door then and said to them, "And how can I be of assistance to you ladies today?"

Arielle wondered how long it took an adult to develop that tone, that body language, that attitude that made a teenager feel like a kindergartner who's about to wet her pants. "Can we come in to discuss a private matter?" Arielle asked, glancing at Rosa.

"Of course!" Mrs. Sherman, dressed in a tailored navy blue suit, stepped aside and ushered the girls into her office. Arielle wondered where the woman shopped for clothes.

Her office, obviously not decorated by school board

63

funds, was done in tones of pale green and gold. Gold woven drapes covered the institutional-looking windows, and a large, pale green area rug covered the bare floor. Decorated with roses and lilies, the room reminded Arielle of a grandmother's parlor, not a school office. A comfortable-looking leather sofa sat on the far side of the room. Dana, November, and Olivia hurried to sit there, looking a little overwhelmed. Arielle took the brocaded wing chair in the front of Mrs. Sherman's desk.

"What seems to be the problem?" Mrs. Sherman asked kindly.

"My iPhone has been stolen!" Arielle blurted out. She didn't want to cry in front of everybody, but she knew what waited for her at home.

Mrs. Sherman scribbled some notes on a yellow pad of paper, then looked up. "Hmm. A cell phone, you say? How can that be when cell phones aren't allowed on campus?"

"Well, you know, every kid at school has a cell phone, and everybody knows that."

Mrs. Sherman nodded. "You're right, my dear. I can't stop progress, but the school board, made up of folks who are older and even more uptight than I am—if you can believe that's possible—is determined to pass laws I can't possibly enforce. Nevertheless, let's at least make a report of this and see if there is anything we can do."

"She's a lot more human than I thought she'd be," Dana whispered to November.

"And her hearing is still pretty good!" Mrs. Sherman said with a smile. "Chill, girls. I'm not here to make your life miserable. Honest."

The three girls on the sofa seemed to relax, but Arielle's stomach still churned with the thought of what would happen if she went home without the iPhone. "Can we search people?" she asked hopefully.

"First of all, we have more than two thousand students in this building, so that would be impossible. But more importantly, it is illegal to search anyone without a warrant. Didn't you learn that in American history class?"

"Uh, yeah, I guess," Arielle murmured. "But I might know who took it."

"And who would that be?"

"Well, it might have been Osrick Wardley."

"And why would you accuse Osrick?" Mrs. Sherman asked, her tone changing. "That young man suffers quite a bit from bullies around here."

Arielle wondered if she should say something about the swimming pool incident. She thought for a moment. No, she'd promised. And Osrick couldn't possibly be the thief—could he?

Arielle blurted out in a rush, "He sits behind me in world history class, and I had my bag on the back of my chair, and it was open, and when I went to lunch, the iPhone was gone."

"Did you see him take it?"

"No, but . . ."

"Did anyone else see him take it, or see him with an iPhone?"

"No, I just discovered it was gone," Arielle replied. "And Osrick is, you know, a little strange."

"That doesn't make him a thief," Olivia interrupted.

"Trust me, I know what it's like to have no friends and not fit in."

Arielle knew that Olivia's comment was in part directed toward her. But she still had to add, "But who else could have taken it?"

Mrs. Sherman addressed Olivia first. "You're right, Olivia, about being the outcast kid at school. I, too, had my share of teenage difficulties."

The girls looked at one another and rolled their eyes as if to say, *Too much information!*

Mrs. Sherman continued, "And unless there are witnesses, there is nothing I can do right now." She stopped and sighed. "I'm sure you girls know that there has been a real increase in petty thefts around our building lately."

"I had ten dollars taken from my purse in the girls' locker room," Dana offered.

"And I had a camera stolen a couple of weeks ago," said Olivia. "Also from the girls' locker room."

"Why didn't either of you report this?" Mrs. Sherman asked.

Both girls shrugged. "I figured nobody would care about a lost ten-dollar bill," Dana replied. "But it was all I had in my wallet, so I know somebody took it. It was there before gym, and not afterward. It was my lunch money. I didn't lose it, and it didn't fall out."

"And the camera was one of those cheapo-drugstore types. It wasn't expensive, but it did have some cool pictures of me and my boyfriend on it," said Olivia. "I hated to lose those."

Mrs. Sherman continued to take notes, then looked up.

"Oh, by the way, welcome back, November. I just received your paperwork from the homeschool teacher. It seems you've worked very hard to keep up with your classes."

"Thanks. Will I be able to graduate with my class in June?" November seemed surprised that the principal knew her by name.

"Well, it's too soon to determine that, but if you continue to do well, it's a possibility."

"Yes!" November said, squeezing her fists together.

Mrs. Sherman put down her pencil. "Okay, then, I have your report. There's not much more I can do right now. I'll keep my eyes open, as should you. Keep your valuables at home, and your money in a jeans pocket. If you hear or see anything else, don't hesitate to come and see me." She stood and made it clear that their time was up.

"Thanks, Mrs. Sherman," said Arielle sadly. "I'm gonna be in big trouble at home."

"I'm sure your parents will understand," Mrs. Sherman told her gently.

"Not likely."

KOFI STOOD IN THE MAIN HALL, SIPPING from a bottle of water, waiting for English class to start. He stayed by the wall, keeping away from the group of guys who circled Eddie Mahoney, guys who spent every morning before class talking smack— about upcoming weekend plans, past weekend victories, and the girls that made all that happen. Eddie had been back for just a couple of days, but since his return, he had become some sort of celebrity to certain kids.

Eddie told his story over and over, each time adding details and making the juvenile detention center sound like the Ritz Hotel. Kofi hated how the younger kids especially seemed to think he was so cool.

"Yo, Eddie, when'd they let you out?"

"Not too long ago. I got to pick my own release date, you know."

"For real, dog?"

"Yeah. The food was great, the beds were soft, and a couple of those female guards were like, hot, you know what I'm sayin'? So I took my time leaving the place."

The guys all elbowed one another, laughing.

"Any girls up there?" asked a wannabe tough-looking ninth grader named Ryan.

"They kept the girls one unit over—just a thin wall separated us. You could *smell* 'em at night," Eddie said, sniffing the air as if remembering.

"What do you mean?"

"Their powder and perfume and girl sweat. Powerful, dude."

"Any of them ever get past that thin wall?" a sophomore asked hopefully.

Eddie motioned them closer. Kofi stretched to hear. "Every Saturday night, man. Heaven came knockin' at eleven p.m. Heaven at eleven. Why you think I stayed up there so long?" He let the lie sink in as the guys high-fived one another.

Kofi shook his head, amazed at what the group would swallow.

"You ever get busted for that?"

"Naw, man. I'm Eddie Mahoney—slick like ice and twice as nice."

His admirers laughed raucously.

"So it wasn't like the jails on TV?" another sophomore asked. A couple of boys punched him in the shoulder for asking a stupid question. But Eddie was cool.

"You're thinkin' about places like Attica where they got

gangs and solitary confinement and killers and rapists and stuff, dude."

The kid nodded, looking fascinated.

"The place they put me was more like one of those vacation villages. We had three meals a day—better than my mama can cook. Steak on Tuesday. Fried chicken on Wednesday. Apple pie and ice cream every night. And a movie every Saturday. With popcorn."

Kofi rolled his eyes. Eddie had left out the barbed-wire fences, the police dogs, the body searches, the locked doors of the cells, and the total lack of privacy. Kofi had spent a weekend at one of those detention centers a couple of years ago, when he'd been picked up for a DUI and no one could locate his parents. It was *not* a hotel. Each cell had bare floors, thin, moldy mattresses and blankets, and a toilet in the corner of the cell that had no seat and always stank. The prison-issue orange jumpsuits, worn and ugly and thin, never fit right, and the food tasted like slop. He had sworn to never again do anything stupid enough to land him back in a place like that.

"For real?" Ryan was asking.

"Yeah, dude. We had a game room with a ping-pong table, a pinball machine, and get this—a huge big-screen TV with all the latest video games. Stacks of DVDs. Headphones and iPods to listen to at night. All the latest tunes downloaded."

Kofi now laughed out loud, but nobody paid any attention to him.

Eddie was on a roll. "During the day we went to school just like you do, except we moved at a faster pace. I'm ahead in most of my classes here, so I got nothing to do but check out the honeys and plan my next move."

"And what's that?" Ryan wanted to know. Kofi caught his breath.

"I got plans, little man. I got some unfinished business around here."

"Like what?"

To Kofi's dismay, Eddie's answer was drowned out by the bell. As the group split up, Kofi put the top back on his water bottle and followed him.

But before Kofi got even halfway down the hall, the sound of Jack Krasinski's crashing cymbals filled the air. Very few kids even looked up. Girls continued their giggled conversations, guys bopped to the music coming from the ear buds attached to their MP3 players, and even teachers just shook their heads wearily. No one told him to stop. Until Kofi.

"Hey, Jack. Can you chill with those things a little? I had a category two kind of headache hurricane, and you just upped it to a category five!"

Jack was sturdy and muscular—Kofi guessed from carrying his heavy bass drum in the marching band. He wore his black hair long and shaggy, the ends matted and uncombed. He was one of the few seniors who sported a full beard. Kofi thought he looked a little like the guy from the *Pirates of the Caribbean* movies.

"My bad. My bad," said Jack as he lowered the two golden disks. "I was just freein' the noise, and colorin' the world a little, you feel me?"

"Yeah, I feel you," Kofi answered. "The whole world feels you, dude."

"The explosion of two cymbals is a splash of color in a dark gray world," Jack told him. "Little kids use crayons. I use sound."

"Deep," Kofi said, "but noisy."

"I'm an artiste," said Jack, "a creator of meaning in a world that makes no sense."

Kofi didn't think Jack was making much sense at that moment, but he didn't say so.

Jack continued, "You know what, man?"

"What's that?"

"In spite of all my noise, nobody notices. Nobody cares."

"You got that wrong, man. Everybody notices!"

Jack shook his head, his hair whipping around like black spaghetti. "No, they don't. Watch this."

He picked up the cymbals and clanged them together with a flourish—two times. Kofi jumped from the sudden sound, and man, his head was pounding, but the two girls walking by didn't even pause.

"See what I mean?" Jack said sadly.

"They hear you every day, Jack. But most of us are so used to it that, well, it's kinda like the morning announcements. Nobody pays any attention to them, either."

"I'm wallpaper." Now Jack sounded despondent.

"Not hardly. You're more like whiskey on the rocks, man!"

Jack looked unconvinced as he ran his fingers over the disks. "Maybe they'd listen better to my drums. Hmm . . . the snare or the bass? Maybe I'll bring both tomorrow."

Kofi hoped not. "Hey, Jack, let me ask you something,"

he began. "You know anything about all these fire drills we been havin' lately?"

"I know I'm tired of freezing my tail off every time we have to go outside," Jack answered.

"You got any idea who's pullin' the alarm?" Kofi pressed. "We've had four in the past three weeks. People are gettin' tired of it."

"Now that can't be true. Every kid wants class messed up, right?" Jack said with a grin.

"Yeah, I guess," Kofi admitted. "You got Fox for history?"

"Yeah. Hatin' it! Sergeant Fox, the king of worksheets and quizzes."

"I got him too—he's a bear. You takin' geometry this year?" Kofi asked casually.

"Yep. Hatin' it!"

"What about band?"

"Lovin' it! Of course."

"Who you got for English?"

"Techno-Spoon. She's cool. I think you're in her afternoon class—I got her first thing in the morning, before the caffeine in her diet Coke kicks in."

Kofi chuckled. "Spoon hates extra fire drills—she says they interrupt her flow."

"But isn't it the fire department who pulls the alarms? Aren't they the ones who decide when we have drills?"

"Yeah, man. I guess so. Later."

Just as Jack disappeared around a corner, he yelled out to Kofi, "I've got a geometry test this afternoon!" Then the sound of his crashing cymbals followed a few seconds later.

Kofi just shook his head. He'd lost Eddie in the crowd, but he brightened when he saw Dana coming toward him. Dressed in tight dark jeans and a pale orange sweater, she looked to him like a sunrise. She was frowning, however.

"Hey, babe," he said softly, reaching for her hand.

She jerked away from him.

"What's the matter?" he asked her.

"I waited for you for over an hour last night! What's up with that? And then you didn't even call!"

"Huh?" He had no idea what she was talking about.

"The library! We were supposed to meet at seven to study, remember? Or have you found somebody else to hang with at night?" He wasn't sure if she was ready to cry or to smack him, but it was clear she was pissed.

He rolled his head back. He'd completely forgotten about her. He'd gone home from school, taken two pills, and slept hard until morning. He hadn't even seen his parents, and he hadn't done any homework, either.

"Oh, snap! I'm sorry, Dana, but you know how it is at my house. Ma was in one of her moods, and she couldn't find my father, and well, you know how it is."

He looked up at Dana and hoped she had believed him.

She seemed to soften. "I'm sorry, Kofi. I sometimes forget you live in Wack City."

"Big-time," he agreed. But his mind was scrambling, trying to figure how he could have been so completely out of it.

"You could have called or texted me to let me know," she reminded him, hands on hips.

"It won't happen again, sugar lips."

"If you want to taste these lips of sugar, it better not!" she teased. Then she got some lip gloss out of her purse and applied it slowly so he could see every stroke. "Suffer!" she said, and then dropped it back into her bag.

He grinned, took a sip of water, and popped an Oxy into his mouth.

"What's that you're taking?" she asked. Her smile had disappeared.

"It was an aspirin—what's the big deal? I got a wicked headache."

"It looked more like one of those pain pills you were taking when you broke your arm."

"It was just a plain old ordinary aspirin—quit sweatin' me."

"Let me see the bottle."

"No! What are you, some kind of narc?" he asked her defensively.

She reached into the outside pocket of his backpack even as he twisted away from her, trying to make her stop. But she was quick. Neither of them said anything for a moment as she held the bottle accusingly in her hand.

"These things are easy to get hooked on, Kofi."

"I'm not jammed."

"So why are you still taking them?"

"They relax me."

"Try taking a hot shower instead."

"You don't understand the stress I'm under, Dana!"

"I know lots more than you think. You better lay off those things," she warned.

"I can stop anytime I want to."

"Prove it."

"No problem. Take them. You can even keep the whole bottle."

Tilting her head quizzically, she stared at the bottle, which contained only two tablets, then tucked it into her purse. "No more?" she asked.

"Straight up," he replied.

But Kofi knew he had a full refill at home.

ARIELLE'S MOTHER WAITED FOR HER OUTSIDE the school in her brand-new, strawberry red Mercedes. Even though it was February and most cars were covered with the muck of dirty, leftover snow, this one gleamed in the afternoon sunlight. Arielle had to admit it stood out and looked really good in the line of vehicles waiting to pick up students.

"Must be nice to have a rich daddy!" somebody yelled as Arielle walked over to the car. She just shook her head and waved. If only they knew.

She tossed her book bag into the back, slid into the front seat, buckled the seat belt, and inhaled deeply. The car enveloped her with a lemony scent.

"Hi, sweetie," her mother said. "How was school?"

"I survived another day," said Arielle with a shrug.

"Talk to any cute boys?"

"Oh, Mom. Give me a break!" Arielle cried. Quickly changing the subject, she said, "The car looks nice."

Her mother beamed. "Chad likes it when I get it cleaned and detailed before I get home."

"Yeah, right. Good old Chad." She stared stonily out the window.

"Why are you so down on him, Arielle? He is *so* good to us."

"Good to you, maybe." She slumped down in the heated leather seat.

"Remember where we came from, Arielle," her mother reminded her gently.

"I know. I know." Arielle crossed her arms over her chest.

"Everything I do is for you and your future, you know. Your college education is secure, and you can go anywhere you choose!"

"Can I go tomorrow?"

Her mother reached over and touched her daughter's hand but had nothing to say. She continued to drive down the winter-dirty street.

"Your nails look nice," Arielle commented, noticing her mother's French manicure.

"Toes, too!" her mother replied. "Next time we'll have to go together."

"Okay. Anything to get out of the house while Chad is around."

"Come on, honey," her mother pleaded. "Remember Ivan?"

How could she forget Ivan? A brooding hulk of a man with thick black hair, he was a chef in a local restaurant and volunteered at the shelter one day a week. Her mother had charmed him and married him before he knew what had hit him. She'd gone back to school and gotten certified as a flight attendant, and things looked hopeful.

But he had a vicious temper, and Arielle grew to fear the knives he used so skillfully in the kitchen as he prepared their meals. He'd lasted three years, until Arielle was eight.

"I was so glad when he left," Arielle told her mother. "But Dirk was even meaner."

Dirk was a dentist and the father of her little sister, Kiki. He kept his head shaved bald, and with his dark, beady eyes, he looked a little like a bowling ball. He made more money than Ivan and could afford a nicer house for them, and Arielle got to wear nice clothes to school. He liked showing off his new wife and pretty little girls. But he, too, had a mean streak. Dirk finally had found someone younger and prettier, and he left, also after three years. Kiki was two, and Arielle was twelve.

"I figure anyone who likes to work in people's mouths with drills and needles has got to be a little sick," Arielle said. "You got issues with men, Mom!"

"Well, I admit I've made a few bad choices," her mother acknowledged.

"I guess you did what you thought was best," said Arielle with a shrug.

They drove without speaking for a couple of miles.

"You want to stop for burgers or something before I drop you off at home?" her mother finally asked. "I've got a YWCA board meeting tonight."

"Yeah, anything so I don't have to sit at the table by

myself with Chad. And Mom? Can we go see Kiki this weekend?" Arielle hadn't seen her little sister since Christmas,
when they all drove to the Cherry Blossom Care Center in
New Jersey. It was supposed to be the best in the country for
kids with severe ADHD. Arielle suspected that Chad thought
it was the best place in the country to keep an eight-year-old
who was prone to spilling things on his white carpet.

"It *has* been a while. I miss her too, sweetheart. But we
have to trust she's getting the best care possible. Chad
did so much research, and this is the best thing for Kiki—
she'll get the emotional behavior adjustment she needs
while she's still young," her mother told her.

"Kiki needs hugs, not doctors," said Arielle dismissively.
"Chad didn't like her from the moment he met her."

"Well, she *was* a mess to clean up after!" her mother
pointed out. "But maybe we can go visit her over spring
break."

They pulled into a Wendy's drive-through. Arielle decided
on broccoli soup and a lemonade, while her mother just
ordered a salad and a bottle of water. That's all she ever ate
now that she was married to Chad. *I guess he likes his wives
thin,* Arielle thought with a snort.

They sat in the parking lot and ate. "Did you save the
receipt?" Arielle suddenly asked.

Her mother nodded and pointed to a stack of receipts
on the windshield visor. Reacting to the fear on Arielle's
face, she said, "You know, I was lucky to meet someone
like him."

"Yeah, bankers are such fun guys!" Arielle shot back
sarcastically.

"He got you that iPhone you'd been wanting, didn't he?"

The memory of the stolen phone made Arielle's stomach churn. She still hadn't told Chad or her mom about the theft. "But Mom," she complained, "he's so *tight* with his money!"

"That's why he has a lot of it, sweetie!"

Arielle tried to explain. "He, well, sometimes he scares me, Mom."

Her mother's fork froze in midair. She turned to Arielle. "Has he ever touched—harmed you in any way?"

"Yeew, no way!"

Her mother cleared her throat. "You'd tell me if Chad was, you know, acting inappropriately, wouldn't you?" she asked carefully.

"I wouldn't let that man touch my unpainted toenails!" Arielle spat out. "If he tried anything on me, I'd have the army, the navy, and the head of every single news station sitting on the front lawn in less than thirty seconds!" She shuddered.

Her mother laughed uneasily but seemed to relax. "So why does he frighten you, Arielle?"

Arielle stirred the clumpy soup and thought for a moment before answering. "I think he's a wack job, Mom. He's not . . . normal. When I'm around him I feel like all the good air has been sucked out and I can't breathe right. You feel me?"

"Yeah, I think so," her mother answered slowly. "But maybe this is just teen tension you're feeling, and it will get better with time."

"Doubt it."

"You're such a tough cookie, Arielle. I know it hasn't been easy for you."

Arielle shifted in her seat. "Sometimes I feel like all I am is the kid of the first husband. I don't even know what that means."

"You're my bright morning star. That's why I named you Arielle, you know."

"I wish it was just us, Mom. And Kiki."

"I love you, sweetie," her mother replied. "Never forget that. It will get better—I promise."

Arielle looked unconvinced. "I wish my father was still alive," she said, sipping her lemonade.

Her mother nodded fiercely. "You know, sometimes I wonder what we'd be doing now if Greg were still here."

"Well, for sure there'd be no Chad in our lives," Arielle muttered.

Arielle's mother reached over and gently touched her daughter's hair. "I loved your daddy so much. I didn't care that we lived in a trailer. I didn't care that we barely had a nickel between us. We had each other. And we had you. And that was enough."

Arielle had heard the story many times, but since she couldn't remember her father at all, she loved it on the rare times when her mother talked about him. But, she thought sadly, this tale would never have a happy ending. A drunk driver took her dad in an instant. What followed was bad luck, lost jobs, lousy apartments, and eventually the homeless shelter.

Arielle sighed. Ivan, Dirk, Chad. What a mess. The only good part had been Kiki, she thought.

Her mother's voice broke through her thoughts. Arielle shifted her focus back to her mom, who was saying, "That's why now you need to learn to appreciate Chad. I still cry to think of you in that shelter—washing you in the bathroom sink, stomping the roaches that crawled the walls. That was no life for you. Can't you see how much better things are now?"

"I guess." Arielle scratched her arm.

"It's not so bad, is it, Arielle?"

"No, Mom. It's okay. Really."

And that was when the dirty brown Ford Escort backed into their car.

THE SOUND OF CRUMPLING METAL AND crunching glass exploded in Arielle's ears as she pitched forward into the dashboard. Soup and salad flew everywhere.

"What happened?" she cried out.

"Somebody just hit us! Are you all right, Arielle?" her mother shrieked.

Arielle sat up straight, wiped soup from her forehead, and blinked rapidly, trying to calm down. After a moment she said shakily, "Yeah, I'm okay—I think."

Bits of salad hung from her mother's hair. She started to cry. "Oh my God! Oh my God!"

"Mom! Are you hurt? What's wrong?" Arielle was really frightened now.

"I'm fine. I'm fine. Nothing bleeding. Just . . . just . . . that really scared me."

Just then an elderly woman, who looked even more upset than Arielle felt, knocked on the window. "I'm so sorry!" the woman shouted. "I'm so, so sorry!"

Arielle's mom, still looking dazed, opened her car door. "What happened?" she asked.

"I meant to hit the brakes, and I hit the gas. Oh my Lord! Is anybody hurt?"

"No, we're okay." Arielle's mom got out of the car slowly. "All in one piece—just a little shaken. But I think you've messed up my new car, ma'am."

"My daughter told me I was getting too old to drive, sugar, but I wouldn't listen. Oh, Lord, look at this mess!"

Arielle heard her mother squeal—a combination of a scream, a screech, and a cry of desperation. "Oh, no, no, no, no, no!"

Arielle scrambled out of the car and gasped. The trunk was scrunched up like a used Kleenex.

"Chad is going to kill me!" her mother whispered, her face a grimace.

"It wasn't your fault, Mom," Arielle said, rubbing her mother's arm. "There are a bunch of witnesses here in the parking lot who will back you up."

"It's not a matter of whose fault it is," her mother tried to explain. "The car's a disaster. He's going to have a coronary!"

"I got insurance, honey," the old woman said, offering a card from her purse. "I'm old, but I ain't stupid!"

Arielle took the card as her mother couldn't seem to stop staring, with her mouth agape, at the crumpled back end of the Mercedes.

"Did you get hurt, ma'am?" Arielle asked the lady. She looked to be about eighty years old, with papery-looking skin and glossy gray hair. Her back was slightly hunched, but her eyes were bright.

"No, honey. I'm fine. But thanks for askin'. I'm Phyllis Simsbury. What's your name?"

"Arielle. Arielle Gresham."

"That's a pretty name, hon. Is your mama all right?"

"She's not hurt, ma'am. It's just that she just got the car for Christmas and it's kind of a shock to see it messed up. My stepfather is gonna be pissed."

"I'm so sorry, sugar. I'd give anything to change the situation." The old woman's eyes got teary. "It was such a pretty car, and now . . . Well, my daughter is gonna give me the blues because of this." She pulled a scarf over her head. "It's a little chilly today."

Arielle felt sorry for the woman. Her mother just kept running her fingers over the ridges of buckled metal.

"Let me write down your insurance information, Mrs. Simsbury, and I'll give you ours, okay?"

They walked over to her Ford, which had only a small dent in its bumper. "I got this car back in the eighties. They don't make 'em tough like they used to," the old woman said, nodding her head toward the crumpled Mercedes.

"Do we need to call the police?" asked Arielle.

"No, honey. The parking lot here is private property. Just make a police report later."

"Okay. It sounds like you've done this before," Arielle said with a gentle smile.

The old woman sighed. "Yeah. A few months ago. Maybe my daughter is right; I should think about givin' up my license."

"I'd hate to see you get hurt, Mrs. Simsbury," Arielle told the woman sympathetically. "Maybe when you get home you can toss your daughter the keys."

"Maybe I will. I'll really miss driving, though. I been doing my own thing for almost sixty years." She touched the car lovingly.

"I understand, ma'am."

Mrs. Simsbury glanced over at Arielle's mother. "I didn't mess up your car too bad, did I? It's drivable, right?" she asked.

"I'm pretty sure it is," Arielle said as she copied the numbers from the two insurance cards. "But we'll have to take it to the shop right away. My stepfather is pretty picky about his cars."

"I thought you said it was your mama's car, honey."

"Well, it is, basically. I mean, she drives it every day. . . ." Arielle stopped. "It's complicated," she said finally.

"Your stepdaddy sounds like my first husband," Mrs. Simsbury replied with a laugh. "Had to send that one to the 'Been there, done that' pile!" She cackled at her own joke.

Arielle laughed and told her, "Don't I wish!" She helped the old woman back into her car. "You drive carefully now, Mrs. Simsbury. I'll make sure my mother files a police report and contacts the insurance companies."

"They'll probably cancel me for sure this time around," Mrs. Simsbury admitted. "It's a bear gettin' old, honey. Have fun while you're young and pretty!"

"I will. I promise." Arielle made sure the old woman had her seat belt on, and then watched her turn out of the driveway of the Wendy's parking lot, jumping the curb and making a deep wedge in the mud next to the street. She waved at Arielle and disappeared into the traffic.

"I hope she makes it home safely," Arielle said, walking back to her mother.

"She seems so sweet," replied her mother. "But what are we going to do about the car?"

Arielle took a deep breath. "I guess we have to go home and face Chad."

"Oh, I just can't face him yet. He's going to go ballistic." Her mother held her hand to her brow. Her hand trembled.

"Mom, he's gonna find out eventually."

Her mother ignored her. "I know what I'm going to do! I'm going to drop you off, then go and do the police report, call the insurance, and take it to a repair shop. Immediately. So at least I can tell Chad it's being taken care of."

"Do you think that will help?" asked Arielle.

"A little." She sighed deeply. "Probably not enough."

"What do you think he'll do?" Arielle wondered.

"Remember the stain on the carpet?"

"Yeah."

"Much worse. Much worse."

They got back into the car then, which fortunately started with no trouble. But as they drove silently out of the parking lot, Arielle could hear an ominous rubbing sound coming from the back of the car that had not been there before.

When they got close to home, her mother did not pull into the driveway but stopped a few houses before theirs. "I don't want him to look out the window and see this yet," she said. "Tell Chad I've got that YWCA board meeting. I'll be home as soon as I can, okay?" She looked really nervous.

"Are you okay, Mom? You look like you're about to throw up."

Her mother gave her a quick, fake smile. "I'm fine, sweetie. I can handle this."

Arielle shook her head, got out of the car, and watched her mother speed off.

I'm gonna need a shrink until I'm old like Mrs. Simsbury, Arielle thought, *to unsort the mess that's my life. It's no wonder I'm so screwed up.*

ARIELLE DRAGGED HER FEET UP THE FRONT steps of Chad's two-story brick house. His shiny black Porsche sat parked in the driveway. Nice car. Nice house. Nice neighborhood. So what.

Chad was sitting in the living room when she opened the door.

She hesitated, then called out as brightly as she could, "Hi, Chad." She hoped he'd let her go right to her room.

"Hello, Arielle," he said in that voice that made investors trust him with millions of their dollars. "How was school?"

"Okay. Same as usual." She forced herself to smile, as if everything really was okay. But she suddenly felt like she had to pee really bad.

"That's a lovely outfit you're wearing," he said. "You look good in yellow."

"Uh, thanks," she said, shifting from one foot to the other.

"What's that you've spilled on it?" he asked, looking more carefully.

"Broccoli soup. Me and Mom stopped at Wendy's on the way home."

"And you decided to wear your soup instead of eat it, I see."

"Yeah, whatever you say." Arielle just wanted to placate him.

"Where's your mother? I didn't hear the car in the drive." Arielle noticed he said "the car," not "her car."

"She had a meeting at the Y. She said she'd be home in a couple of hours." Arielle hoped his interrogation was over, and she moved toward the stairs.

"Not just yet, Arielle. I'm wondering where you bought the outfit you're wearing."

"Uh, T.J. Maxx, I think."

"And when did you buy it?"

"A few days ago."

"I find that very interesting," said Chad. "Because I know you have no money."

"You don't know everything," Arielle said sullenly.

"I see you have new shoes as well."

"Yes, sir."

"And where are the receipts for all of this?"

"I think they're in my purse." Her hands started shaking.

He eyed her closely. "How much did the outfit and shoes cost?"

"They were on sale," Arielle said evasively.

Chad paused, as if he were waiting to reel in a wriggling fish. "Arielle, you had no allowance last week. How did you pay for the clothing and shoes? Did you steal them?"

Arielle stared at him in disbelief. "Did I—did I—*what*?" she sputtered. "Are you accusing me of—Who the hell do—"

"Watch your mouth, young lady!"

"Well, you watch yours! I didn't steal any clothes!"

"Then give me the receipts."

"I'll show you!" She dug down in her purse, muttering curses under her breath. But she couldn't find them! She thought back to when she'd dumped out her purse looking for the iPhone the other day. She kept searching, growing more frantic by the second, but both of them was gone. They must have fallen on the cafeteria floor.

"The receipts, Arielle," Chad ordered, ice in his voice.

"I can't find them!" she had to admit. "But I paid for everything I have on! I swear I did."

"With what money?"

Arielle hesitated.

"With what money?" he asked again.

"I charged it," she whispered finally.

"You what?" he thundered.

"Since I shop there so much, they gave me an instant credit card," she hurried to explain.

"In whose name is the card?" asked Chad. "You're a minor."

"Mine," she said. She backed a step away from him.

"And whose credit history did they use to allow the privilege of charging at their store?" His voice cut like razors.

"Uh, yours." Arielle lowered her gaze.

"And at whose home will the bill arrive?"

"Yours."

"How do you plan to pay when the bill comes?"

"I'll pay it when I get my allowance again."

"You mean if you get your allowance back."

"What?" Arielle yelped.

"I can't have irresponsible women spending my money recklessly—do you understand?"

"Yes, sir." Arielle felt her confidence ebbing quickly.

"First of all, that charge account will be canceled. You haven't got the sense of a goose. You can't possibly handle credit and finances."

"But I—"

He continued as if she had not spoken. "Secondly, you will pay me back the amount charged for those clothes, plus the interest. I will pay it, clear my credit, and deduct the amount from your allowance after the expense for the carpet. It should only add a week or so to your payback plan. You'll survive."

"Can I go now?" Arielle asked. She didn't think she could share one more breath of air with Chadwick Kensington O'Neil.

"No. I'm not finished. It seems a punishment is in order," Chad said quietly.

"For what?"

"You've stolen my good name and good credit. You've deceived me. You failed to keep a record of your own purchases. Haven't I taught you *anything*?" He sighed with disgust.

Arielle looked up. "What are you going to do?" she whispered.

"You must learn order and responsibility, Arielle. I'm trying to teach your mother the same thing."

"What else can you do to me?" she asked.

"I'm suspending the use of your iPhone for two weeks. Hand it over!" He held out his hand.

"But you gave it to me for my birthday!" Arielle desperately tried to think of a way to get out of this.

"I am aware of that. It was mine to give and mine to take back. Now give me the cell phone."

"Please, not my iPhone," Arielle pleaded. "I really like it, Chad." She wrung her hands; her palms felt moist and clammy.

"That's why I'm taking it. Give it to me."

"Please?" Arielle fought back tears.

"It's only for two weeks. By then you'll have learned your lesson. Now give it here!" He snapped his fingers.

Arielle gritted her teeth. "I can't," she said, bursting into sobs.

"And why not?"

"It . . . it . . . it got stolen two days ago."

"Stolen?" he roared. "What do you mean, it got *stolen*?" He stood up, nostrils flaring.

Arielle stepped backward again, cringing. "Some kid from school went into my backpack and took it. When I went to look for it at lunch, it was gone."

"How could you be so careless!" he shouted. "I was right! You're an irresponsible ninny!"

"How was I supposed to know?" Arielle yelled back.

"You were supposed to keep up with your property! If you had valued it, you would have kept an eye on it."

"I *loved* it, Chad. You know that," she pleaded. "I never even left it on my desk at school. I hid it at the bottom of my bag."

"Obviously not safely enough! And you had no business taking it to school anyway! Isn't there a rule against cell phones at that school?"

Arielle closed her eyes. "Yes, sir."

"Rules are in place for a reason, young lady! But you seem to think rules don't apply to you. You are in for a rude awakening when you realize the world does not revolve around Arielle Gresham!" Chad's face was red with anger.

"Yes, sir."

"You can bet I will never buy you *anything* else as long as I live!"

"I understand. I'm so sorry." She wiped her tears with the sleeve of the yellow sweater.

"Did you call the police?" Chad asked.

"No, but I reported it to the principal. There wasn't a whole lot she could do," Arielle told him. "I'll pay you back, Chad. I promise."

"Yes, you will. Every cent I spent on that thing, you are going to reimburse me for—with interest." He paused for a moment, then added, "And your allowance? Forget about it. If you need spending money, you can work for it. I should have known better." He glanced at a picture of her mother on the mantel above the fireplace.

"Yes, sir. Can I go now? I *really* have to go to the bathroom."

He nodded, frowning still.

She scurried upstairs, sat on the toilet, and cried and cried and cried.

KOFI GLANCED OUT THE WINDOWS OF Mrs. Witherspoon's class and wished he were at home, in bed, snuggled under something like a hundred blankets. Maybe with Dana.

Fat, lazy snowflakes fell, covering the already snowy ground. It would be cold and wet on the way home tonight.

Shortly after class began, Eddie called out in his gravelly voice, "May I be excused, please?"

"Please remember to take care of bodily functions before my class, Mr. Mahoney," Mrs. Witherspoon said, giving him the hall pass. "If I can run to the bathroom in the five minutes they give us between classes, you can too." The class giggled, but Eddie only narrowed his eyes as he left, pausing only at Dana's desk to give her a long look.

Kofi could feel Dana tense up, in the same way some people reacted to a snake—with great fear and the need to put distance between themselves and the reptile.

"I wish I could get my classes changed," Dana whispered to him.

"He's the one who needs to leave—not us," Kofi fumed.

Mrs. Witherspoon drew their attention back to the lesson. "Well, group," she said cheerily, "let's continue with the life of our hero Beowulf. Is he a hero because he's big and tough, or because he kills monsters?"

"Maybe both," Jericho replied thoughtfully.

"So what makes a person a hero?" asked the teacher.

"He saves the world," Susan suggested.

"What if he just saves a kid from drowning?" Arielle wondered.

"He's gotta be strong," Kofi added.

"Who says it's gotta be a dude?" asked Dana.

"Women back then just served the wine, and then they served the men," Cleveland said with a laugh, "like they're s'posed to do!" Dana threw a notebook at him, but he ducked.

"Can't a woman be a hero?" Dana asked again.

"Heroine," November corrected.

"Changing the name makes her sound weaker," Dana argued. "I think if a lady saves a baby from a burning house, she ought to be called a hero, not a wussy-sounding heroine."

"Good point," Mrs. Witherspoon said, encouraging the students to talk. "But do you have to save somebody to be a hero?"

"Maybe you have to kill somebody, like Beowulf did," Cleveland said.

"Killers aren't heroes, stupid," said November.

"Beowulf was," Roscoe insisted.

"But he killed monsters like Grendel!" Eric added.

"Grendel's mother musta loved him an awful lot," Roscoe answered. "After Beowulf killed her son, she came back and kicked butt! So maybe monsters have feelings too."

Then Osrick, who rarely spoke up, raised his hand.

A couple of kids giggled. Mrs. Witherspoon silenced them with a dagger look.

"Yes, Osrick," she said with an encouraging smile.

"Grendel's mom just wanted revenge," Osrick said in his soft voice. "The people who listened to this story would have understood that." Osrick bowed his head then, as if he were embarrassed. "Sometimes people just have to get even for bad stuff," he added even more softly.

"Great observation!" Mrs. Witherspoon noted.

"Which proves my point that women are strong," Dana insisted.

"But she was uggg-leee!" Cleveland replied. "Green and slimy."

"Sounds like your prom date," Jericho teased.

"Enough, enough," Mrs. Witherspoon said. "Let's read that line about how big and bad Beowulf was." She began, without the crown and cape this time:

That shepherd of evil, guardian of crime,
Knew at once that nowhere on earth
Had he met a man whose hands were harder;
His mind was flooded with fear . . . . .

*In the darkness, the horrible shrieks of pain
And defeat, the tears torn out of Grendel's
Taut throat, ... caught in the arms
Of him who of all the men on earth
Was the strongest.*

"Now is *that* a hero or what?" Spoon asked the class triumphantly. "I might want to marry this guy!"

"He couldn't handle you, Spoon!" Roscoe teased. The class laughed.

Jericho raised his hand. "Yeah, but at the end Beowulf died! What good was all that hero stuff if he gets killed anyway?" The look in Jericho's eyes was intense. Kofi figured he must be thinking about his cousin Josh.

Mrs. Witherspoon paused and looked thoughtful. "Even heroes die, Jericho," she said sadly.

"Maybe a dude's gotta kick it before he can be called a hero," Cleveland suggested.

"Or maybe it just makes the story better," said Rosa.

"Lots of stories end when the hero marries the girl and they live happily ever after," Olivia said, shooting a glance at Jericho.

"Aw, people think that stuff is real, but it's only in fairy tales," Cleveland scoffed. "That's why there's so many divorces." He got more than a few approving nods.

"Trust me. 'Happily ever after' is not what it's cracked up to be," Arielle said with a frown. "Sometimes the good-looking hero turns out to be the beast."

"Could the beast be the hero?" Spoon asked.

"Not in my house," said Arielle quietly.

Mrs. Witherspoon looked at her strangely. "Let's have a little talk one day soon, Arielle, all right?"

"Okay," Arielle replied, but she didn't look up.

Spoon then asked, "Does the monster get to have feelings and desires and live a nice, long life gobbling people up?"

Susan raised her hand. Everything about her was graceful, Kofi noticed, even her arm movements. "I don't think so," she said clearly. "Bad guys need to be punished."

The teacher nodded with approval. "Let's take a look at the section where the dragon takes a bite out of crime, a.k.a. Beowulf." She read:

> Then the monster charged again, vomiting
> Fire, wild with pain, rushed out
> Fierce and dreadful, its fear forgotten.
> Watching for its chance it drove its tusks
> Into Beowulf's neck; he staggered, the blood
> Came flooding forth, fell like rain.

The class, stunned into silence, said nothing for a second. Then another fire alarm shattered the mood and power of that moment. Everyone jumped, including the teacher.

"I've had about enough of these interruptions!" Mrs. Witherspoon cried out in frustration as she gathered her grade book, her coat, and her purse. "How am I supposed to teach? We may as well hold class out in the snow! Let's go, pups. Out the door, down the hall, and outside. Don't forget your coats."

"You think it's another false alarm?" Dana asked Kofi as they hurried out, holding hands.

"Probably."

"What does Crazy Jack have this bell?" she wondered.

"Math, I bet," Kofi replied, remembering what Jack had told him earlier.

Roscoe trotted up to them. "Hey, didn't Jack have a French test today?" he asked.

"Aw, man! Every time that dude has a test he can't pass, he pulls the alarm. What's up with that?" Cleveland complained.

"Do you think the teachers know?" asked November.

"Probably not. And ain't nobody gonna narc on Crazy Jack. He's just silly." Cleveland buttoned up his coat.

"What about Eddie? Could it be him?" Dana suggested.

"The fire drills started way before Eddie got back, but you never know. He might be messin' with everybody's minds."

"Well, at least we're on the first floor, and I can roll out by myself this time," Eric said, relief in his voice.

"You can carry *me* if you want," Jericho teased him.

"I'll pass on that one, dude. But Olivia might want the job," Eric said with a laugh.

"Hey, don't be messin' with Olivia the Superwoman," she said as they got to the end of the hall. "You make me pull out my red cape and I'll dust the floor with both of you!" They all laughed as they headed outside.

Thick snow fell on the students as they milled outside the building, stomping their feet and cursing the weather.

"It wouldn't be so bad if it was spring," said Jericho, shoving his hands into his pockets.

"This *sucks*!" Cleveland grumbled. "It's, like, the coldest day of the year."

Kofi wondered if it was the cold that was making his head suddenly start pounding. *Doesn't matter—pain's the same!* he reasoned. He thrust his hands deep into his jeans pockets—partly for warmth, but mostly to locate the bottle of pills he'd hidden there. Just touching the container made him relax.

"Kofi. Dana. November. Jericho. Eric. Luis. Olivia. Susan. Osrick. You okay, sweetie?" she asked. Osrick nodded. Mrs. Witherspoon took attendance on a handheld Blackberry device, which was awkward through her gloved hands. "Rosa. Arielle. Brandon. Roscoe. Cleveland. Eddie." She paused and looked around, concern and suspicion on her face. "Where's Eddie?" she asked.

"Right behind you, Spoon," Eddie said into her ear.

The teacher gave Eddie an uneasy look, but made no further comment.

Once again the classes waited for twenty minutes for the all-clear bell and finally went back into their classrooms, frosty and bitter.

Kofi's head still throbbed. As they hurried down the hall, he popped a pill into his mouth, chewing it dry and making sure Dana didn't see him do it.

"HAVE YOU SEEN IT?"

"Girl, that was too funny!"

"I almost peed my pants!"

"No, but I bet the little weirdo peed on the floor!"

"What you talking about?"

"Weird Osrick's butt cheeks!"

"For real?"

"How do you know it's him?"

"I'd know that hoodie anywhere."

"Shut up!"

"Check out YouTube, man."

"He's got his pants down and you can see *every-thing*!"

"Everything?"

"Well, almost. Skinny little legs. Skinny little thighs. Skinny little butt!" The laughter was loud and raucous.

"I gotta see this!"

"Who filmed it?"

"I don't know. But somebody is holding him down. You can only see their hands."

"Poor little geek."

"Ah, he probably liked it—he got to be the center of attention for a change."

"Show it again! Show it again!"

Three girls huddled around an iPhone and laughed so loudly that the bus driver glanced back to see what they were up to. They passed the phone around to almost everyone on the bus, and everyone who watched the video seemed to think it was the funniest thing they'd ever seen.

Arielle, who was riding the bus because the Mercedes was still in the shop, sat two seats behind them. She listened to the conversation helplessly. She knew that by the end of the day the video would have gone viral and there would be nothing she could do about it.

And she knew she should say something to defend the kid—she felt so sorry for him—but what could she say that would stop the video?

She hadn't noticed Olivia, however, sitting near the front of the bus. When someone passed the phone to her, she looked at it briefly, then immediately tossed it back and stood up, outraged.

"No standing on the bus," the driver said mechanically.

Olivia ignored him. "You think that video is funny?" she bellowed. Her eyes were narrowed slits and her nostrils flared. She looked like a bull about to charge.

Nobody answered.

"How would you like it if it was *you* being embarrassed

like that? You think it feels good to be laughed at?"

"Aw, get over it, Olivia," a burly sophomore replied carelessly. "Nobody got hurt, and it really *is* funny. You can't even see his face."

"Why don't you come up here then and let me toss you up and down the aisle of this bus?" Olivia replied, her voice a challenge. "And maybe we'll film it, just for fun," she added.

"Ooh!" came the whispered response from the group.

The boy, however, seemed to decide that ignoring Olivia was the wisest choice. He just shrugged and turned back to his friends.

Without an audience any longer, Olivia, still clearly very angry, glanced down the aisle and made eye contact with Arielle, then looked beyond her to the very last row. She picked up her book bag and stomped angrily toward the back.

And I once tried to get up in this girl's face? Arielle thought. *What was I thinking?*

Olivia stormed past Arielle, ignoring her and stopping instead at the seat of . . . oh, no! Osrick! Arielle had been so caught up in her own thoughts that she hadn't even noticed him sitting there.

He heard everything they said, she thought in dismay.

Olivia plopped down next to Osrick and exhaled loudly.

"It's pretty funky on this bus, huh, Osrick?" she began.

"Yeah, I guess." His voice was so low, Arielle could barely hear him.

"You ever need me to tighten somebody up for you, let me know, you hear?"

"I need to fight my own war," Osrick replied quietly.

"Nobody goes into battle alone," Olivia told him.

Wise advice, Arielle thought.

"One day I'll get even," Osrick murmured. "They'll be sorry."

Arielle felt like she had to speak up too. She turned around and said softly, "You got friends, Osrick. Remember that."

"Who? You?" Osrick sounded doubtful.

"Yeah, me. For real," Arielle said with more confidence. She glanced at Olivia, who, amazingly, nodded.

"You don't usually ride the bus," Osrick pointed out.

"My mom's car is, uh, in the shop," she said.

"I just want to graduate," said Osrick, "and have this all be over."

"When we come back for our ten-year reunion, you'll be a rich and famous scientist and getting the red carpet treatment. No joke!" Arielle told him.

"I'll never come back to this place!" Osrick exclaimed fiercely. "They can kiss my skinny butt that they think is so funny!"

As the bus continued to roll, Olivia looked up. "Wasn't that your stop, Osrick?" she asked. "I know you get off before I do."

"Yeah, it was."

"Why did you ride past it?" Arielle asked him.

"Sometimes I wait until everybody is off and the bus is empty. The driver circles around and takes me back to my stop." He sighed. "I couldn't walk past them today. I just couldn't." He gave a halfhearted grin. "I'm a jellyfish."

"I think you're pretty brave," Arielle told him. "I don't know what I would have done if they had posted me like that."

"They e-mailed the video to me, you know. Twenty-seven different people sent it," Osrick said. "Twenty-seven." He seemed overwhelmed at the enormity.

"Is there any way to get it removed from YouTube?" Olivia asked.

"It's already all over MySpace and Facebook and a dozen other sites. It's there forever until they get tired of it and move on to something else," Osrick told her.

The bus rumbled on.

IT FELT SO GOOD TO HAVE FRIENDS TO EAT lunch with once more. Arielle hadn't realized how lonely she'd been. Dana sometimes ate with Kofi, since they had only a couple of classes together. But November, who always had new baby pictures with her, and Olivia, who was surprisingly laid-back and friendly, were becoming regular lunch partners.

They'd dealt with one another slowly and carefully at first, each cautious about what was said, but Arielle realized she'd really underestimated Olivia. She was smart and witty and clever. And she was *really* hooked on Jericho, who seemed to be just as into her. And Arielle could finally begin to see why.

I can live with that, Arielle thought.

"Did you hear the latest?" asked November as Arielle walked over with her tray.

"You mean the YouTube video?"

"No, not that, but it is *so* not fair what they did to Osrick!" November exclaimed.

"Did they ever find out who did it?" Olivia asked, her voice as cold and angry as it had been on the bus.

"I don't think so."

"At least nobody could see his face," said November.

"Still sucks," Arielle said.

"I heard Mrs. Witherspoon tried to get it removed, but it was too late. Everybody has a copy of it, and they've sent it to everybody they know," Olivia said. "It's like spreading a disease. Once you sneeze, you can't suck it back in."

"Thanks for the nasty image while we eat," Arielle teased gently. She still wasn't sure how far to go with Olivia.

But Olivia just grinned and pretended to sneeze on Arielle's sandwich.

"So what's your news?" Arielle asked November.

November smacked her forehead. "I almost forgot! Susan Richards got fifty dollars stolen out of her wallet today! It was her deposit for her class ring."

"Shut up!" said Arielle. "When did she realize it was missing?"

"Right after gym class. She was going to pay for the ring at lunch. You know, from those geeky guys who sit there and sell you stuff."

"I let them sell one of them to me!" Olivia said, showing off the shiny ring on her right hand.

"I was going to order one," Arielle said, "but my allowance has been cut off—permanently, I guess."

"Just 'cause of the stolen iPhone?" November asked incredulously. "Your stepfather seems like one cold dude."

Arielle nodded. "You don't know the half of it." She narrowed her eyes. "He made me get an after-school job."

"That's not so bad. Lots of kids have jobs. At least you'll have your own spending money," Olivia reasoned.

"No, you don't understand. I have to give him my whole paycheck. All of it."

"Until you've paid off the cost of the phone?" November asked.

"Until he thinks I've been punished enough," Arielle replied. She couldn't tell them the rest of what her stepfather made her pay for at home.

"But I thought it was a birthday present," Olivia said, frowning. "You shouldn't have to pay for your own gift."

"Obviously, you haven't met Chadwick Kensington O'Neil," said Arielle, squashing a cube of Jell-O.

"I don't think I want to." Olivia shook her head.

"What about your mom? Won't she back you up?"

"She's afraid to make him mad. He might cut off *her* allowance! And then I'll have both of them mad at me."

November and Olivia looked at each other, eyebrows raised.

"Where are you working?" November asked then.

"At that Smoochie's Boutique at the mall. If I had money, I could get clothes at a twenty-five percent discount."

"Bummer. They got nice threads there. The other week I saw—" November was interrupted by voices shouting. Teachers yelling.

The girls looked up. Some kind of commotion was going on at the far side of the lunchroom. Then, unusual quiet. "Probably a fight," November said in a bored voice.

But Dana came running over to their table. "Guess what?" she said, breathing hard.

"Kofi proposed," said November with a smirk.

"Get a life, girlfriend," Dana said, laughing at her. "No, there's been more thievin' around here. Somebody took Mrs. Sherman's wallet!"

"The principal? Who'd have the balls to do that?" November asked.

"When did it happen?"

"Just now! She was in here, doing lunch duty like she always does during fifth bell. She set her purse down to talk to a couple of teachers, and when she picked it up to buy her lunch, her wallet was gone!"

"Well, putting her purse down was dumb," Olivia pointed out.

"Did anybody see who did it?" November wondered.

"Nobody's talkin' if they did."

"I bet she's about to clock some folks!" said Olivia.

"She's locked down the lunchroom—nobody in or out until that wallet shows up," Dana said.

"Where's Osrick?" Arielle asked, then hated herself for wondering.

"Sitting where he usually does—by himself in the corner," Dana reported.

"Was he . . . was he . . . close?" She couldn't bring herself to say what she meant. But Dana got it.

"Actually, he was. He always waits until the end of the

line to get his food, so he was standing right by Mrs. Sherman when it happened."

"Don't go accusing him yet," Olivia warned. "What about Eddie Mahoney? He seems a more likely suspect, if you ask me."

"Well, he *is* in the cafeteria," Dana reported. "Kofi keeps tabs on him all the time—like a GPS system."

"Was he anywhere near Mrs. Sherman?" asked Olivia.

Dana thought for a moment. "Close enough," she decided.

"But my phone was stolen *before* Eddie got out of jail," Arielle reasoned. "He couldn't be the thief."

"No, your phone was stolen on the *exact same day* that Eddie came back to school," Olivia reminded her.

"Hey, you're right," Arielle replied. "But wouldn't I have noticed him hanging around?"

"Not if he didn't want you to," Dana said thoughtfully.

Mrs. Sherman marched to each table like the tank she looked like. She had a megaphone in her hands. "We will stay here until midnight if we have to, but nobody is leaving this lunchroom until my wallet shows up!" she announced. "I hate to do this, but I am asking each person to voluntarily show me the contents of your purse and book bag. If you have not taken the wallet, you have nothing to hide, and I apologize."

"Big difference between her reaction when my stuff was stolen and when hers was," Arielle noted ruefully.

"Principals got the big guns," said November.

Ms. Hathaway, Miss Pringle, Mrs. Witherspoon, and Mr. Tambori, who all had lunch that bell, as well as Officer

Hammler, the school police resource officer, helped with the search. Kids at every table spread their stuff out and were then dismissed. Arielle wondered if Mrs. Sherman was checking for iPhones as well. Probably not.

"The wallet could just as easily be in a pocket or a bra," November reasoned.

"Yeah, but I guess if she starts with strip searches, the news folks will show up," said Dana knowingly.

Arielle noticed that the teachers seemed to take extra time going though Osrick Wardley's things, even though the pile in front of him seemed to contain only his dirty Kleenex and scribbled math equations on sticky notes.

They did the same with Eddie Mahoney, who had a smirk on his face through the whole process. He even emptied out his jeans pockets. All he had was Spoon's zip drive and what looked like, from Arielle's vantage point across the room, a handful of change.

All of a sudden Miss Pringle shouted out, "I found it!" She had been digging in the garbage can next to the table where Osrick had been sitting. Her hand was covered with ketchup and mustard, but in it she held a slightly soiled leather wallet.

Mrs. Sherman sighed with relief as she took it.

"Is all your stuff in there?" Mr. Tambori asked.

"Driver's license. Credit cards. All there," Mrs. Sherman said as she thumbed through her wallet. "But my money's gone," she reported. "I had about twenty dollars in there. I don't carry a lot of cash."

She picked up the megaphone and announced, "We have an all clear, students. The wallet has been found.

My valuables are intact, although the cash is gone." She paused. "This has been very difficult for me, as I know it has been for you. I apologize to all the honest students, I appreciate your cooperation, and I grieve for the student who needs some serious help. We've got to stop this! If anyone saw anything, or knows the identity of the thief, please don't hesitate to contact me."

She made the same announcement twice more before school let out—once on the public address system, and again through the closed-circuit television system.

But no one seemed to know anything.

Or no one was willing to tell.

KOFI SAT IN DR. STINSON'S OFFICE, TAPPING his feet nervously. He flipped through a few pages of a men's health magazine, tossed it aside, then picked it up again.

What is taking this dude so long? he thought, checking his watch for the fifteenth time.

"Kofi Freeman?" a nurse finally called from a doorway.

Kofi jumped up. "That's me! I'm here."

"Great," the nurse said, looking as if she boiled teenagers in her basement. "The doctor will see you now."

It was another fifteen minutes before the doctor finally sauntered into the examining room. Kofi had looked through every drawer and cabinet in the little room, trying to kill time. He figured if he ever ran short of cotton balls, he'd know who to rob.

Dr. Stinson, a tall, brown-skinned, broad-shouldered

man, entered the room with an air of authority. He wore his graying beard neatly trimmed. It made him look distinguished, Kofi thought. "How's it going, young man?" he asked as he checked the chart.

"My head hurts," said Kofi right away. "All the time. It keeps me awake at night, and I can't concentrate at school."

"Hmm," the doctor replied. "I thought it was your arm that was broken last year."

"Oh, that hurts, too!" Kofi added quickly. He rubbed his arm for effect.

Dr. Stinson took Kofi's pulse and temperature, then carefully examined Kofi's injured arm. "How are your grades?"

"Well, pretty good, most of the time. I just got accepted into MIT," Kofi told him.

"Good job! Proud of you, son," the doctor said, clearly impressed.

"But I'm having trouble concentrating," Kofi admitted.

"Because of the pain?" asked Dr. Stinson.

"Uh, yeah, I guess."

"I see."

Doctors always said that, Kofi thought, but did they *really* see?

After listening to Kofi's heart with his stethoscope, Dr. Stinson looked pleased. "I hear no murmurs at all. That happens sometimes with maturation," he explained. "Your heart rhythm sounds great today."

Kofi smiled. "That's 'cause my girl Dana isn't in the house! She rocks me, you know what I'm sayin'?"

The doctor smiled. "Ah, yes! I remember when a sweet young thing could rock my world and make my heart do flip-flops!"

"Back in the day?"

"Not so long ago. You'd be surprised." He continued his examination. "Any other symptoms? Fever? Rashes?"

"No, not really," Kofi replied.

"What about nausea or swelling?" The doctor was checking his eyes with a tiny flashlight. "And does anything seem to trigger the headaches?"

"Stress, I guess. I got a lot on my mind these days," Kofi answered slowly.

"Anything else?" asked the doctor.

Kofi wasn't sure what the doctor was thinking. So he just said, "Uh, noise, maybe." He thought about Crazy Jack and the pounding in his head that always followed Jack's adventures in the hall. That, at least, was very real.

"I'm ordering another set of X-rays on that arm, son," Dr. Stinson said. "Let's see if we can get to the source of your pain and get rid of it. Your arm should be fully healed by now, and you should not be in any pain at all."

"Okay, that's cool, but, uh, my prescription has run out," Kofi said as nonchalantly as he could.

"I'll give you one more refill, but this'll be the last one. You shouldn't need these anymore," the doctor said firmly. He scribbled the magic words on the small white square and handed it to Kofi, who stuffed it into his jeans pocket right away. Then Dr. Stinson gave him another sheet. "Take this to the lab to get the X-rays. I'll call you with the results as soon as they come in."

"Thanks, Doctor S. I'll get right on this." Kofi slid off the examining table with a smile on his face.

The doctor, however, did not smile. "This is your last refill, Mr. Freeman. I don't want you getting hooked."

"Aw, you don't have to worry about me, Doc," Kofi said as he pulled his shirt over his head. "I got everything under control!"

But the way the doctor was looking at him made him uneasy . . . as if he didn't quite believe Kofi truly did have everything under control.

Kofi bounded out of the office, stopped by the drugstore, got the prescription filled, and swallowed one of the little white pills before he even left the store. *Gotta make these babies last,* he reminded himself.

He still managed to get to his job at McDonald's on time. He hated the smell of the skimpy brown burgers, the sight of piles of pickles and onions, and the artificial glop of milkshake as it fell into the paper cups from the dispenser. The place was always full of screaming kids and tired parents.

"I ordered this cheeseburger without cheese!" one lady shouted at him.

"Yes, ma'am," he said as he tossed the perfectly good burger into the trash. "One hamburger coming right up."

"I do NOT want a hamburger, young man! Can't you hear? I want a cheeseburger without cheese!"

"Yes, ma'am," Kofi replied with a large, fake smile. "One cheeseburger without cheese, coming right up." He typed "hamburger" into the machine.

"My son says his fries taste funny," another lady complained. "I want a refund."

"No problem, ma'am," Kofi told her cheerfully as he returned her money. What he wanted to say was, *If your kid hadn't poured syrup all over them, they wouldn't taste like that!* But he didn't.

I gotta get a better job quick, Kofi thought, *before I toss one of these kids into the french fry grease!* But he knew that no after-school job was going to be enough to pay for a school like MIT. He needed big money and soon.

When he got off at ten, his head throbbed and he was starving. Even though he'd been surrounded by food, he hadn't eaten a thing. He stopped by Skyline Chili, where the sauce was thick, the pasta was buttery, and the cheese was real. He ordered a five-way with everything, including onions. *I can't really afford this, but man, I'm starved!*

He sat inside, sipped on a Coke, and munched on the food. He started to take another pill, then reminded himself that this was the last refill, and tossed the bottle back into his backpack. *I can handle this,* he thought. *No sweat.*

He opened his cell phone and hit number one on his speed dial. "What's up, my sweet?" he said smoothly when Dana picked up.

"Nothin' happenin'. Doing homework. Where are you— eating at the competition again?"

"Nobody can compete with Cincinnati's most famous chili place, babe! I bet they serve Skyline in heaven!"

"And all the angels probably have onion breath!" she joked.

"I'd like to share some of my onion breath with you."

"You turn me on even when you're being disgusting!" Dana replied softly.

"For real, girl. You know you're my only."

"I know. I better be." She laughed. "You always know just what to say to me."

"That's 'cause *you* turn *me* on, just by the sound of your voice."

"What can I say—I got the power!" she said.

"You got more than that!" he told her.

"Hey, didn't you go to the doctor today?"

"Yeah, I went."

"He didn't give you any more of those pills, did he?"

"Nope. I'm clean," Kofi lied.

"What did he say about your arm?"

"He said I'm Superman, and I got arms of steel."

"Well fly on over here, put those steel arms around me, and kiss me good night."

"Wish I could, sweet thing, but I gotta fly home. I still got homework to do. Besides, your mama would kill me if I came over this late."

"I can handle my mother. But can you handle *me*?" she asked, her voice deep and inviting.

"Ooh, girl! You're one hot mama!" Kofi breathed into the phone.

"I gotta go, Kofi, before we burn up the phone," she said. "I can't wait to see you tomorrow. Love you."

"Love you back." He closed the cell phone and smiled. Dana made his screwed-up life make sense. Without her, he didn't think he'd make it to graduation, maybe not even to the end of the week. Sometimes it scared him, how much he needed her.

When he opened the front door, he was surprised to see his mother at home, acting like a real mom. She had cooked dinner—it smelled like chicken with onions, his favorite—washed the dishes, and swept the kitchen floor. Her eyes looked bright and clear, and they reminded him of times when she always looked like that, when she went tromping through the woods helping him find buckeyes for a school project on Ohio. When they'd made a red-green-blue-purple mess of the kitchen table and floor when they dyed Easter eggs one spring. The times before she lost her job . . . two babies to miscarriages . . . the times before the liquor bottles started piling up.

"Hey there, Kofi," his mother called out, bringing him back to the present.

"Hey, Ma," he said as he tossed his book bag into the closet. "Something smells good." He kissed her on the cheek and sniffed. All he smelled was Shalimar cologne, her favorite. He sighed with relief and surprise.

"I fixed dinner for you," she said, a hint of annoyance in her voice. "But it's cold now."

"You never cook, Ma. How would I know you had food waiting for me?" he replied as he grabbed her and gave her a hug. "But I really appreciate it—honest. I'll take it to school for lunch tomorrow. Kids at school will be jealous 'cause I have a home-cooked meal!"

That made her smile. "I wanted to celebrate your college acceptance. I really am proud of you, you know."

Kofi blinked. "I told you about that almost two weeks ago," he said, trying to be patient.

"Oh. I guess you did." She checked her nail polish. "Well, you know how busy I've been," she replied. "I can't believe you'll be leaving us to go off to college in just a few months!"

Kofi shook his head. He truly didn't know how his parents were going to manage without him.

"I have to mail the letter back to MIT real soon, Ma, to let them know whether I'm gonna show up in the fall. But . . . well . . . I'm not sure how to answer it."

"Why? They should be proud to have my sweet, smart son showing the rest of the kids how it's done!" His mother reached out and touched him on his cheek, like she used to when he was a little boy.

Kofi jerked back. "Ma! How are we gonna pay for it?" he said, exasperated. "Have you thought about that for even one minute?"

"Yes, actually, I have."

Kofi looked at her, stunned. "For real?"

"Have you already applied for the scholarship that's given through the post office for children of employees?" she asked.

"Yep. Filled out the application online and sent it a couple of months ago."

"My boy, you're really on the ball," his mother replied admiringly. "And what about the McDonald's scholarship for students who work there after school?"

"Yeah, I applied, but there's, like, a million kids on that list. It's a long shot."

"Did you check with your guidance counselors? I bet they'd know about other available scholarships," his mother said hopefully. "Don't smart kids get to go to school for free?"

"Not anymore," Kofi told her ruefully. "I've applied for several grants and loans, Ma. But I don't know if I got any of them, and even if by some magic they come through, it still won't be enough."

"We'd better speak to your father when he comes home. I'm sure he'll have some suggestions."

"Like rob a bank?" Kofi said sarcastically.

"Kofi!" His mother scowled. "Your dad can be very resourceful. And who knows? He might just win the lottery between now and the time you start packing your bags."

"Are you *serious*?" Kofi stared at her.

"Hoo-boy! I need a drink." She went to the cupboard to find a clean glass.

Kofi slumped into a chair, knowing serious conversation with her would disappear into that glass of brandy. "Ma, should I mail the acceptance letter, or just go to one of the community colleges here?" He dreaded her response.

"Mail the letter, Kofi," she said. "Tell them you proudly accept their invitation to enroll in their fine institution."

"And the money?"

"We'll find it somehow. Have faith, son. Now get to bed—you have to be up early for school." She poured three inches of brandy into a wineglass and took a sip.

Kofi trudged upstairs to his room and quickly finished his homework. As he brushed his teeth, he heard his cell phone ring—he'd downloaded a really cool ring tone last month.

"What's up, man?" said Jericho when Kofi flipped open the phone.

"Nothin' happenin'," Kofi replied. "Just talking to my ma about all the college stuff."

"How's it look?"

"Pretty grim right now. I live on the Cartoon Network, man. Except the 'toons got more sense than my folks do sometimes."

"Do they know you got accepted to MIT?"

"Yeah, but I may as well have been accepted to college on the moon. I don't know how I'll get there, or how I'll pay for it."

"You can't turn down MIT, dude."

Kofi flopped on his bed. "I haven't mailed the letter back yet—I'm still hoping for a miracle. That's what my father's praying for."

"I feel ya."

"What about you? Did you ever get that Juilliard audition rescheduled?" Jericho had missed his chance to try out for a spot at the prestigious school when he chose to go to the initiation activities of the Warriors of Distinction instead. "I know your dad was pissed at you for blowin' that off."

Kofi heard Jericho sigh. "Yeah, lookin' back, it was pretty stupid, missing that shot, you know. So I called the man and he let me have a private audition a couple of weeks ago."

"That's cool. How'd you do?"

"Do you even have to ask?" Jericho replied with a laugh. "I played my trumpet so sweet and so good they wanted to change the name of the school to Jericho University!"

"You crazy, dude. So is that where you're going in the fall?"

"Well, I also had a football scout from Michigan State come talk to me."

"Shut up!"

"He's offerin' me a full ride—books and everything," said Jericho.

"Man! You think it's too late for me to learn to play the drums or get good at ping-pong or something?"

Jericho laughed. "You got straight As, Kofi. That ought to get you something. And I've seen you play ping-pong, so forget that one!"

"So what are you gonna do? Which one are you gonna take?"

"I don't know yet, man. I applied to a couple of other schools too. Olivia says go with my heart and trust my gut, but I don't know what that is. I just don't know."

Kofi was quiet for a moment. "Funny. Dana tells me the same thing. Holler back tomorrow, man. Peace out." He shut the phone.

Kofi lay restlessly on the bed, thinking about his parents. He knew he'd have a hard time falling asleep. The prescription bottle in his pocket started calling out to him. *Boy, if I don't get out of this house soon, I'll end up just like them.*

ARIELLE PADDED DOWN THE HALL IN HER bare feet to shower and brush her teeth before bed. She loved the feel of the thick, cushioned carpet between her toes.

I'm beat, she thought, stretching her arms above her head. *I could sleep for a year.* She yawned.

Like a bad dream, Chad came out of the bathroom, startling her. He wore a lush black silk bathrobe with matching slippers. "Did you finish your homework?" he asked her.

"Yes. All of it." She hoped his interrogation would be brief.

"Dinner dishes washed and put away?"

"Yes."

"Kitchen floor swept?"

"Yes." Chad employed a maid service that came in twice a week, but she couldn't figure out why. It seemed like he made her do all the cleaning before they even got there.

"You have exactly three minutes in the shower," he said, glancing at his watch. "The water bill was a little high last month."

"I know," she said with resignation. She started to ask him how long *he'd* taken in the shower, but she didn't want to get into another confrontation.

"You are so wasteful. I left you a bar of soap from one of my hotel trips and a half inch of toothpaste on your brush."

Arielle hated that hotel soap—it was harsh, didn't lather, smelled like perfumed medicine, and made her skin dry and itchy. Plus, it was so small it barely filled the palm of her hand.

But all she said was, "Thanks, Chad. Good night."

She closed and locked the bathroom door and leaned against the cool yellow tiles. Egyptian cotton towels and rugs the color of buttercups decorated the room. But like all the other rooms in the house, it seemed to Arielle to be just another pretty prison.

She stayed in the shower a full ten minutes, just to spite Chad, and took her time drying off and putting on her pajamas and robe. The bathroom, warm and steamy, was a pleasant respite from the rest of the house, which Chad kept on the chilly side. She unlocked the door and headed to her room.

The door of the bedroom her mother shared with Chad was slightly ajar, and she could hear their animated, agitated conversation. She knew she shouldn't listen, but, well, they should have shut the door if they didn't want her to hear, she reasoned.

"Don't tell me how to run my business or my house-hold!" she could hear Chad saying.

"I don't care how you treat your clients, but this is our *family*, Chad."

"Even a family needs structure, Michelle."

"But . . . somehow it feels like . . . you're using a ham-mer instead of a hug to control things," her mother said hesitantly.

"Hugs are a waste of time." Chad's voice was gruff.

"Not to me." Her mother was silent for a moment.

Arielle tiptoed closer to the door.

Chad said suddenly, "You should have met my father."

"You hardly talk about your dad."

"Army general. Tough. Hard. Proud. I felt his iron fist many nights." Chad's voice sounded tight and tense.

I bet his dad was a real piece of work! Arielle thought, shaking her head.

"That must have been rough for you as a kid," Michelle said gently. "But surely he had a soft side too."

Yeah, right—Chad the huggable baby. Hah!

"Heroes don't hug."

"Daddies do."

Good one, Mom!

"Perhaps. But fathers do not."

"Oh Chad, in some ways I feel sorry for both of you."

"I don't need your sympathy, Michelle."

Then her mother asked, "Do you think Arielle is as strong as you were as a child?"

Arielle leaned forward to hear better.

"Arielle? She's a puff of smoke."

So that's what he thinks of me? Not that she was surprised, but it still hurt to hear him talk about her like that.

"If that's true, do you think maybe you're too hard on her?"

Good lookin' out, Mom!

"She needs discipline."

"Give her a chance, Chad. She's just a kid."

Thanks, Mom.

"By the time I was her age, I had a straight A average and I'd been accepted at West Point."

"She's not you."

"Look, I don't ask for much—just do things my way."

Of course! Because your way is the only way! What a narrow-minded piece of scum. . . .

"I know, but—"

Don't cave in, Mom. Stand up for me!

"Aren't you happy here?" Chad interrupted her.

"It's lovely. I love this house, the roses in the yard, the furniture, the paintings, even the plates and glasses. Every time I come in the front door, I take a deep breath and smile with pleasure."

Me too, but I'd never admit that to him.

"Doesn't all that make you happy?" asked Chad.

"I can't hug the carpet, Chad. It's people who make happiness, not furniture."

Another good one, Mom!

"I've never been one to show emotions, Michelle. You knew that when you married me. I've given you all I can. If that's not enough, then . . . then . . . maybe it's time to move on."

What? Uh-oh! But maybe this is a good thing.

Her mother exhaled loudly. "Are *we* happy, Chad? When's the last time we went out and did something just for fun?"

"The office Christmas party," Chad replied.

"That wasn't fun—that was a required appearance."

"You looked drop-dead gorgeous that night." Chad's voice went low.

"Thanks, but what was I—just another holiday decoration?"

Mom sounds sad, Arielle thought.

"Michelle, what do you want from me? I've given you and Arielle so much."

"And we appreciate it, Chad."

"It can all go away, you know."

"Is that a threat?" her mother asked.

I woulda asked the same thing.

"I need to get some sleep," Chad said, his voice dismissive and final. "I have to be at the gym at six. Turn off the light, Michelle. We'll discuss this more at a later time."

"Should I make an appointment?"

Good final jab, Mom.

"I'll ignore that. Go to sleep."

Arielle tiptoed back to her room, but it was a long, long time before she fell asleep.

"QUIT HOGGIN' ALL THE PIZZA!" DANA SAID with a laugh, grabbing the warm, greasy slice from Kofi.

"Girl, don't be messing with me and my food!" he said, snatching it back.

"You had six pieces!" she cried out, pulling it away from him while he was in mid-bite.

"Don't you want me big and strong so I can protect you from monsters and dragons and stuff?"

"I might need protection from your dragon breath!" she teased, holding her nose. "That garlic is kickin'!"

He leaned over and breathed heavily in her face. "All to keep you under my spell, my princess!"

"You're wack, Kofi." She snuggled closer to him on the sofa.

"Seriously, I'm glad you stopped by, Dana. You always know when I need company—or food!" He grinned.

"Where's your mom?" Dana asked.

"Who knows? Thursday is ladies' night at lots of the clubs, and she gets in free. She'll probably hit several of them before she drags in here." He picked up a frayed sofa pillow and punched it.

"And your dad?"

"He's at work, I think. He's been taking late shifts at the post office. I gotta admit—he seems to be trying."

"I like your dad," Dana said.

"You do?"

"Sure. He looks like you—only a little grayer and fuzzier. And he's got a great sense of humor. He cracks me up with his corny jokes."

"Yep, that's my pop. Always ready with a funny line and a tip on which horse is sure to win at Turfway." Kofi sighed.

"Does he still spend a lot of time at the track?"

"There, and at the casinos. Time and money," said Kofi. "Way too much of both. Every credit card we have is charged up to the max, plus he has several of those payday check-cashing loans to pay back."

"Does he ever win?"

"Sometimes. He comes in whooping about how he won a thousand dollars at the slots. But he forgets that he lost two thousand trying to do it." He took a bite of the slice Dana held out to him.

"Just think, in a few months you'll be far away from all of this," Dana reminded him.

"But what's going to happen to them if I leave? They'll end up evicted in no time."

"You're the kid, *not* the parent here, Kofi!" she told him

sternly. "It's *not* your responsibility to take care of them! They're adults!"

"If I go off to college, I'll probably come home and find them living in a cardboard box downtown."

"Well, if they are, you just stop by the box and say hello, kiss them both on the cheek, then leave them there! You're not responsible for what your parents do . . . or don't do."

Kofi looked up at the cracked ceiling. "I guess you're right," he admitted.

"I know I am."

Sitting on the worn, lumpy sofa with Dana, listening to the rain outside, made Kofi feel better than he had in a while.

"My parents love me, you know," he said finally.

"Of course they do."

"Maybe I'm having second thoughts," he said, rubbing the fuzz on his chin. "It wouldn't hurt for me to stay home for a couple of semesters and keep an eye on them. Maybe I can get a better job, a full-time job, and save more money for school."

"Kofi Freeman! If you give up on MIT, I will break up with you—no lie!" she warned.

"You wouldn't!" he said, checking her face to see if she was serious.

"No more of these sweet, juicy kisses. No more hugs on this hot, sexy body!" Her words were teasing, yet her tone was not.

"I couldn't handle that. I'd go flush myself down the toilet!" He leaned over to kiss her, putting his hands around her waist.

She pulled back, however. "I'm dead serious, Kofi."

Then she looked thoughtful. "Have you checked your mail today?"

"It's raining, girl. Gimme some of them lips."

"No. That letter might have come from the McDonald's scholarship folks. Go check your mail."

"You cold, Dana."

"Mailbox first. Dana body next." She folded her arms across her chest and grinned at him.

"Do you know how many teenagers work for McDonald's?"

"Thousands, I'm sure."

"And how many do you think applied for that scholarship money?"

"Lots."

"So what makes you think I have a shot at it?"

"Because you're cuter than the rest of them! Now go check the mail!"

He pulled his long body up from the couch, stretched, and gazed at his saucy girlfriend. *I'm the luckiest dude in the world,* he thought.

"Why are you cheesin' like that?" she asked.

"Just thinkin' about you and me."

She smiled. "I can't wait for prom," she said. "I already bought my dress. It's white and slinky and cut down to here, and up to there," she said, pointing to her upper thigh.

"Aw, man! I'm gonna need a million dollars just to graduate!" He slapped his forehead.

"I don't need a limo or a fancy dinner for prom. Just you. Only you."

"Girl, you the bomb!"

"Go check the mail, silly."

Kofi shivered as he ran out to the edge of the porch, where the mailbox hung by one rusty nail. He lifted the lid and pulled out a handful of damp envelopes. He did not look at them. Instead he saw the sagging wooden porch beams, the blistered, peeling, faded blue paint, and the door that barely closed on rainy days like this one. It looked like crap.

"Anything good?" Dana asked as she took the pizza box to the kitchen.

He ripped open the first one. "Well, it looks like we have three days to pay the electric bill, or they cut off the power."

"Can you pay it?" she asked.

"The folks at the electric company billing office downtown office know me by now. I'll give them a little something when I get paid tomorrow and work out a payment plan—another one."

"You sure got a handle on that one," Dana told him.

He shrugged. "I figure it out as I go." He opened another envelope. "Here's an offer for a credit card for my dad. Are these people stupid?"

"We get those things at our house all the time too. Don't they check credit records or stuff like that?" Dana asked him.

"I think they just get names out of the phone book." Kofi ripped the letter into little pieces. "They should send me a medal and thank me for saving them the trouble of chasing down my father every month for their money!"

Then he paused at the next envelope. The return address simply had those familiar golden arches in the upper left-hand corner.

Dana looked over his shoulder. "Didn't I tell you?" she said excitedly.

Kofi grinned, put down the rest of the mail, and ripped open the envelope. His heart beat fast as he hurriedly unfolded the letter. "Oh, Dana!"

"Read it! Read it!"

Kofi read the first paragraph. "'Dear Mr. Freeman: The McDonald's National Employee Scholarship Program is one of many examples of McDonald's commitment to employee development and recognition. The program recognizes and rewards the accomplishments of McDonald's student-employees who excel in their studies, serve their communities, and work hard to deliver an outstanding experience for our customers.'"

"We knew all that already," said Dana. "Get to the good part!"

Kofi's face fell as he read the next paragraph. "'Although we admire your dedication to your studies and excellence as an employee, we regret to inform you that your application was not chosen as a winner this year.'" He tossed the letter and the rest of the mail on the coffee table.

"Well, that sucks," Dana said, dropping back onto the sofa.

"I told you. It was a million-to-one chance."

"You applied for other grants and stuff, didn't you?"

"Yeah. But all of them have hundreds of kids like me with their hands out for help."

"Don't give up hope, Kofi. I believe in miracles," Dana told him.

"You sound like my mother," he replied glumly.

But Dana picked up the rest of the mail and proceeded to go through it. "What's this one, Kofi?" she asked, sliding an envelope from the bottom of the ads for home-goods and hardware stores. She passed it to him.

Written on thick, cream-colored stationery, the letter was addressed to Mr. Kofi Freeman. He rubbed his fingers across his name.

"Who's it from?" she asked.

"The Freedom Achievers Association in Washington, DC."

She inhaled. "Is that the group that picks one student from each state?"

"Yes," he whispered.

"Just fifty kids from the entire United States who will get a full ride to the college of their choice?"

"Yeah," he whispered. He held the letter like it was breakable.

"When did you apply?"

"I guess I filled out the application last year. Actually, I forgot I even sent it in."

"So open it!" she implored.

"I'm afraid to read it," he admitted.

"I have a feeling this is good news," she said softly.

"McDonald's just blew me off," he reminded her.

"What does McDonald's know?" Dana urged him again, "Open it!"

"Nah, one disappointment a day is about all I can handle."

"Kofi, open it! Or I will."

"Chill, woman." He slid his finger under the flap and

pulled out a sheet of the thickest stationery he'd ever seen. His hands shook.

"Kofi?" she whispered. "Read it to me."

He cleared his throat. "'Dear Mr. Freeman.'" He looked up at Dana. "See, it's just like the other one. There's no point—"

Dana bopped Kofi in the head with a sofa pillow. "Tell me what it says!"

Slowly, Kofi continued. "'It is with great pleasure that we inform you that you have been selected as the Freedom Achiever Scholarship Award recipient for the state of Ohio.'"

He could barely breathe.

"Keep reading!" Dana insisted.

"I'm reading! I'm reading! 'Only one student from each state is chosen for this prestigious honor. This award will provide full tuition, as well as room and board and books, to the college or university of your choice. If you maintain a 3.5 average in your college studies, the award will be renewed for up to four years.'"

Dana pounced on Kofi, causing both of to them fall off the couch. "Oh my God! Kofi, you did it! You did it! They're going to pay for everything! It's gonna happen!"

Kofi sat on the floor and finished reading the letter, which talked about the necessity of high grades for the rest of the senior year, an awards ceremony in Washington, DC, and tons of paperwork to be filled out in the next few weeks.

He gulped, then gasped. Then he hollered "Whoopee!" and leaped onto the battered sofa and started jumping up and down like a little kid. He grabbed Dana's hand and pulled her up next to him, and the two of them jumped and bounced like jelly beans and hugged and kissed and jumped some more.

"I'm goin' to MIT!" he said, dumbfounded.

"I'm so proud of you I could just scream!" she replied.

"So scream, baby! There's nobody home but you and me."

She shrieked. She screeched. She hugged him again. Gasping and out of breath, they flopped back down on the sofa.

"We oughta call Natasha Singletary, that reporter on Channel Five who wears too much lip gloss!" Dana suggested with enthusiasm.

"Why would she care? And who notices lip gloss?"

"Me and my girls in the fashion police," she told him with a laugh. "But your scholarship is big news, Kofi! The only award given in the whole state? Everybody in town ought to know!"

"Naw, no reporters. It's enough you're proud of me," Kofi told her.

"Well, okay—if you say so. But read it again!" she said. "I want to hear every beautiful word one more time."

Relaxed and grinning this time, Kofi started to read the letter once more.

"Dear Mr. Freeman," he began, trying to make his voice sound deep and dignified. "It is with great pleasure—"

"Kofi, what's this?" Dana asked, interrupting him.

The mood of the room changed as quickly as a summer storm changes the day from sunshine to thunder clouds.

Dana held a small amber container with the childproof white cap.

"Uh, nothing." He hadn't even noticed that the bottle had flipped out of his pants pocket. He tried to grab it back from her, but she angrily held it away from him.

"You told me you quit." Her voice was dangerous.

"I did!"

"These are half gone and . . ." She paused and looked at the date on the label. "This was just filled last week!" Her words were like sharp knives.

"I spilled some."

"You LIE!"

"I don't really need them," he told her, looking down at the floor.

She turned to him, lifted his chin with her fingertips, and looked him directly in the eye. "You are about to screw up the rest of your life!" she growled.

"I know," he said, his voice quiet.

"You just got a free ticket to the Superbowl and you're peeing on it!"

"Dana, I don't *want* to take them, but I can't help it," he protested. "It's not my fault."

"That's the dumbest thing I've ever heard in my life." She looked at him again—this time with a frown.

"It's just that my parents are *so* hard to deal with."

She poked him hard in the chest. "Don't you *dare* blame this on your parents! Do they beat you with a stick and force those pills down your throat? I love you, Kofi. But if you don't get control of this, *you* will end up living with your parents in that cardboard box! Is that

141

what you want?" He had never seen her so angry.

"I'm not going to be able to get any more meds anyway," he told her. "Dr. Stinson told me no more refills. He figured out I was using them as a crutch. He's no dummy."

"Neither am I," Dana said. She took Kofi's hand and pulled him to her. He tried to kiss her, but she turned her head. Instead she walked him over to the kitchen sink.

"We gonna wash dishes?" he asked with a small smile.

"Nope."

"We gonna fix the leaky faucet?"

"Guess again."

"We're gonna put my pills down the garbage disposal?"

"Nope. *You* are." She handed him the bottle, put her hands on her hips, and waited.

Kofi hesitated for only a moment. Then he opened the container, dumped the pills into the drain, turned on the cold water, and flipped the switch for the disposal.

Kreak-a-kreak-a whirr. The drain gargled and chewed, then spun clear and silent. Kofi flipped the switch to the off position.

"You got any more hidden in your jeans or your book bag?" asked Dana.

Kofi started to say no. He *wanted* to say no. But he couldn't lie to Dana again. He went up to his room and found four more pills that he had hidden in a bedroom drawer. "I swear this is all of them. I swear," he told her as they churned those up as well.

"I believe you," she said. This time she let him kiss her with all the pain and passion he felt.

ARIELLE, DRESSED IN A DARK BLUE BLAZER, gazed out the window at the end of the hallway at the rapidly melting snow as she waited with the other students for Miss Pringle to show up. The store where Arielle worked after school was having a March Madness clothing sale, and she knew she'd end up mopping all the March footprints off the floor before she got to go home tonight. She sighed.

Where was that woman? Probably at the cafeteria getting another cup of coffee to fill her ever-present mug.

Kids sat on the floor or leaned on a wall, checking their watches and deciding, Arielle knew, whether to skip class or not. Room 317 was unlocked, but only a few kids had bothered to go in.

Eddie Mahoney, who had ended up in this class as well, sat waiting alone at the other end of the hall. Drumming two pencils on the floor, he challenged everyone with his eyes.

Arielle thought he always looked as if he was up to something. Nothing specific, but he threw off all kinds of bad vibes. If he'd been a painting, she would have drawn him in shades of deep purple and indigo.

She shivered. Even though March had arrived, it still got really cold at night, but Chad had turned off the heat in the house. "No need for heat. It's almost spring," he'd announced last night. Arielle slept in a sweatshirt over her pajamas, and she still hadn't warmed up.

Lost in thought, she was surprised to notice Osrick standing next to her. He looked scared.

"Uh, can I ask you something, Arielle?" he began, his voice high and thin.

"Sure, Osrick. What's up?" She still wasn't sure whether she felt more sorry for him, or suspicious of him.

"Did you ever find your iPhone?"

Arielle tilted her head sideways. "No, I didn't. Do you have any idea what happened to it?"

"I know you think I took it, but I didn't," he told her.

"I never said that," she said.

"I know, but everyone else does. And I've seen how you watch me."

Arielle didn't know what to say. She couldn't deny it. "I, uh—"

Osrick interrupted her. "I've never stolen anything in my life. But even if I had, I'd never touch that model iPhone. It's flawed. I've examined the specs." He spoke with an authority that erased their mutual embarrassment.

She believed him, and she was glad about it. "Now you're sounding more like the Wizard of Osrick we all know," she said with real relief.

"Well, that's one of the nicer things they call me," he told her. His braces gleamed in the sunlight. "You buy like the usual consumer—because it's pretty. Apple will improve the defects in future versions of the device."

"I thought it was pretty cool for the short time I had it."

"When they fix the glitches, maybe then I'll buy one. I have money, you know."

"I'm sure you do," said Arielle, still not sure where Osrick was headed. "So what does this have to do with my phone getting stolen?"

He looked around carefully to make sure no one else could hear him. "I think I know who took it, and the other stuff that's been disappearing as well," he whispered.

Arielle looked surprised. "Who?" she asked.

"People treat me like I'm invisible, so I notice things," Osrick said with a shrug.

Miss Pringle hurried up the steps then, balancing coffee, grade book, and papers. Osrick abruptly stopped talking.

"Who unlocked this?" Miss Pringle demanded, seeing her classroom door standing ajar.

"The custodian," Kofi told her.

She frowned and indicated that the students should enter the classroom. They filed in slowly.

As Arielle picked up her book bag, pondering what Osrick had said, November, Dana, and Olivia walked over to her.

"What was little Osrick sayin'? Tryin' to get a date for the prom?" Dana teased her.

"No, leave him alone. He's okay. None of us have ever tried to talk to him or get to know him."

"Yeah, it must really suck to be Osrick," November mused.

Arielle started to tell them what Osrick had hinted about the thefts, but just then Brandon Merriweather sauntered over to her. November and Dana stepped back and watched with raised eyebrows.

"Hey, Lollipop," he called out, using the nickname he'd made up for her when they were together.

"Hey, yourself," she replied.

"You look kissable today, but then you look like that every day!"

Arielle gave him a look. "Wow, you don't waste any time!" she said. "You haven't talked to me in months, and all of a sudden I'm kissable?"

November and Dana giggled. Brandon ignored them.

"I've missed you, Lollipop," he replied.

"Coulda fooled me. It's been a while."

"I tried to call you, but your cell phone doesn't answer."

"It's a wonder your sweet Nikki didn't delete my number out of your phone," Arielle said.

"Nikki is bad news and very old news. Trust me."

I wonder what's up with this. Is he for real? Still, she told him, "My phone got stolen, and my stepfather canceled the service."

"Bummer about the phone. Who pinched it?"

"How am I supposed to know?" she replied, frustration creeping into her voice. "The school thief, I guess. Me and a bunch of other kids have been ripped off—everyone knows that."

"I tried to call your landline, too. All I get at your house is a recording that says, 'This phone line is temporarily unavailable.'"

"Long story. Wicked stepfather," she replied tersely. "I'm on punishment—for the next hundred years, I think."

"It couldn't be that bad," said Brandon as they walked into the classroom.

"Yeah, it could," Arielle replied, not willing to say more. "I've got a job at Smoochie's Boutique at the mall. I'm on tonight. Stop by if you want to talk."

"I might just do that," Brandon said, giving her the up and down. He wandered on into the classroom. Eddie followed behind him.

Arielle wasn't sure whether Eddie had overheard her conversation, but she didn't trust the look on his face, as if he was gathering information to put in a large, dirty sack to be used later to hurt people.

Dana and November cornered Arielle before she could take another step, however. "So, Brandon's back?" November asked with a sly grin.

Arielle shrugged. "Maybe. He's kinda shaky. One minute he's all up in my face, and the next minute he's drivin' somebody else in that BMW."

"Tell us if he stops by the mall tonight!" Dana said.

"Yeah, sure. I hope he does, just so I can get a ride home. I don't have bus fare."

"Won't your mom pick you up?" Olivia asked.

"My stepfather locked her car in the garage," Arielle told them.

"What! How come?"

"Somebody backed into the Mercedes in a parking lot and dented it. It cost a lot to get it fixed."

"Wasn't it insured?" Dana asked.

"Yes, but that's not the point."

"So what did he do?" asked Olivia.

"He put my *mother* on punishment!"

"Shut up!" November put her hand over her mouth.

"That's not possible, is it? Can a grown-up get put on punishment?" Olivia said, shaking her head in disbelief.

"He took away her keys!"

"But if someone backed into her, it wasn't her fault!" November insisted.

"Tell that to Chadwick Kensington O'Neil. He can do anything he wants. He's got all the power and all the money in the family. Me and my mom just live there."

"Is he as super rich as folks say he is?" Olivia asked. "I've read articles about him in the business section of the newspaper."

"Well," Arielle began, "I watched him pay cash for a Hummer he never drives, and two years ago he bought a boat that he's taken out only once—so we could see the fireworks on the river for Labor Day."

"Man!" November said. "And I thought I wanted to be rich so Sunshine could have nice things."

"You know that saying, be careful what you wish for?" said Arielle. "Well, it's true. My mother thought she'd be hot and happy forever when she married Chad. But money is cold, cold, cold."

"But why is he so hard?" Olivia wondered.

"I don't know. I try to keep out of his way."

"So what kind of punishment has he put *you* on?" Dana wanted to know. "You don't have a car for him to take away."

"He's removed all my privileges. Everything," Arielle admitted.

"Everything?" November asked.

"Everything."

"Allowance?"

"Hah!"

"Video games?"

"Packed in a box."

"CDs and DVDs?"

"Same box."

"Radio?"

"Locked away."

"Television?"

"Gone. And he told the cable company to disconnect the service."

"Laptop?"

"He took it. I have to use the computers at school to do homework assignments and research. My mother's desktop at home has been shut off as well. No Internet except on his personal computer."

Dana frowned. "This sucks, Arielle."

"Big, pretty plasma-screen TV in the living room—unplugged."

Olivia scratched her head. "He sounds like a control freak."

"Actually, he sounds a little bit like a psychopath," said November.

"Why is he doing this? What did you *do*?" Dana asked.

"I refuse to obey him, to bow down and suck up, so he punishes me. It started when I dropped a Coke on the carpet and made a little stain. Then I got a store credit card without getting permission first. But lately it's been getting crazy—almost like we're at war," Arielle explained.

"He hits you?" November asked carefully.

"I wouldn't let him get close enough to touch me," Arielle replied angrily. "But now he makes me pay for everything, even what I eat," she admitted with embarrassment.

"Huh? I don't get it," Olivia said.

"This morning I had a small container of blueberry yogurt, a banana, and a glass of orange juice for breakfast."

"Yeah, so?"

"He tallied up the cost of each item and gave me a bill for three dollars and seventeen cents."

"Shut up!"

"He subtracts the cost of my food from my Smoochie's paycheck, which I have to give him."

"That's crazy!"

"I try to eat just a little, but dinner last night cost almost twelve dollars. He decides the prices."

"Girlfriend, you have to report this to somebody!" November cried out. "This is, like, child abuse or something."

"It's not like he beats me or tries to sleep with me or something nasty like that. He's just mean," Arielle tried to explain.

"Shouldn't you tell somebody?"

"Tell what? That he put me on punishment? Every kid in school would have to get in line if that was a crime." Arielle was afraid she'd said too much already. He'd ease up eventually. He just had to.

Dana said, "You're just a prisoner in paradise, girlfriend. This is really messed up."

"Please don't tell Kofi or Jericho," Arielle pleaded.

"Okay, but you holler if you need help, you hear?"

Arielle nodded.

Just as the girls finished their conversation, Miss Pringle, who'd been going from desk to desk checking each student's homework, paused at November's desk. She looked carefully at November's papers and smiled. "Good job, November," she said. "I think you're going to do just fine."

November beamed. "I just *gotta* graduate! I still want to try to go to college."

The teacher nodded encouragingly, then stopped at Roscoe's desk and seemed to be trying to stifle a laugh. "Roscoe," she began, "your homework is certainly the prettiest I've seen all day—printed up in color ink and everything."

"Hey, I worked all night on that thing, Miss P," Roscoe asserted. "Hours and hours of hard work." He seemed to be pleased with himself.

Miss Pringle continued, "Well, perhaps you should have

deleted the author's name and website before you down-loaded it from the Internet!"

"Oops! My bad. I didn't think you'd notice," Roscoe replied with an embarrassed grin.

"That's copyright infringement. Theft of another's work. You know better than that, Roscoe," she told him.

"Can I have a do-over?" he asked.

"Just this once. But it better be all Roscoe this time!"

"Gotcha!"

As Miss Pringle finally began class, Olivia reached over and put five dollars on Arielle's desk. "Bus fare and dinner," she whispered. Arielle nodded, her eyes welling with tears.

Not even sure what words to say, she opened her mouth to thank Olivia, but just then Paula Ingram screamed out, "My Game Boy is gone! It was in my backpack this morning before school. And now it's gone!"

Miss Pringle looked up in concern. "Oh, no! Not again! Did you have it when you got to class?"

"Yes, I think so. I'm not sure," Paula said, her voice sounding frantic. "I didn't notice if it was there or not."

"When did you last see it?" asked Miss Pringle, hurrying over to where Paula sat digging fruitlessly through her book bag.

Arielle saw Paula peer over at Eddie, who looked as if he dared someone to accuse him, and at Osrick, who hid under his hood. Of course, nobody was blamed. The game player could have disappeared at any time that morning.

"For sure? Uh, this morning, down in the cafeteria."

Paula looked like she was about to cry. Or hit somebody. Arielle understood the feeling.

Miss Pringle frowned. "Go right down to Mrs. Sherman's office and report this, Paula. I'm so sorry, sweetie. The administration has got to get to the bottom of this— soon!" Paula left in tears.

When the bell finally rang for class to be dismissed, everyone gathered their belongings and checked carefully to make sure nothing else was missing. Before he zipped up his winter coat and scurried out of the room, Osrick caught Arielle's eye. He mouthed some words to her.

She wasn't sure, but he might have whispered, "I know who it is."

KOFI'S HEAD FELT AS IF IT WERE FULL OF large, jagged rocks. It throbbed to the rhythm of a dark, horrible symphony. He could feel his bones and even his muscles, and everything ached. His body felt like a broken wind-up toy, just about ready for the trash. He had almost no appetite, but he couldn't keep anything down anyway. He'd thrown up twice already that day, and when he wasn't letting it all out that way, he was sitting on the toilet with diarrhea.

But he was determined to beat the pills. In his throbby head they were a monster—one that was trying to eat him from the inside out.

I am Beowulf. I am powerful. I rule.

Then he wiped his runny nose and eyes and breathed deeply, waiting for the hot and then cold sweats to subside.

I'm pudding, and I'd kill for one little white pill, he thought helplessly.

But even though he felt like his guts might do a tap dance on the outside of his body, he was glad the pills were gone. He felt free.

He headed to Spoon's class early, hoping she had a Coke in the classroom refrigerator. All the vending machines in the building had recently been switched over to fruit juices, which pretty much everyone hated. Kofi need caffeine—lots of it—and maybe some Tylenol or Advil to quiet the storm in his head and the queasiness in his gut. Spoon kept stuff like that in her desk, he remembered, even though it was technically illegal for teachers to give a student anything stronger than a candy bar.

When he got to the door of the classroom, he heard scuffling, a male voice gravelly and demanding, and the sound of a girl crying. He paused—it sort of sounded like Dana! He tried the knob. The door was locked, and the window had been covered from the inside by a poster or something.

The male voice said, "I just want the chance to be alone with you for a minute—make you see how I've changed. Just let me talk to you—"

The girl's voice, louder now, cried out, "Leave me alone, Eddie!" Kofi heard chairs falling. Now he was sure it was Dana. Then she screamed. "Stop! Let me out of here!"

Kofi yanked on the locked doorknob and pounded on the door, adrenaline fueling his fury. "Open this door! Don't you touch her! I swear I'll kill you!"

He heard Eddie laugh. "I ain't gonna hurt her. I just wanna talk to her. How you like that, my man with the weird African name?" Kofi could hear more desks falling over.

"Kofi!" Dana screamed. "Go get help!"

Kofi didn't know what to do. He didn't want to leave Dana for a single second, but he knew he couldn't get the door open.

"I'm not gonna hurt you, baby," he heard Eddie say. "The whole time I was gone I was thinking of you. I just want you to get to know me better. I just wanna talk. Relax."

His aches and chills forgotten, Kofi raced down the hall, looking for help, but it was lunchtime—the wing was deserted.

Then Mrs. Witherspoon turned the corner, and the smile she greeted Kofi with turned to concern when she saw his face. "What's wrong, Kofi?"

"Help!" he shouted. "Spoon! Quick! Open your classroom door! Eddie. Dana. Hurry!"

Spoon hurried. She ran down the hall, whipped out her keys, and unlocked the door. Kofi almost knocked her down getting into the room.

Dana sat on the floor, hugging her knees to her chest. Her face was a mask of tears and anger.

"Are you okay?" he asked, pulling Dana to him.

She breathed a sigh of relief and let herself be folded in his arms. "He didn't hurt me. He didn't touch me. But I did manage to get in a good kick," she told Kofi triumphantly.

Eddie sat on a chair near the door, where he'd been blocking Dana's exit. He looked oddly calm. "I just wanted to talk to her," he explained. Kofi thought his voice always sounded like he was gargling marbles.

"What's going on, Eddie?" Mrs. Witherspoon asked, her voice cautious.

"Nothin' at all, Spoonie. Just a private conversation with my girl Dana."

"She is NOT your girl!" Kofi shouted. He started to get up, but Dana pulled him back.

"Don't let go of me," she whispered. Kofi held her, but his eyes shot bullets toward Eddie.

"Did he touch you, Dana?" the teacher asked carefully.

"No, ma'am. He didn't."

"I'm the one who's injured," Eddie said with a laugh. "She's a little ninja warrior!"

The teacher ignored him. "How did your blouse get torn?" she asked Dana.

"I ripped it on the edge of the bulletin board," Dana explained. "I was trying to get out of the room, and he blocked my way. He wouldn't let me leave!"

Kofi held her tighter. "I was havin' a really bad day when I got here." He spat out the words to Eddie. "And you just made it worse. It won't take *nothin'* for me to clean Spoon's floors with your face!"

Eddie laughed again. "I didn't do nothin'! I didn't put one single finger on her pretty little body. I mighta wanted to, but I didn't."

"You have no right to hold a student unwillingly in a classroom!" Mrs. Witherspoon told him.

"She coulda left any time she wanted," said Eddie. "The door wasn't locked on this side."

"That's not true!" Dana spat. "Your ugly face blocked the door!"

"What were you doing here so early?" Mrs. Witherspoon asked Dana.

"I came to ask you to read a poem I wrote," Dana said. "I guess he followed me here."

"Was the door unlocked when you got here?"

"It was standing open, so I don't really know." She was still shaking.

Eddie turned to the teacher. "Just to save you the trouble, Spoon, I'm going home early today, so we can let things calm down a little. But I'll be back tomorrow!" He strolled out the door as if he were leaving on vacation. He paused in the doorway, however, and added, "Oh, you might want to pick up those chairs. Miss Dana made a mess." Then he disappeared.

Kofi was about to explode. He knew that one day—very soon—he would have to settle with Eddie.

Mrs. Witherspoon sat down on the floor with Dana and Kofi and rocked them both in her arms. Except for Dana's angry sniffling, the room was quiet. "Do you want to go home, Dana?" the teacher asked gently.

"No, ma'am. I'm not hurt—I'm pissed! Can I say that in front of a teacher?"

"I've said worse," the teacher admitted with a slight chuckle.

"I'm not letting her out of my sight, Spoon," Kofi said. "I'll make sure she gets home safely."

The teacher took a deep breath and nodded. "I'm filing a report with the office immediately. And I'll call your mother tonight, Dana, just to make sure she understands what happened and to check that you're okay."

"What's going to happen to Eddie?" Dana asked, as she got up from the floor and brushed herself off. Kofi peeled off his sweatshirt and handed it to her to cover her torn blouse.

"I don't think Eddie belongs in a public school setting anymore," the teacher replied quietly as she started picking up the chairs. Kofi and Dana helped her.

When the bell rang for class, Spoon didn't call out jokes and greetings as she usually did. She gave everybody seatwork and a reading assignment, and never even turned on any of her computers.

Kofi seethed throughout the period, trying to figure out when and where he'd beat the crap out of Eddie Mahoney.

When class ended, he and Jericho walked Dana to her European history class. "Is Eddie in your last period?" Jericho asked Dana.

"No, he's not."

Kofi hated hearing her voice sounding so thin and nervous, not her usual bold and brazen tone.

"He said he was going home," Kofi said. "I know *I* better not see him!"

"You can't be gettin' into fights and kicked out of school," said Dana, trying to calm him. "You gotta keep your nose clean. You got MIT *and* the Freedom Achievers depending on you. Me too," she added.

"Don't worry. I'm straight. If I see him, I'm just gonna *talk*, like he said he was going to do to you," Kofi spat out.

"What do you think would have happened if you hadn't shown up?" Dana asked.

"I can't even let myself think about it," Kofi told her. "Don't leave this room until I get back, okay? I'm not leaving you alone for one second."

"I'll wait for you." She kissed him lightly on the cheek and went into the classroom.

As he and Jericho continued down the hall, Kofi suddenly felt weak and chilled, as if someone had opened a refrigerator door, then hit him with the whole icebox. He shivered. His arms were covered with goose bumps. He felt like he might throw up again. He stopped, leaned against a locker, and took several deep breaths.

"You okay, man?" Jericho asked.

"Not really. You got any Tylenol or maybe something stronger?" Kofi asked hopefully.

"Do I look like a drugstore?" said Jericho.

"How about a Coke?"

"Yeah, I got one, but it's warm—been in my bag all day."

"I don't care."

Jericho dug in his bag and pulled out the Coke, and Kofi almost snatched it from him. He wished fruitlessly for a pain pill, then swallowed the warm drink in a few gulps.

"Chill, dude," Jericho warned. "You saved her. She's fine. You're, like, the hero, man."

"I don't feel like a hero—I just feel pissed," Kofi admitted. The cold flash had subsided, but his muscles cried out for more than Coca-Cola.

"That's probably pretty normal," Jericho told him reasonably.

"What would you have done if it had been Olivia in there?" Kofi asked.

"Stomped him. Unless she had already stomped him first!" Jericho replied with a grin.

"You two gettin' pretty tight?" asked Kofi, feeling himself relax a little.

"Yeah, I guess."

"Olivia's a lot, uh, different from Arielle, who had you dancing on your tippy-toes last year," Kofi said carefully.

"You mean 'cause she's not a twig like Arielle?" Jericho's voice took on an edge.

"I ain't sayin' nothin' against her, man. I think she's cool," Kofi told him. "But Olivia doesn't look like any girl I've ever seen in one of those fashion magazines that Dana reads all the time."

Jericho slowed his walk and looked thoughtful. "I quit lookin' at the package, man. All I see is the gift inside."

"You got it *bad*, dude! She got your nose on a hook!" Kofi slapped Jericho on the shoulder and hooted with laughter.

Jericho shrugged him off. "Have you *ever* met a girl who really does look like one of those models in those mags?"

Kofi laughed. "Never! You're right about that, man! But don't tell Dana I said that," he added.

"It is what it is, man. Olivia brings out the best in me. When I'm down on myself, she knows just what to say to make me feel like I could climb a mountain."

"Dana does that too. You think girls take classes or something in how to wrap a dude up tight?" Kofi asked.

"Yeah. When they all get together at their sleepovers,

when they got their hair all up in curlers, and they smell like seventeen kinds of perfume, and their toenails are all polished all red and pretty, they sit down and discuss the secrets of the Female Power Society. They make up the rules, they always win, and we just lucky they let us sniff some of that perfume!"

"You crazy, dude."

Kofi's craving for the pills had diminished a little, but his anger at Eddie had not.

"CAN YOU FINISH HANGING UP THE NEW box of sportswear that came in, dear?" Mrs. Petrie asked Arielle. "And don't forget to attach the Smoochie's security tags to each one. Many teenagers are thieves, you know."

"Most teens never steal stuff, Mrs. Petrie," Arielle replied with a sigh. They'd had this conversation many times.

"You're one of the good ones, dear," Mrs. Petrie told Arielle as she patted her on the back. "I can't trust the others."

Arielle knew she'd never win the argument, so she just said, "Sure, Mrs. Petrie. I'll hang the shorts and tag them." Arielle glanced at the clock. It was almost eight thirty. There was no way she'd finish before closing. That meant leaving the store long after the mall closed at nine, walking through that dark parking lot by herself, and waiting for a bus that came only once an hour.

She grabbed the box from the back storeroom, pulled out the shorts and matching tops, and stacked them on the counter. Green. Red. Purple. Yellow. Some with sparkles, some with appliqués. Sizes from zero to fourteen.

"Do you have anything in Lollipop red?" a deep voice asked, jarring Arielle from her thoughts.

She looked up with pleasant surprise to the chiseled face of Brandon Merriweather. "We have anything you need," she said softly. She hoped she wasn't blushing. "Are you shopping for a friend?"

"I sure hope so," he replied. He picked up a bright red T-shirt and caressed the fabric.

"That's a nice shirt," she told him. "I like the sparkles on it."

"Then I'll buy it," he said, pulling a wallet out of his pocket.

"It's thirty-nine dollars plus tax." She thought Mrs. Petrie charged way too much for the clothes in the place, but nobody seemed to complain.

Brandon gave her a fifty-dollar bill. She took it with shaking hands and rang up the sale on the register. As she gave him his change, he grabbed her hand and held it. He opened his mouth to speak, but then Mrs. Petrie, dressed in a silky turquoise top and boot-cut jeans, emerged from the back room. Tall and willowy, she looked as if she could wear most of the teen clothes she sold, even though she had to be at least fifty, Arielle figured.

"Thanks for shopping, my dear. May I interest you in some accessories—a bracelet or some earrings?" For some

reason Mrs. Petrie seemed to look at Brandon as a cus-
tomer instead of a thief.

"No, ma'am," he answered smoothly. "But I'll be back.
I like everything in this store." He gave Arielle the briefest
of smiles, sauntered out the door, and disappeared into
the mall.

Arielle, breathless for the moment, could only stare in
amazement. *What was that all about?*

Mrs. Petrie headed back to the storeroom. "Are you
finished with that box?" she asked Arielle, even though it
was obvious that the stack on the counter had diminished
only a little.

"I'm on it, Mrs. Petrie," Arielle said, returning to the
tedious process of sorting and tagging. *Brandon Merriweather. Should I get my hopes up?*

"Way cute," another familiar voice said.

Arielle looked up, glad for another interruption. She
grinned when she saw November, and when she saw
that she had the baby with her, she ran from behind the
counter.

"Am I glad to see you!" she whispered, glancing at the
back room to make sure Mrs. Petrie was still back there.
"And welcome, little Sunshine!" Arielle knelt down in
front of the stroller. "You look so beautiful in your little
yellow outfit!"

The baby gurgled and smiled, kicking her little feet.
November smoothed the child's hair and brushed a speck
off her bib. "I needed some air, and Sunshine decided she
wanted to check out the latest fashions," she explained.

"These will be way out of style by the time she gets old

enough to wear them," Arielle said with a laugh.

"Well, maybe Sunshine's mom can sport something new. I want *nothing* that's loose and roomy at the top." Both girls cracked up. Even the baby seemed to get the joke as she cooed and reached her hands out jerkily toward Arielle.

Arielle touched the child's fingers, amazed at how tiny and soft they felt. Looking closer at the baby's face, Arielle noticed that one eye seemed to be slightly turned in.

As she stood up, she asked awkwardly, "How's Sunshine doing—her, uh, health problems?"

"Well, at six months old she should be sitting up and turning over. She's not—yet. The doctor tries to warn me that she might have trouble walking or talking, but I have to believe she'll be just fine."

"And if she isn't?" Arielle was almost afraid to ask.

"I'll deal with it," November replied briskly. She picked up a pair of shorts and checked out the stitching.

"I really admire you, November," Arielle told her. "You've got everything so under control."

November touched little Sunshine's face and sighed. "You don't see me when it's three in the morning and she's screaming her head off, or when I'm so tired I can't stop crying myself. You don't see the stacks of poopy diapers, or the baby vomit all over my new T-shirt. All you see is the baby in the stroller my mother bought, dressed in a cute little outfit that Olivia got for her."

"I guess I never thought about it like that," Arielle admitted, picking up another pair of shorts and sticking a security tag on them. "You make it seem so easy."

"Ha!" November retorted. The baby jumped at the noise, and Mrs. Petrie peeked around the corner.

"My boss doesn't like it when friends hang out here, so pretend you're shopping if she comes out here," whispered Arielle. "But you might find something you really like . . ."

As if on cue, Mrs. Petrie, marched out into the store, folding shirts and rattling clothes hangers. "May I help you, dear?" she asked November. Arielle noticed she called everybody "dear," even the male customers.

"I'm looking for jeans," November told her.

"They're in the front of the store—left-hand side," Mrs. Petrie said.

"Thanks," said November. She pushed the stroller to that area and picked out a pair of jeans.

Arielle figured Mrs. Petrie was satisfied that November was not a thief—yet—so she returned to the back room, where she could watch the closed-circuit television she'd had installed. She seemed to really enjoy staring at its grainy images.

"How'd you get to the mall?" Arielle asked as she rang up November's purchase. "You driving?"

"No, I got no wheels, girlfriend. Dana dropped me off. She and Olivia went to Macy's to return a pair of shoes and use Dana's gift card. They'll be up here in a hot minute."

When Olivia strode in a few minutes later, the store seemed somehow smaller. Olivia filled a room with the power of her personality. *She's not just a tuba player, she's the whole band*, Arielle thought, *full of booming, powerful music.* Dana hurried behind her, dragging a huge Macy's bag.

"What's up, Miss Saleslady?" Olivia asked loudly. Mrs. Petrie's head appeared for a moment, but didn't come out this time.

"Hey, Olivia," said Arielle. "Thanks for stopping by."

Dana asked, "Where are all the customers?"

"I guess you're it for now. But guess who stopped by the store a few minutes ago?"

"Who?"

"Brandon Merriweather!"

"For real? Was he shopping for clothes or women?" Olivia asked.

"I don't know. He bought a T-shirt and split. But I could still smell his aftershave after he left," Arielle replied, trying not to feel hopeful.

"Sounds serious," said Dana. "Kofi's got this one cologne that turns me on big-time!"

Arielle, needing to change the subject, asked Dana, "Are you okay after what happened today?"

"Yeah, I'm straight. But earlier today I wanted to bite something. You feel me?"

"Trust me, I do," Olivia told her.

"What did you buy, Dana? That bag is huge!" Arielle asked.

"Guess." A big smile erased the shadow from Dana's face.

"A hundred pairs of shoes?" Arielle offered.

"Girl, you're not even close," said Olivia. "And when Dana isn't buying shoes, you know there's some serious stuff goin' on."

"A dozen boxes of Pampers?" November guessed.

"Nice try," Dana said. She kneeled down and tickled Sunshine under her chin.

"Tell us!" Arielle insisted.

Mrs. Petrie peeked her head out again. She seemed to be curious about Dana's bundle as well.

Dana stood up and unwrapped the package. They all looked inside.

"You bought sheets and blankets?" Arielle said in amazement. "Why?"

"I got a gift card for my birthday, so instead of buying clothes, I bought stuff I'll need for my dorm room," Dana explained. "I am *so* out of here come September!"

"You're shopping to get over what happened at school today?" November asked Dana. "I used to do that when I got upset with my mother, or with Josh."

Dana sighed. "Yeah, I guess. But this was so much worse than a fight with your mom or your boyfriend."

"I heard Eddie only got three days' suspension," Olivia said in disbelief.

"That's it," Dana confirmed.

"That's crazy!" said Arielle, her voice full of outrage.

Mrs. Petrie had moved out of her storeroom. She stood a few feet away from the counter, listening intently to the girls' conversation.

Dana looked defeated. "Mrs. Sherman told my mother that since he had only scared me, and hadn't really hurt me, that was the max the school laws allowed."

"That's messed up, girl," November said.

"You know what I hate?" said Dana.

"What's that?" Arielle asked.

"I'm basically pretty tough. I passed a Girl Scout endurance test last summer—out in the woods, eating berries and stuff."

"Yeah, so?" Olivia didn't seem to be impressed.

"What I mean is—when Eddie cornered me, I couldn't even think straight. I felt like a little first-grade sissy girl with pink bows—scared and stupid. I should have fought back."

"You kicked him, didn't you?" November asked.

"Yeah, but not hard enough. I was scared and stupid." Dana looked down.

Olivia put her arm around her. "You weren't stupid, Dana, you were smart. Survival has nothing to do with eating berries. It's about using your head to get out of a bad situation."

"She's right," Arielle said. "You had no idea what that crazy fool was going to do."

"I guess," Dana said. "But I sure wish I'd had on my heavy boots—I woulda aimed that kick higher and landed it where the sun don't shine!"

The four girls cracked up at that. Even Mrs. Petrie laughed.

"What's gonna happen when he gets back?" November asked.

"Kofi might do a little kickin' of his own!" said Dana. She sounded concerned. "He's been real edgy lately. Any little thing sets him off. And Eddie is huge in Kofi's mind. Huge."

"Will he come back to Spoon's class?" Arielle wondered.

"My mom and Spoon got Eddie moved into a different

English class, so at least I can breathe in there," Dana told them.

"What other classes you got with Eddie?" Olivia asked.

"Just Pringle's chemistry. It was the only one my mom couldn't get switched, but I got Kofi in there with me, so I'm not so worried."

"We got your back, Dana," Olivia assured her.

"Yeah, we'll put a force field around you like they do in those sci-fi movies," November added. "Eddie won't even get close."

"That's cool, but you guys can't be there all the time," Dana reminded them.

"Maybe they'll transfer Eddie out of the school," Arielle offered. She hoped it was at least a possibility.

"People like Eddie fall through the cracks," said Olivia. "He's not bad enough for the school to kick him out, but he's scary enough to make kids fart when he passes by."

"For real." Dana put her hands on her hips.

"Well, my dears," Mrs. Petrie said as she folded one last shirt, "it's nine o'clock and we're closed. I must admit, I enjoyed eavesdropping on your conversation. I had forgotten how hard it is to be a kid. You girls stay safe, you hear?"

"Yes, ma'am," said Olivia.

"And take care of this little one, dear," she said to November.

"I promise," November replied with a smile.

Arielle was shocked to see Mrs. Petrie take a soft yellow scarf from the shelf and tuck it around the baby.

"For luck," she said. "No charge."

"Thank you," whispered November. She and Olivia rolled the baby out of the store and into the mall, where lights were being switched off in many of the stores.

"You need a ride home?" Dana asked Arielle.

Arielle glanced at the pile of sportswear she had not yet tagged. "I have to finish here first," she said reluctantly.

"Go on home, dear," Mrs. Petrie said. "This can wait until tomorrow."

Before her boss could change her mind, Arielle grabbed her purse from under the counter. "Thanks so much! I'll come in early tomorrow."

Mrs. Petrie just waved her off, and Arielle raced gratefully out of the store. She turned to see the mechanical door begin to roll down.

"What a nice lady you work for," November said, stroking the yellow scarf. Sunshine had fallen asleep clutching the fabric in one hand.

"I think my boss got abducted by aliens and they replaced her with that nice lady!" Arielle joked. "She's usually grumpy and really suspicious of teenagers."

"And Dana and I didn't even buy anything!" Olivia reminded them.

As they headed out to the car, Arielle said, "I really appreciate the ride, Dana. It's rough taking the bus home this late."

"When is your punishment over?" Dana asked as she tossed the bag of blankets and sheets into the trunk.

"I have no idea. Whenever my stepfather gets tired of making me miserable, I guess," Arielle replied.

November placed Sunshine into her car seat, then

deftly folded the stroller with one hand and placed it into the trunk.

"Impressive," said Arielle. "There ought to be a one-handed stroller toss in the next Olympics. You'd take the gold, November."

November just shrugged. "Sunshine is my gold."

"I HOPE SPRING GETS HERE IN A HURRY," Kofi said with a shiver. "The sun is bright, but it's not working very hard." He put his arm around Dana as they stood together outside in the area behind the cafeteria called the Commons. Only juniors and seniors were allowed to use the area, so many of them went out after lunch just because they could.

"Yes, but the fresh air feels so good," Dana said, inhaling deeply. "The cafeteria always smells like old onions and boiled tomatoes."

"Isn't that what was on the lunch special today?" he teased.

"Yep. I had two servings."

Students sat in groups of two and three, talking, listening to music through ear buds, or texting with the phones that nobody was supposed to have.

Kofi tried to hide the chill bumps, but his body shuddered involuntarily.

"Are you shivering from the weather, or because you need a pill?" Dana asked him matter-of-factly.

"You cold, girl," Kofi replied. "You don't give a dude no slack!"

"You didn't answer my question," she said. Her tone was serious.

"I'm straight. Promise. I have not taken anything."

"For real?"

"Every day gets a little easier," he told her. It was true. His appetite was returning, and his frequent visits to the toilet had slowed almost to normal.

She turned, twisting from his embrace. "You know I love you, Kofi."

"'Cause I'm so fine?" he asked her, patting his cheeks.

"No, 'cause you so crazy!"

He put both arms around her then and pulled her close. "You dare me to kiss you right here in front of a hundred kids?"

"Hey, they don't get a free show," she whispered in his ear. "Save the good stuff for when we're alone."

"Bet." Kofi hugged her tightly. Then he asked, "Are you worried about Eddie . . . when he gets back?"

"I refuse to walk around scared. I'm not gonna let Eddie mess up my life," she proclaimed. But he could feel her tense up.

"He better not touch you," Kofi said, menace in his voice. "I'd have to light him up."

"Don't do anything stupid," Dana warned. "If you get suspended for fighting, who's gonna protect me?"

"Well, can I squeeze him into goo?"

"Probably not." Dana giggled.

"I can't stomp him into muddy molecules?"

"Nope!"

"Then he better stay outta my way and keep himself far away from you." Kofi's voice trembled. "Besides . . ."

But Kofi stopped as Jack Krasinski, wearing a snare drum around his neck, a book bag on his back, and a fuzzy purple hat on his head, began beating out a series of loud and complicated cadences on the drum. He seemed to ignore everyone around him as he marched from the cafeteria and out to the center of the Commons. Pounding away, he chanted, "Flamadiddle, flamadiddle, bop, bop, bop! Flamadiddle, flamadiddle, bop, bop, bop!" His forehead and face, beaded with sweat, looked strained.

A few students laughed at him, and some marched with him for a moment or two, but most students just shook their heads. Jack played for a full five minutes, alone in the center of the Commons. Only Dana and Kofi clapped when he finished with a flourish and took an elaborate bow.

Jack looked around, like he was maybe searching for more attention, but most kids continued to chat and text and treat Jack as if he were invisible.

"He looks sad," Dana said.

Jack continued to march and mumble until he disappeared into the building. "Now *that's* marching to the beat of a different drummer!" Kofi told her.

Dana looked concerned. "Olivia told me Jack's usually the life of the band, but lately it seems like he's got some issues."

"We all got issues," said Kofi with a shrug. The bell rang, indicating the end of lunch, and they headed into the building. Kofi looked around, but didn't see Jack anywhere in the crowds of kids.

"You walkin' me to class?" Dana asked as Kofi passed by his math classroom. "I'm okay—Eddie's not back yet."

"Every day. Every class, my sweet. Eddie or not." He bowed like Jack had done.

"Where are your drums?"

"Can't you hear my heart beating for you?" he asked her with a laugh. "It's pounding louder than any drum!"

"You're *really* full of it!"

He made sure she got to her history class, and later to Spoon's class, which he always enjoyed. He knew he'd like it even better without Eddie.

"Hey, Spoon," Kofi said as he and Dana walked in together.

"You two all right?" the teacher asked, peering over her glasses.

"Yeah. Thanks. We're in this together," Dana told her.

After all the students had checked in through her computer system and everyone was settled, Mrs. Witherspoon stood up.

"You know I call you guys my puppies. It's a term of endearment."

"Yeah, we know, Spoon. You cool. Even if you *do* give too much homework!" Cleveland said.

"Yesterday's incident was very unsettling for me, and I want to make sure that all of you are safe. I don't want anyone in here, or any other classroom, alone anymore, okay?"

"Gotcha, Spoon," said Jericho.

"My room is open for you, however, any time I'm here."

"Well, we all know you ain't got no life outside of school, so that must mean day and night!" Roscoe said with a laugh.

"Hey, don't dis me, kid. I have a cat who loves me very much!"

"We love you too, Spoon," Dana said. "You saved my butt yesterday."

"I'd jump through fire for each and every one of you. You know that, don't you?"

"Even me?" Roscoe asked from the back of the room.

"Especially you, Roscoe, my man," she replied with a grin. "Seriously, if you've got stuff going on that you need help with, just holler. You got that?"

"Eeeeeeee!" Roscoe cried.

"What was that?"

"I'm hollering out for help!" His classmates chuckled.

"The last time I heard a noise like that, my microwave was overheating," Spoon replied. "I had to toss it and get a new one. You reading me?"

"Yeah, I feel you. I was just playin'." Roscoe gave Cleveland a high five.

"Each of you," Mrs. Witherspoon continued, "has the capacity to be a hero, a winner, a champion. You know of heroes in your own lives, and you've studied heroes in history class."

"Sounds like an assignment comin' up," Jericho whispered to Kofi.

"Yep."

"Since we have just about finished our study of *Beowulf*, it's time for our annual Hero Project."

"I knew it! What is it with teachers and projects?" Kofi complained to Jericho.

"I'm dividing you into study groups," Mrs. Witherspoon went on, "different from what you'd choose yourselves."

"That's no fun," grumbled Roscoe.

"Sure it is," Mrs. Witherspoon said. She turned on her computer, and an elaborate chart describing the project was displayed on the whiteboard in front.

"She's been plannin' this all along!" Kofi said as he realized what she was doing.

"What a slick way to slide into makin' us do a whole lotta work!" Jericho whispered back.

Mrs. Witherspoon ignored the grumbling. "Check this out," she said. "I'm dividing you into teams of two."

"Can I be with Dana?" Kofi asked.

"No, Dana is teamed with Jericho."

"Why can't I be with my girl?" asked Kofi. "I need to be with her—I'm her bodyguard."

"I want you to concentrate on Beowulf, not on Dana the Wolfe," Spoon replied. "Jericho will keep an eye on her."

"Ooh, she got you, man!" Roscoe hooted.

"No fair," Kofi grumbled.

"The next team is Cleveland and Roscoe," the teacher announced.

"How come I can't get a fine girl to work with?" Roscoe complained.

Mrs. Witherspoon kept reading the teams from her list. "Rosa and Ram. Charles and Luis. Arielle and Kofi."

Kofi watched as Dana looked quickly at Arielle, but both girls smiled, so he relaxed.

"Hey, I'll take Arielle off your hands, man," Roscoe offered. "I'll sacrifice to work with that taste of honey."

Arielle tossed him a dirty look. "You couldn't handle it," she said softly.

"Oowee! Gotcha, man. Sizzle!" Jericho chuckled.

Spoon continued. "November will work with Eric. Susan and Osrick. Olivia and Lisa."

"So what we s'posed to do, Spoon? Why you mix us up like that?" Cleveland frowned and crossed his arms.

"I know your learning styles and your strengths. I put together teams that will make the very best Hero Projects. You can focus on a fictional hero, or someone in your own life. I'm looking for the *essence* of heroism," she explained.

"You are such a *teacher*!" November said.

"Is that a compliment?" asked Spoon.

"I'm not sure yet. I'm waiting to see how hard this thing is gonna be," she replied with a laugh.

"Fair enough," Spoon said. "Okay—here we go. You are to create an interactive, multimedia hero project. I want bells and whistles, rhythm and rhyme. I want music, pictures, video. Internet links and webisodes. This is to be a twenty-first-century project. Your grandfather couldn't do this assignment. This stuff didn't even exist thirty years ago."

"My grandma got a MySpace page!" Cleveland told the class with a laugh. "She rocks!"

"Well, she might be able to help you then," Spoon retorted.

"When is it due?" asked Olivia.

Spoon grinned. "Specifics and details are on our class website. Pop the data in your zip drive, and you're good to go. You guys are the children of the future, and you're bringing it home to me in two weeks." She paused for effect.

"Two weeks?" Kofi groaned.

"If you need to use school equipment, I have laptops you can take home, or you can use the stuff in my room from six a.m. until six p.m. I'll come early and stay late if you need me to."

"You're too good, Spoon. I can't even use no computer as an excuse," Cleveland said.

"Break into your teams now and start to plan," the teacher told everyone. "You've got the rest of the class to start getting it together."

Kofi and Arielle searched the Internet for twenty minutes or so, but nothing seemed to jump out as perfect.

"We need more time to plan this thing," Kofi said. "Spoon's rhythm and rhyme is gonna take some time. More than we can do in class. When can we get together?"

"I work every night but Thursday. Hey, that's today," Arielle said.

"I'm off today too. You wanna do something after school and get it over with?" Kofi asked.

She paused. "Dana gonna be cool with this?"

"Yeah, we're straight."

"Okay. I'll meet you by your car at three."

ARIELLE
CHAPTER 23
THURSDAY, MARCH 3

ARIELLE HURRIED ACROSS THE PARKING LOT to Kofi's ancient, dirty gray Ford Taurus. Kofi stood by it with Dana, shielding her from the brisk winds.

"I think you must drive the very first Taurus ever made," Arielle teased him. "Ford should send you a prize or something."

Kofi brushed a leaf off the hood and pretended to shine the rusty door handle. "Naw, this is a 1992. It's special to nobody but me. Runs on rubber bands and bacon grease!"

"What's up, Dana?" Arielle said, rubbing her ungloved hands together. Her face was pink from the cold. "You two look warm and snuggly."

"You look like a popsicle, girl," Dana told her. "Get in the car. Kofi's got it all warmed up." She untangled herself and slid into the front seat next to Kofi.

"Thanks." Arielle opened the back door and got in. "You comin' with us, Dana?" she asked.

"I don't have to be at my job until six, so I figured I'd hang with you two until then. That all right with you?"

"Sure. I just want to get the project done in a hurry."

"Gotcha," Dana said.

"So, where can we do this?" asked Arielle.

"The library?" Kofi suggested. He pulled out of the school parking lot.

"Bells and whistles are pretty noisy. Spoon wants techno-dazzle," Arielle said.

"What about the food court at the mall?" Dana suggested. "I'm hungry."

"No computer access there. What about your house, Kofi?" asked Arielle.

He exchanged a look with Dana. "Probably not a good idea," he said slowly. "My mom is wobbly and Dad is shaky. I love 'em, but they're Pop-Tarts, if you know what I mean."

"Believe it or not, I really do," Arielle said. "For real."

Kofi asked, "How 'bout your house? I've driven past there—it looks like a street on some TV show."

"It's not what you think," said Arielle.

"You know what? As long as I've known you, I've never been inside your house," Dana commented.

"You want to talk about a parental Pop-Tart? My stepfather beats them all," Arielle told them. "He doesn't like visitors."

"Aw, I know you got the hookups in that big old pretty house," Kofi said.

Arielle hesitated. "If my stepfather isn't home, I guess we can use the TV in the great room, as long as you have your laptop. When he went off the deep end, he killed the Internet except on his personal stuff."

"My laptop is old, but I've got broadband and all kinds of techie hookups I designed myself," Kofi boasted.

"We have to finish before he gets home," Arielle told them nervously.

"You have a great room? I'm not even sure what that is," Dana said with a laugh.

Arielle didn't smile. "It's not so great—just a big living room."

"You're really lucky, Arielle," said Kofi.

"No, I'm not. Let me ask you something. When you go home and flop on your sofa and turn on your TV, who do those things belong to?"

Kofi scratched his head. "Me and my folks, I guess. But I think the TV belongs to Rent-A-Center," he added with a grin.

Arielle said softly, "Everything in *our* house belong to Chadwick Kensington O'Neil, my stepfather."

"What difference does it make?" Kofi asked.

"Lots. He just lets us use his stuff. It's not ours."

"Deep," said Dana.

"And I'm still on punishment. It's been, like, a month now," Arielle admitted.

"Still? Jeez—it's not like you robbed a bank!" Dana said.

"What's so bad about being on punishment?" Kofi asked. "Parents do that all the time. It's some kind of power trip."

"Chad's different," Arielle replied quietly, as they reached the driveway. Then she said with relief, "His car's gone! Good, we'll be able to work, but you two have to be

really careful not to get anything dirty or mess up anything. He freaks."

"I feel sorry for you, girl," Dana said with a shake of her
head.

Kofi pulled into the driveway. Arielle hopped out of the
car and tapped in the alarm code by the front door.

"That's odd," she said, re-entering the code. "He
always sets the alarm when he leaves. He's anal about
stuff like that."

"He didn't set it?" Dana asked as she and Kofi got to
the front door.

Arielle frowned. "I don't believe this. He didn't even
lock it!"

As she pushed open the heavy oak door, Kofi and Dana
walked into the house with her.

"Oh my God!" Arielle said breathlessly.

"I don't get it," Kofi said, confused. "This is where you
live?"

"Where *is* everything?" Dana asked. Her voice echoed
off bare walls.

Arielle felt faint. The house was empty, completely empty.
No sofas, no chairs, no tables. Nothing.

"Where is everything?" Arielle asked in a whisper. "You
guys . . . I think we've been robbed!"

"Maybe we'd better not go in," Kofi suggested, pulling
both Arielle and Dana back. "We should call the police!"

But as Arielle looked around, she realized that if they
had been robbed, the house wouldn't be so completely,
utterly bare. She shook herself free from Kofi and walked
into the kitchen, her mouth agape. She opened a cupboard.

No plates. No dishes. Every single can and box of food had simply vanished.

She opened a kitchen drawer. The spoons were gone. So were the forks, the knives, and the rest of the utensils.

She turned slowly as Kofi peered in the refrigerator. It could have been sold at an appliance store. It was that clean and empty.

"You gotta call the police, Arielle!" Kofi said again.

Arielle had started to cry. Dana put her arm around her shoulder. "This is unbelievable! We gotta call your mom, too, Arielle."

Arielle gasped. "My clothes!" She took the stairs two at a time, Kofi and Dana right behind her.

The pretty pink carpet remained, as well as the indentations where the bed and the chest of drawers had once stood. But Arielle's room, like the rest of the house, was completely bare.

A few hangers dangled in the empty closet. Everything else was gone.

Arielle let out a wail, then fell onto the floor in a heap, her shoulders heaving with sobs. She felt Dana's hand on her back, but she couldn't stop crying. "I hate him! I hate him!" she repeated over and over. "How could he *do* this to us?"

Kofi and Dana exchanged glances. Finally Kofi said, "Arielle, we *have* to call the police."

Arielle sniffed and said, "Can I borrow a tissue? He probably took the Kleenex box, too."

"Who did?" Kofi asked. "You know who did this?"

"My stepfather," Arielle replied with conviction.

"But . . . but . . . why?" asked Dana.

Arielle didn't answer. "Can I use your cell phone?"

"Sure." Dana flipped it open.

With trembling fingers, Arielle punched in the number of her mother's job at the Delta desk. "Mom?" she cried. "You gotta come home—now."

"Tell her to hurry," Dana whispered.

Arielle continued, her voice shuddering with disbelief. "No, no, I'm fine. But everything's gone, Mom. Chad took everything." She paused, listening to her mother's outcry. "Mom, he took every belt and bottle. My clothes, even my underwear. My books and pictures. All your stuff too. The furniture. The food. Gone. Please hurry. I'm scared."

Arielle snapped the phone shut and handed it back to Dana.

"Your stepfather really did this?" Dana asked incredulously.

Kofi walked down the empty hall and peeked into a couple of the other rooms. All empty. Not a thing was in any of them. Even the toilet paper was gone.

"Can a dude do that?" he asked.

"I guess he already has," Arielle replied sadly.

Dana's phone shrilled loudly in the empty room.

"Hello," she said. She tossed the phone to Arielle. "It's your mom."

"Are you on your way, Mom? I don't know what to do!"

Dana rubbed Arielle's arm as she and Kofi listened to Arielle's side of the conversation.

"Your car's been stolen?" Arielle cried out. "Are you sure?"

Kofi exchanged a knowing look with Dana.

"Mom, I bet it wasn't stolen—at least not by an ordinary thief."

"Her stepfather?" Dana whispered to Kofi.

He nodded.

"I bet Chad took it, Mom. He took everything else. Why would he leave you the car?"

"What a low-life piece of trash!" Dana muttered as Arielle clicked off the phone.

"Kofi, I hate to ask, but do you think you can drive me to my mother's job? She has no way to get home." Arielle looked around the room and shook her head. "Well, I guess she has no home to go to anyway."

"Sure, Arielle. Let's get out of here. This place is givin' me the creeps!"

As they closed the front door, Kofi watched Arielle give one last look at the large, empty house. Her eyes welled again with tears. She was quiet as she got into the backseat.

"Does your mother still work at the downtown Delta office?" Dana asked.

"No, she's at the Kenwood office. It's right off Montgomery Road, ten minutes away from here," Arielle answered, her voice hollow. "Across the street from the mall."

Kofi drove quickly to the circular parking lot of the glass-enclosed building. Arielle's mother waited outside. She waved and hurried to the car, sliding into the backseat next to Arielle.

"Thank you so much," she said. "I really appreciate this, Kofi."

"No trouble at all," said Kofi.

Arielle thought, *What does a dude say to somebody's*

mother who has lost everything—I mean everything? She
was beyond embarrassed.

"How've you been, Dana? It's great to see you again,"
Arielle's mom said, her voice oddly hyper.

"I'm good, Mrs. O'Neil," Dana replied. "We, uh, just
left your house. I'm, like, really sorry."

"This is simply unbelievable," Arielle's mom whispered,
hugging her daughter.

"Where do you want me to take you, Mrs. O'Neil?" Kofi
asked.

"Well, I guess there's no need for me to go to the house,
huh?"

"It's slick as glass, Mom. He took everything but the wallpaper and the carpet." Arielle felt like she might cry again.

"Can you drop us at the Holiday Inn down the street,
Kofi?" her mother asked. "We'll stay there for a day or two,
then we'll just have to figure out plan B."

"Sure thing."

"Do you have any money?" Arielle whispered to her mom.

"I have enough for now, and I switched the direct deposit
of my check before I left work. We'll be okay, sweetie."

Kofi pulled into the parking lot of the motel. The car was
strangely quiet. "Uh, is there anything else we can do?" he
asked.

"We're all set for now, but I appreciate your kindness and
understanding, Kofi," Arielle's mom said as she opened the
back door.

Dana turned around and told Arielle, "If you need to
borrow a couple of outfits next week, let me know."

Arielle burst into tears.

KOFI HAD THE ITCHES. MILLIONS OF INSECTS crawled on the insides of his arms and legs, it seemed. He couldn't stop scratching. His fingernails left long, ashy marks on his arms as he tried in vain to make the itching stop.

It had started early that morning, and by lunchtime, Kofi wanted to jump in a pool of lotion or salve or something to make the itching stop. After he gulped down a burger, he stopped by the school nurse's office.

"Hey, Miss Thornton," Kofi said, just peeking inside her door.

"Hi Kofi, come on in," she said cheerfully. Barely five feet tall, Miss Thornton wore high heels every day, in spite of the slippery hall floors. "Are you feeling okay?"

"Uh, I'm fine—not sick or anything. I just want to know if you got some ice I can borrow," Kofi said. It took all his effort not to scratch as he stood there.

"Borrow?" Miss Thornton asked with a lilting laugh. Kofi thought her voice sounded like a bird's—almost musical. "It's going to melt, you know."

Kofi grinned. "You know what I mean, Miss Thornton."

"Do you have a headache?" she asked, sounding concerned. She walked over to a small refrigerator.

"Yeah. It's nothing serious."

"Well, you know I'm not allowed to give out meds without a doctor's scrip. Not even colas with caffeine anymore. Just Band-Aids and Jolly Ranchers and ice packs." She sighed. "I wish I could do more for you kids."

"I'll take the candy if it will make you happy," Kofi told her as she handed him a plastic bag full of ice.

She reached into a dish on her desk and gave him a handful of candy and gum. "Now get to class!" she said.

"Can I have a hall pass back?" he asked her.

"You clean me out of candy and ice, and now you want a reason to be late to class?"

"Yep!" he replied, grinning hopefully.

She scribbled off the pass and sent him on his way. "Seniors!" she said with a shake of her head.

Kofi thanked her, waved, and darted out of her office. The halls were deserted. As soon as he was around the corner, he leaned against a wall and rubbed the ice pack up and down his arms. "Ahh!" The ice cooled his arms, soothing the unbearable itching.

But by the end of his last class, the ice had melted and the itching had returned. He didn't have the nerve to go back and ask Miss Thornton for more ice. He waited for Jericho by his car.

"What's wrong with you, man?" Jericho asked as he unlocked the car. "You scratchin' like you got chicken pox or something." He tossed his books and his trumpet in the backseat.

Climbing into the front seat of Jericho's car, Kofi didn't answer right away. He tried rubbing his arms, but that only made the irritation increase. "It's nothing," he said finally. "And thanks for takin' me over to the Medi-Center. My car decided it was gonna sleep in this morning."

"I feel you. Your car and my car together don't make one good vehicle," Jericho joked.

"I got rotten brakes," said Kofi.

"And my front fender's more rust than fender," Jericho continued.

"My radio won't work on Tuesday and Thursday!" Kofi was trying not to scratch.

"How come?"

"Old age. Same reason you've had a CD stuck in your player for the past two years!"

"My back door doesn't open," Jericho went on.

"And my back door won't lock!" Kofi said with a grin.

"We need to junk both cars and start over. I think I'll get me a Maserati," Jericho said dreamily.

"A hundred thirty-five thousand to start, my man," said Kofi.

"Chump change!" Jericho joked. "I plan to be both rich and famous one day."

"Like Arielle's stepfather?" Kofi kept scratching.

"No, man. From what you told me, he's like the demon seed or something."

Kofi nodded. "It was plain crazy, man. He stripped the house clean. I never seen anything like it."

"Yeah, everybody at school's talkin' about it. How's Arielle doing?" Jericho asked.

Kofi glanced over at his friend. "Why? You worrying about her?"

"Be for real, man. You know Olivia's my only squeeze."

"Just checkin'. Dana told me Arielle and her mom are staying at a homeless shelter."

"Shut up!" said Jericho. "Must be rough for Princess Arielle."

"You got that right." The itching increased, and so did Kofi's scratching.

"Does this X-ray have anything to do with all that scratching?" Jericho asked as they pulled into the parking lot of the Medi-Center on Montgomery Road.

"Nah. My doctor just ordered some more X-rays on my arm—the one I broke when . . ." His voice trailed off.

Jericho was silent for a moment. "We were so stupid that night."

Kofi nodded. "My arm is fine, Jericho. And I'm pretty sure my doctor knows that."

"So why the X-rays?"

Kofi continued to scratch his arms. Then he looked at Jericho and said, "I been takin' Oxy like a madman, Jericho. Ever since the accident. Even after my arm stopped hurting."

"Every day?"

"Sometimes several times a day," Kofi admitted. "I been makin' up reasons for my doctor to give me more pills."

"That's some serious stuff, man."

Kofi rubbed his arm. "But the doctor figured out what I was doin', and even worse, Dana found out, so my supply is dry. She made me put them down the garbage disposal."

Jericho chuckled. "Sounds like Dana. No half-steppin'!"

"The X-ray is so the doctor has medical proof my arm is healed, so I can't ask him for one more pill. But I won't. I'm comin' clean."

"Is it rough?"

"Well, if you don't count the vomiting and diarrhea, and the chills and the sweats, it's a piece of cake!" Kofi thought back to the sleepless nights, the dizziness, and the deep, gnawing hunger for the drug. He exhaled. "I guess the last step is the itches. If I don't pull my arms off and use them as matchsticks, I think I'll be straight," Kofi told him.

"You're a better man than me," Jericho said.

"Everybody got messed up some kinda way because of that night," Kofi said as he got out of the car. "You. Me. November. Dana. Even Arielle."

"Yeah, I know."

Kofi slammed the car door. "You got your issues, and I got mine. I'm doin' the best I can. I'll be out in twenty minutes. Can you wait?"

"I'll be here."

Kofi disappeared into the huge glass doors of the out-patient treatment center.

ARIELLE
CHAPTER 25
WEDNESDAY, MARCH 9

STARTLED BY LOUD COUGHING COMING from across the room, Arielle woke up stiff and confused. As her eyes adjusted to the dim light in the room, she remembered where she was. On a thin mattress. Under a thinner blanket that smelled of Clorox. Close to her mother, who slept in the bed beside her. At the Hillside Valley Shelter on Vine Street.

She had seen no hillsides and no valleys since she and her mother had arrived three days ago. Only cement sidewalks. Outside, cars zoomed past, music from the apartments nearby played loudly, and police sirens shrieked most of the night.

"This is just temporary," her mother had whispered as they had filled out the paperwork to enroll.

Arielle, almost numb, had merely nodded. The walls were painted a bright blue, as if someone had tried to add artificial cheer. But the faces of the women who wordlessly watched Arielle and her mother from the plastic chairs in the recreation room were drawn. Their children, instead of running and chasing one another with loud games, played quietly and stayed close to their mothers. No amount of color would change anything.

"My name is Sarah Toth," the gray-haired intake woman had told them. "I want to welcome you two to Hillside Valley." She shook both their hands warmly. Arielle liked her immediately.

"We just need a place to stay for a few days," her mother had explained. "We've . . . we've no place else to go. It's because—"

"Explanations are not necessary around here," Mrs. Toth had said briskly. "You're here because you're here, and we'll take good care of you. It's not the Ritz, but it's clean and safe."

Her mother had relaxed then, but Arielle looked around in dismay. A well-worn sofa sat in the center of a recreation room. A TV was chained to the far wall.

"The last television walked," Mrs. Toth had explained. "I really hate when I'm forced to decorate like the prison of a medieval castle."

"How many residents do you have here?" Arielle's mother had asked as they walked up a flight of barren stairs.

"It varies, depending on the weather and the date. We tend to get a few more around the first of every month— evictions. And around the full moon—no kidding. Men who batter often increase their violence when the moon is high and full in the sky."

Arielle and her mother had looked at each other knowingly.

"Ordinarily I'd try to give you two a private room, but we're pretty full this week, and all I have is dorm space," Mrs. Toth had explained. "Can you share with two other women? Alice and Margaret are kind old souls. They're sisters—both have been battered all their lives. Both of their spouses have been incarcerated. They're too old to get jobs, so I expect they'll be here for a while."

Arielle and her mother had been introduced to the two elderly women, both in their seventies. Alice was as soft as a pillow when she hugged Arielle in welcome, while her sister Margaret was as thin and brittle as sticks. Except for Alice's constant coughing at night, they were pleasant roommates.

"If you need clothes, we got something called the Clothes Closet downstairs," Margaret had told them. "Go first thing in the morning before the good stuff is gone."

"They've got a general store down there too. Tooth-paste, deodorant, stuff like that. All free. Set up like a real store, so you don't feel like you're a beggar, you know what I mean?" Alice had explained.

"Y'all runnin' from a bad daddy?" Margaret asked gently.

"Yes, he was pretty bad," Arielle's mom replied. She gave no further explanation.

"Understatement of the year," Arielle muttered.

"We all been there. Talk when you got a mind to," said Alice, touching Arielle and her mother on their shoulders.

Arielle's mother had thanked them and immediately began covering their plastic mattresses with the clean sheets they'd been given. Arielle, still stunned at where they had landed, checked out the room.

Four beds had been set up, with a small wooden table next to each. A pair of windows let sun into one side of the room. The bottoms of the pale yellow curtains were frayed, but they were clean.

No rugs decorated the floor. No pictures hung on the blue walls.

The whole far wall had been divided into four sections, with two cabinet drawers at the bottom and poles for hanging clothes at the top of each area. Arielle had nothing to hang.

She sighed deeply. *This is so unreal. I want to go home.* But she didn't even know what that meant anymore. Home, for now, meant breakfasts of runny oatmeal and powdered eggs sprinkled with parsley, a shared bathroom, a cold linoleum floor, and nothing, not even her underwear, to call her own.

Arielle got up and squeezed into the narrow bed next to her mother. "You smell like baby powder," she whispered.

"You sleep okay?" her mother asked softly as they snuggled.

"Yeah. Alice needs to get that cough checked," Arielle replied.

"I hope to get us out of here in a week or two," her mother promised. "I'm so sorry, Arielle."

"It's not your fault, Mom. This is all Chad."

"Chad. What a huge mistake *that* was!"

"I'm not gonna fight you on that one."

"You and I started here, you know," her mother admitted. "Well, a place just like this. I feel like such a failure, bringing you back to a place like this once again. It's like I'm going backward instead of forward in my life."

Arielle bit her lip, aching over her mother's pain. She thought for a moment, then said, "I don't really remember it much. But as long as I'm with you, Mom, everything is gonna be okay."

Her mother hugged her close. Then she said, "Gee, you feel thin."

Arielle pulled away from her mom a little. "I haven't been eating so good, I guess. I'm just so glad it's over, Mom."

"I put up with that man way too long."

Arielle sat up on one elbow. "Mom, you're a grown woman, and you let a smooth-talking, good-looking man put *you* on punishment! How messed up is that? What was *wrong* with you?"

Her mother sat up on the bed. "Even moms make mistakes, sweetheart," she said finally.

"I'd rather live forever in this shelter," Arielle said with finality, "than ever have to see the face of Chadwick Kensington O'Neil again."

They slapped palms. "For real!" Then, her voice serious, her mother promised, "We'll be out of here soon."

"I don't care, Mom. They have hot meals and free toilet paper!" They both laughed a little.

"And I want my Kiki back," her mother added. "I'm getting her out of that place as soon as I can. She needs her mom."

"So do I," Arielle whispered.

Her mother kissed her forehead. "You've got to go back

to school today, Arielle. They'll provide a bus for you."

"I know. I know. What will I wear?" Arielle asked grumpily.

"Let's go downstairs and do some early morning shopping at the Clothes Closet," her mother suggested. "I hear they're having a big sale!"

"May as well," Arielle agreed, getting up and slipping into an oversize sweatshirt. She and her mother crept down the steps, arm in arm, trying their best to pretend they were heading to a fancy boutique. At the bottom of the stairs they met Mrs. Toth, who was just unlocking the door to the clothing area.

"Good morning, ladies," she said. "I'm glad someone is in a good mood today. How can I help you?"

"I need something to wear to school," Arielle said quietly. She glanced at the piles of faded T-shirts with the logos of various stores or sports teams or cartoon characters, at the rack of dresses that she'd seen old ladies wear to church, and the slacks that were cut too high, or too wide-legged, or too plaid to be worn by anyone she knew.

Mrs. Toth looked at Arielle's face and said, "I'm afraid that when people give clothes to shelters, they give up the ugly clothes first, then the old-fashioned stuff, then the ridiculous items." She picked up a gold feather boa. "Now, who needs this to keep her warm on the streets?" she asked.

"I guess if she wanted to feel fancy for a few minutes, it might help," Arielle offered.

"You're right, my dear," Mrs. Toth said with a wink.

"Does anybody ever give away cute jeans or tops that

teens would wear?" Arielle asked, her voice only faintly hopeful.

"Have you ever donated any of your nice clothes to us?" asked Mrs. Toth gently.

"No, ma'am," Arielle admitted. "When I had a closet full of sharp outfits, well, I just never thought about a kid like me who might need something to wear. It honestly never crossed my mind." The realization made her feel like pond scum.

Mrs. Toth patted Arielle's back. "Well, fortunately for you, somebody *did* think about it. We just received a large donation from a high school across town. Jeans and tops and such. Not new, but they'll do. They also give us prom gowns every year for kids who don't have one."

Arielle's eyes grew wide. Man, in all the years of spending Chad's money, she only ever thought of herself and her own racks of clothes. She felt humbled when Mrs. Toth unlocked a small area in the back room. "Oh, my," she breathed. The small closet was full of up-to-date, stylish clothes for teens.

Mrs. Toth looked pleased. "I saved these back here for you. I had a feeling you'd be needing school clothes pretty soon."

Arielle thanked her profusely, then picked out a pair of blue denim capris, a red top with only a few of the sparkles missing, and a neat white sweatshirt—just her size. She even found some socks and a pair of tennis shoes that were almost new. The soles weren't even scuffed.

"Oh, thank you, Mrs. Toth," Arielle said again, giving the woman a hug.

Mrs. Toth shrugged her off. "Just remember us when you get back on your feet, kid."

"Oh, I will!" Arielle told her.

"You sure you don't want the feather boa?" Mrs. Toth asked, teasing.

"Maybe tomorrow!" Arielle replied with a laugh.

Her mother dug through boxes and found underwear for Arielle, and Mrs. Toth brought her a nice-looking canvas book bag.

"Now hurry and get dressed and grab some breakfast. The bus will be here at eight!" her mother reminded Arielle.

The bus, a battered yellow one with the words HILLSIDE VALLEY SHELTER on the sides, stopped at several elementary schools, dropping off the younger kids who lived at the shelter before it lumbered to the high school. As Arielle got close to her school, she knew that she was probably the guts of everybody's gossip this week. But she didn't care anymore. She was grateful for the smallest things these days. Shoes. Deodorant. Underwear.

Arielle hesitated before she stepped off the bus. She hoped she wouldn't see anyone she knew, but standing right by where the bus pulled up were November, Dana, and Olivia. She cringed only for a moment.

"Hey, Arielle. What's up?" Dana greeted her.

"Believe it or not, I feel great," Arielle told her. "Better than I've been in a long time." And she wasn't kidding.

"You sure you're handlin' all this?" asked November.

"I'm taking one day at a time, but I'm okay. Really. Thanks for asking. How's Sunshine?"

November grinned and pulled out a new picture. "She sat up yesterday! All by herself! I must have taken a million pictures. She sat there grinning, like she knew she'd done something special."

"That's really great," Arielle said, smiling at the tiny face in front of her. "One day she's gonna be running all over your house, and you'll need track shoes to keep up with her!"

"I sure hope so," November told her, tucking the picture back into her purse.

"How is it at the shelter?" Olivia asked carefully. "You hanging tough for real?"

Arielle furrowed her brow. "You know, the ladies who end up at a shelter for battered women have been through so much—tons worse than me and my mom. I've learned a lot just by listening to their stories."

"Deep," Olivia said. "Is it, like—depressing?"

"It's not as bad as you think," Arielle replied as they headed toward the school. "It's real basic, kinda like the army—no frills. But my stepfather's not there, so it's like heaven!" The other girls relaxed as they laughed with her.

"But you're not battered, are you?" November asked.

"No, but I guess we've been abused—mentally, the woman who runs the place says—big-time. Mom's had time to see things differently. She said she never dreamed she'd be staying at the place she only thought about once a year when she wrote a check to support it."

"Um . . . so . . . what's it like there?"

"Small, but clean. As soon as Mom gets a couple of paychecks under her belt, we're gonna look for an apartment."

"For real now, Arielle," Dana told her. "I was serious about letting you borrow some clothes. I just didn't want to, you know, embarrass you."

"I think I could walk in here butt naked and not be embarrassed after all that's happened," Arielle said with a laugh.

Roscoe, who'd been walking near them, hollered out, "Go ahead, baby cakes! Do your thing if that's what you need to do."

Olivia, Dana, and November all groaned and popped him on the head at the same time.

"Pervert!" November said.

"No, I'm just a healthy boy!" Roscoe called as he ran toward the building.

"It feels so good to have friends again," Arielle told the girls. "And I *really* appreciate your offer of clothes. I might take you up on it this weekend."

"Just say the word."

"How about that green suede outfit?" Arielle asked, her tone playful.

"Not a chance. That's Kofi's favorite!"

Arielle touched Dana on the arm. "I was just teasing. I'd never accept your really cool clothes. But some leftover jeans or old T-shirts might help out."

"Bet."

"Did you ever find out what happened to Chad?"

"His office moved him to California, my mother found out. He'd been planning this for *months*!"

"What about your clothes and stuff?"

"You're not gonna believe this. He told the movers

to put his belongings in the truck, and our stuff in a Dumpster."

"No way!"

"My mom went to Legal Aid and got a lawyer."

"I hope she's careful," November said. "The last time me and my mom had to tangle with a lawyer, I felt slimy every time I was in a room with the dude."

Arielle nodded. "I guess the lady my mom found handles divorce and whatever else Chad can be charged with."

"Sounds good," said Olivia.

They got to Miss Pringle's class a few minutes before the bell rang. Arielle slid into her seat, happier than she'd been in a long time, which seemed so odd to her, considering the mess she and her mother were in.

Jericho jogged in then, grabbed Olivia, and twirled her around in a little dance step. She laughed and let him swing her around.

"What's got into you?" Kofi asked. "You practicin' Pringle's periodic table dance again?"

"Naw, man. I got my letter yesterday. College!"

"MIT?" guessed Kofi.

"Be for real, man. I can't even pronounce some of the courses you'll be taking!"

"You took the Michigan State offer?" Roscoe asked.

"Nope. I turned them down," said Jericho, his voice pumped with excitement.

"You turned down a full football scholarship to a Big Ten school?" Roscoe said in amazement.

"True that."

"So you gonna toot your trumpet in a tutu at Juilliard with the rest of the ballet dancers?" Cleveland asked with a laugh.

"No tutus. I'm not going to New York."

"Your dad musta freaked out. That's where he wanted you to go, wasn't it?"

"It ain't my dad's life," Jericho said.

Arielle thought about her applications to Stanford and Cornell and her heart suddenly sank. They were meaningless pieces of paper without Chad's financial backing. *I'd better start looking for scholarships at state schools,* she told herself.

"So where you gonna go?" Luis asked. "Too bad you can't go to a school where you can play football, then switch uniforms at half time and play in the band. You're pretty good at both things."

Jericho exchanged glances with Olivia, who obviously already knew what he was going to say. "That's exactly what I'm doing, my man! I'm going to Shenandoah University. It's in Virginia."

"Huh? I never heard of it," said Roscoe.

Jericho continued, "It's got a good football team, and a great music program. So I can major in music and play ball for fun. I can't be in the marching band, but I'll be in the orchestra."

"You get the best of both worlds," Cleveland said, getting it. "How'd you find a place like that?"

"Olivia," Jericho replied simply.

"So is that where you're going too, Olivia?" November asked her.

She beamed. "Yeah, I think so."

"Ooh, gag me with the cuteness!" Roscoe said, grabbing his throat and pretending to choke himself. "Are you sure you wanna be with your girl every single day?"

"You just jealous, man," Jericho replied with a laugh, "that no girl wants to be with you *any* day!"

The bell rang then, Miss Pringle began the class, and everyone settled down.

Arielle sketched drawings of Jericho and Olivia in her notebook, marveling at, and a little bit jealous of, the magic they had together.

AFTER CLASS, OSRICK APPEARED AT Arielle's side.

"Do you have a second?" he whispered, glancing at Miss Pringle, who was busy in the back room.

"Sure," Arielle replied.

"I ordered something off the Internet," Osrick confided.

"Great," said Arielle, looking at him strangely. "I order stuff all the time—at least I used to."

"You don't understand. I ordered a secret weapon!" His little-boy voice sounded really excited.

"What's all this mystery, Osrick?" Arielle said, trying to be patient. "I've got to get to class."

He reached down into his bag and pulled out a small white jar. The label read ANTITHEFT POWDER. "This," he whispered, "is going to catch the school thief. But I need your help."

"How is that going to catch the thief, and why me?" Arielle asked.

Osrick blinked rapidly several times and ducked his head. "Well, you've always been nice to me," he finally said.

"I have?"

"You never laugh at me, and you kept your mouth shut about the poolside thing." He paused, looked up at her, then continued, "And you once stopped a kid from tossing me in the Dumpster out back."

"I did?"

"You don't remember?" Osrick looked disappointed. "It was two years ago, in May. It was a hot day, and the garbage was real stinky."

Arielle thought, but the event that stood out in Osrick's mind had faded from hers. "Well, at any rate, I'm glad I did. Okay, what's that stuff?"

"If you put it on an object and a person tries to steal that object, their hands get stained a bright blue!" he explained with glee.

"So they wash their hands."

"It stays on for three days. Even if you wash your hands lots of times."

"Wow. That's really cool. How did you discover this stuff?"

"I spend lots of time on the Internet—it's what I do," he said simply.

"So what's your plan?" she asked, starting to get intrigued.

"We go to Mrs. Sherman and let her set up the 'sting.'" He sounded like a cop from one of those crime TV shows.

"Why do you need me?" Arielle wondered. "You're the brains of the operation." *Now* I'm *sounding like a TV cop*, she thought, rolling her eyes.

"If I go to the principal, it's just Weird Osrick talking. But if we both go, she'll listen. Please?" he added. "You might get your iPhone back."

The thought of perhaps getting back the one item Chad had missed helped her decide. "Okay," she said. "I'm in."

"Can we go now, before I lose my nerve?" Osrick asked.

Arielle had gym class next bell, and the chance to skip the sweating and jumping was a no-brainer. She picked up her bag. "Let's do it."

"Thank you, Arielle," Osrick said softly. As they headed out the room he said, "You know, your name means 'brave and beautiful one.'"

"Really? How do you know?"

"Internet." They said the word at the same time and laughed. He seemed giddy with excitement.

"I've never walked down the hall with a pretty girl before," he admitted shyly. "Not with an ugly girl either!" He laughed again.

"So . . . you know who the thief is, Osrick?"

"Yeah. At least, I'm pretty sure I do."

"Who is it? Tell me!"

"I can't, not yet."

"So why don't you just tell Mrs. Sherman who it is and be done with it? Why do we have to do all this secret spy stuff?"

"Because nobody will believe me, and we have to have proof."

"I guess you've got a point there."

They entered the main office and told Rosa that they needed to see Mrs. Sherman right away.

"Another theft to report?" she asked, almost hopefully.

"Not exactly," Arielle replied. "But it's really important."

"Did you hear about Paula Ingram's Game Boy? And Carlos Burke's cell phone? And Susan's money?" Rosa asked.

"Yeah. Everybody is getting real tired of this."

As they waited for Mrs. Sherman, Arielle turned to Osrick. "I know you don't want to talk about this, but during the last fire drill I saw the guys who made that video." She made sure her voice was low and Rosa could not hear.

"You're right. I don't want to talk about it."

"But I found out their names! Don't you want them to get punished?"

"I told you, Arielle," he said urgently, "leave it alone!" Rosa looked up from her desk. Arielle knew her ears were attuned to any notes of discord.

"I'm going to tell Mrs. Sherman who they are," Arielle told Osrick.

"Please don't. At least not yet. Can't you wait until this is over?"

Arielle frowned. But it *was* his decision, she supposed. "Okay. You win. I guess I'm into revenge these days."

Mrs. Sherman appeared then and escorted them into

her office. Arielle found herself sitting in the same spot she'd been in when she reported her phone stolen.

Osrick wasted no time. "I'm almost positive I know who the thief is, and I know how to catch him," he said breathlessly.

Mrs. Sherman sat up straighter. "You do? I'd give anything to be rid of this problem person in our school. Who is it, Osrick?"

"I can't tell you right now. When you see who it is, you'll understand."

"Is it someone who is bullying you again, Osrick?" the principal asked gently.

Arielle gave Osrick a quick look, but he shook his head no.

"And do you know anything about who the thief might be, Arielle?" the principal asked.

"No, I'm just here for moral support."

Osrick showed Mrs. Sherman the antitheft powder.

"Hmm. I'm not sure about this," the principal muttered as she read the directions. "I don't think I want to deal with lawsuits about entrapment and such. You know how parents can be these days." She pressed a button on her intercom and asked Rosa to get Officer Hammler right away.

"Didn't your wallet get stolen, Mrs. Sherman?" Osrick asked her.

"Yes, it did. And you're right. I felt so violated, so I know how the students must feel who've had their property taken. It's a pretty long list of stuff that has disappeared the past couple of months."

"Like my iPhone," Arielle reminded her.

Officer Hammler knocked and walked into the principal's office. Tall and stocky, he wore the full regulation navy blue uniform of the Cincinnati Police Department, including a walkie-talkie, a Taser, and a gun.

"How can I help?" he asked in his deep voice.

Mrs. Sherman showed him the antitheft powder and explained how it worked. "What do you think?" she asked him.

"I've used it before. It can be very effective," he said. "I think it may be our last resort here."

"Don't you have security cameras around the building?" Arielle asked.

"Yes, but not nearly enough. Not one camera has captured a theft," Officer Hammler replied.

"School-board-affordable technology?" asked Osrick.

"If you mean the cheapest stuff available, of course!" Mrs. Sherman answered with a laugh.

"Everybody knows where they are—they're pretty obvious," Osrick said.

"Plus, we've got teachers watching the classrooms and the gym locker rooms."

"And I'm doing all I can—talking to kids about leads, checking lockers, and patrolling the hallways from dawn to dusk," the police officer said. "But we've come up with nothing. Zip."

Mrs. Sherman nodded. "I have to admit—I'm stumped."

Osrick spoke up again, sounding more sure of himself than he ever did in class. "What we need to do is set a trap. The thief takes money and cool electronic gadgets.

We put some of this stuff on some money or a cell phone, leave it out as a temptation, and see whose hands turn blue."

"That's smart thinking, Osrick," the principal said. "But the directions say here that you need one of the UV/black lights for the blue gel to show up on the thief's hands."

Osrick dug down into his bag once more and pulled out a small UV light. "Runs on batteries," he explained. Officer Hammler grinned.

Boy, people sure have underestimated Osrick, Arielle thought as she listened to his plan. She agreed to let them put a fifty-dollar bill—to make it a greater temptation—and an electronic gadget in her purse. The purse would be placed in the girls' locker room, where many of the thefts seemed to have occurred. The rest would be up to the thief.

"If we hurry, we can plant my bag down in the gym right now," Arielle said. "That's what class I'm supposed to be in."

"This better work," said Mrs. Sherman as she took a fifty-dollar bill out of the petty-cash box in her office. "These babies don't grow on trees, you know." Then she pulled an iPod out of a box by her desk.

"Is that an iPod?" Arielle asked. "It looks like a brick! I've never seen one so huge." She and Osrick both laughed at the ancient-looking device. "No kid will steal that thing—it's a dinosaur!"

Mrs. Sherman said, "I have to agree, but it's all we have to use as bait. I don't think it even works—it was in that box of lost items when I got here."

Officer Hammler put on a latex glove from the first-aid kit, scooped some of the powder out of the jar, and rubbed it all over the money and the iPod. Neither item looked any different when he'd finished.

"Let's check it," Arielle suggested, "just to make sure it works."

Osrick turned on the black light. Both the money and the device glowed an odd, iridescent blue. "Awesome," he said.

"You're pretty cool, you know that, Osrick?" Arielle said with a slow nod.

"I know," he said, blushing.

Officer Hammler carefully placed both articles in Arielle's purse, right on top.

"Hurry, now," Mrs. Sherman told Arielle. "Let's see if we can catch this thief."

"Can I get a pass to class and a note that says I don't have to dress for gym today?" Arielle asked.

Mrs. Sherman smiled. "Just for today," she said. "Now, go! And where are you headed, Osrick?"

"I have computer class last bell," he explained. "I'm not missing anything. In fact, I could probably *teach* the class!" he joked.

"I believe you," Mrs. Sherman replied. "Do you want to wait here to see if anyone takes our bait?"

Osrick nodded eagerly.

As Arielle dashed out of the office, Rosa leaned her chair back, clearly trying to figure out what was going on, but Mrs. Sherman firmly shut the door.

Arielle rushed down to the gym, wondering if the trap

would work. Officer Hammler followed Arielle at a distance, acting as if he wasn't paying attention to her. The plan was for him to observe the few students with passes who were in the hall and near the gym so they could be questioned later.

The locker room was deserted. Arielle breathed a sigh of relief and carefully set her purse on a bench near a wall of lockers. She lifted the top flap so the money was in plain view. The iPod lay right beneath the cash. Then she checked her watch, realized she had about fifteen minutes of class left, so she grabbed the note and headed into the hot, smelly gym. She did not look back at the purse.

November was already seated on one of the bleachers, watching a volleyball game.

"Looking at gym class is *so* much better than doing it," Arielle said as she slid onto a bench next to November. Her heart was beating fast, but she tried to act relaxed.

"I feel ya," November agreed. "They scheduled me for two gym classes. How dumb is that? But they wouldn't change my schedule. What a waste of time. I could be out of here and with my baby. How'd you get an excuse to miss class?"

"I told them I was sick," Arielle told her.

"Actually, you don't look so good. You feelin' okay?" November asked. "You're not pregnant, are you?" she said jokingly.

"Not hardly!" Arielle laughed. "I got enough problems!" She didn't want to talk about herself, so she changed the subject. "What's Eddie's excuse to sit out?" she asked, pointing toward the other side of the bleachers.

"I don't know, and I don't care. That dude makes me itch!" November replied.

"Dana's really spooked by him," said Arielle. "Her mother's looking into getting a restraining order against him."

"Yeah, I heard. But that's gotta be almost impossible to enforce inside a school."

"True that."

"At least she's got Kofi and Jericho as her unofficial security guards. They've worked it out so that one of them or the other is with her between every class."

"That's cool."

"There goes Pringle out to run around the track," November said as the skinny teacher jogged through the gym toward the outside exit. She waved at the girls as she headed out—earphones on her head, keys jingling around her neck, a bottle of water strapped to her waist, and a determined look on her face.

"Every day like clockwork, just before the bell rings at the end of the day. The woman must run on batteries. Did you ever see her do the dance of the chemical elements?"

"No, I missed that while I was out," November replied with a chuckle. "Lucky me."

Arielle watched Olivia swat the volleyball across the net. She was sweaty and looked like she was having fun. "You know, I really underestimated Olivia," she said.

"Yeah, you did."

"I'm sorry."

"Tell her, not me," November said.

"I will."

"She's a bigger person than you are, Arielle, and I'm not talking about her weight."

"I know," Arielle whispered. "I know."

The gym teacher finally blew the whistle. November sighed with relief, told Arielle good-bye, and left to go pick up her baby. Eddie, Arielle noticed, had disappeared. *Good riddance,* she thought.

Arielle waited so a few girls got to the locker room before she did. Then, slowly, she turned the corner toward the row of pale green, rusty lockers. Her purse was sitting on the bench exactly where she'd left it, with the flap up and the insides clearly visible. But the fifty-dollar bill and the ancient iPod were gone.

ARIELLE SHIVERED IN THE CHILLY CLASS-
room—partly from the cold and even more
from nervousness. She and Osrick, who sat
up tall without his hoodie, sat in the front
row and waited quietly. She had no classes
in this room; it felt odd to be in someone
else's space. The faded posters of American
heroes and the vocabulary words on the board
in an unfamiliar handwriting all added to the
tension of the morning. Officer Hammler stood in
uniform by the front door, his face stern.

It was the first bell of the day, the time when
students got books from lockers, teachers ran off
tests on the copy machine, all school attendance was
taken, and announcements were made. Home Base,
the time was called, and it really did serve as a relaxed
launching point for most school days. But not today.

Arielle usually used this as her own personal quiet
time—to scribble out some lines to a poem, finish up her

chemistry homework for that next class, or grab a dough-nut and some juice from the free breakfast line. But today was different. When the morning announcements came on, she jumped, startled by the sudden noise on the TV monitor.

The student camera operators had chosen to use a close-up lens this morning, so Mrs. Sherman's large face and body filled up the whole viewing area. She was dressed all in black and looked every bit as stern as Officer Hammler. *"The following students should please report to room 123 for a special meeting. Repeat. If you hear your name called, please bring your books to room 123 for a special meeting IMMEDIATELY.*

Eddie Mahoney
Olivia Thigpen
Arielle Gresham
November Nelson
Jack Krasinski
Jericho Prescott
Kofi Freeman
Dana Wolfe
Roscoe Robinson
Rosa Gonzalez
Luis Morales
Osrick Wardley
Rudy Amadour
Cleveland Wilson
Jesse Smith
Burton Johnson

Carlos Burke
Susan Richards
Paula Ingram
Wendy Bartles
Brandon Merriweather."

In addition to those who'd had items stolen, or who had been impacted by the thefts, she had also read off the names of all the students who were enrolled in that last-bell gym class. *"Additionally,"* Mrs. Sherman continued, *"I'm requesting all teachers who are not assigned to a class the last bell of the day or the first bell of the day, to come to room 123 to assist with this very important meeting as well. It should take only a few minutes of your time. I appreciate your swift response."*

Arielle could imagine the whispers that would be flying around the school as students whose names were called packed up their gear and headed to room 123.

"What's up with this?"

"Anybody know what the meeting is for?"

"Is it time to announce who got into National Honor Society?"

"Not with Eddie Mahoney on the list!"

"Somebody's in trouble, that's for sure."

"Weird Osrick? What could he do bad?"

"Maybe he sneezed on somebody."

"Maybe it's a bunch of people who treated the little dude bad."

"That would be a much longer list, man!"

"Maybe they're prize winners."

"Scholarship announcements, you think?"

"Naw, some of the kids whose names she called are not the tallest trees in the jungle. You know what I'm sayin'?"

"Well, maybe they're checkin' for drugs. I saw Officer Hammler down by Room 123 early this morning."

"He got the drug-sniffing dog with him?"

"I don't know. I didn't see the dog."

"I guess we'll find out soon enough."

The teachers who walked into the room looked annoyed, because they'd probably been preparing for their morning classes.

"What's this all about, Thelma?" Mrs. Witherspoon asked Mrs. Sherman. "I'm trying to calibrate my computers for the day, and I really need this time."

"Give me five minutes, Maggie, and I'll explain it all. I promise," Mrs. Sherman assured her.

Miss Pringle came in next, carrying her ever-present mug of coffee, then Mr. Tambori, the music teacher, and Ms. Hathaway, another English teacher.

Eddie was the first student to arrive. He sat in the back of the room and folded his arms across his chest. Then came Jericho and Olivia, along with Kofi and Dana, all dressed alike in red and white school sweatshirts.

Arielle smiled at them as they sat down next to her. "Did you guys plan that?" she asked.

Kofi rolled his eyes. "When you let your girls be your fashion planners, there's no telling what they might make you do!" Dana just punched his arm.

"You know why they called this meeting?" Dana whispered.

Arielle shook her head, feeling bad that she'd had to keep all this a secret from her friends.

November slipped into the next row of seats, along with Roscoe and Luis and Cleveland. "Maybe we all won scholarships!" she whispered.

"Not likely," Kofi replied.

"Maybe they're sending us all to Disney World!" suggested Luis.

"You trippin', man. You know how cheap the school board is. They wouldn't send us to the corner drugstore!" Cleveland told them.

"For sure."

When Brandon walked in, wearing tailored slacks and a cashmere sweater instead of the jeans and sweats that most of the kids wore, he winked at Arielle. She could swear she caught a whiff of that cologne he wore. *He looks out of place here—as if he should be in some private boarding school instead of raggedy old Douglass. I can't believe he's making my gut do flip-flops!* she thought.

Mrs. Sherman checked off each student's name on her clipboard list as they arrived. Susan Richards, still wearing her dance clothes from morning rehearsal, slipped in quietly. The last student to arrive was Jack Krasinski. His hair was uncombed, and he looked as if he'd slept in his clothes—they were wrinkled and slightly sour smelling. But then, sleeping in one's clothes is sometimes necessary, Arielle thought ruefully. *Who am I to talk about somebody else?*

"Crazy Jack is here and the party can begin!" he announced, loudly crashing his ever-present cymbals,

223

startling everyone. "Who brought the chips and dip?" He laughed loudly at his own joke, but nobody else seemed to think it was very funny.

"Put those things away, Jack," the principal said sternly. "Now!"

Arielle and the other students turned to see what he would do.

He cocked his head, stared hard at Mrs. Sherman with red-rimmed eyes, then dropped the cymbals to the cement floor with a loud clattering commotion. She chose not to challenge him further.

"That's crazy, even for Jack," Kofi whispered to Arielle.

Mrs. Sherman closed the door to the classroom and began the meeting. "All of us here at Douglass High School have been concerned with the recent thefts of money and property."

"You find my stuff?" Cleveland called out, interrupting.

"Please let me finish," the principal said tersely. "We have called you here this morning to do a routine check. No one is under suspicion, and no one is being accused."

Officer Hammler spoke next in his gruff, no-nonsense voice. "Please understand that this is strictly voluntary, although we are fully within our rights to conduct this search. We are not looking in your personal property—just checking your hands. All we are asking is that you pass your hands under this black light. If nothing appears, you are free to go back to class."

"What's supposed to show up?" asked Jericho.

"Dirt if it's *your* hands!" Roscoe said jokingly.

Officer Hammler did not answer. "Let's begin," he said.

"Please walk to the front, pass both hands under the light, then get your gear and head back to your class-rooms," Mrs. Sherman instructed. "Would anyone like to volunteer to go first?"

The room was silent for a moment, then Eddie stood up and slung his backpack over his left shoulder. He walked slowly and deliberately to the front, everyone seeming to squeeze tighter into themselves as he passed. "I know everybody thinks I'm a thief and criminal, so I'm goin' first to show you how wrong you are!" He dropped his book bag on the floor and passed both hands under the UV light. Nothing showed except for the line markings on his palms. Eddie then turned to face the class. He stared directly at Dana and said, "I'm outta here. Later, losers." The door slammed as he left.

"Why am I in here?" Paula Ingram asked. "I got my stuff stolen! I'm not the thief." She put her hands under the light and left angrily.

When Kofi walked to the front, Arielle remembered what Dana had told her about Kofi's receiving the Free-dom Achievers Scholarship. He deserved it, she thought with pride. She'd known him since seventh grade—he was no thief. His hands tested clear as well.

One by one each student passed their hands under the strange blue light. Roscoe. Jericho. Cleveland. Dana. November. Olivia. Brandon. All were clean.

Dana waved at Arielle as she left. "See you in chem," she said.

Luis Morales, Wendy Bartles, and Rudy Amadour were next. Clean. Susan Richards's hands also came out clean.

225

Arielle noticed that Osrick bit his fingernails as that group hurried out of the room. No one who had that last-bell gym class, and no student aides who had been in the hall that bell, had shown any signs of the antitheft powder on their hands.

Most of the teachers were checked. Mrs. Witherspoon hurried out to finish setting her computers, Mr. Tambori left for the band room, and Ms. Hathaway said she had to finish grading a set of tests.

Just four students remained—Rosa Gonzalez, Arielle, Osrick, and Jack, who stomped up next. "I *hope* you find something on my hands," he shouted, much louder than necessary for the small room, Arielle thought. "It's just first bell and already I've had a *really* bad day!"

Here it is! Arielle just knew Jack would prove to be the thief.

Jack placed his hands under the ultraviolet light, screamed as if he were in extreme pain, and pulled them away violently. "Eeeeeeh!" he yelled. "What did you put in that blue stuff? It burns! It burns!"

Mrs. Sherman, her eyes wide, reached out to touch Jack on the shoulder, but he jerked away from her. "Jack," she said calmly, "it's just light. It can't hurt you." She put her own hand under the light to show him. "See? It's okay."

He looked at her warily, then let her guide his hands under the glow. Jack's hands tested as clear as the others, but Arielle continued to watch him. His reaction to the light was way weird in her book. He looked like he hadn't slept for days. But he seemed to have calmed down, and he stuffed his hands in his pockets.

But then he shouted, "Don't *ever* accuse me of anything again! I am *not* a thief!"

"Jack, stop by the cafeteria and get some breakfast before you go on to second bell," Mrs. Sherman suggested gently. "Sometimes a little food in the morning helps me manage my day so much better. And stop by Nurse Thornton's office as well, you hear?"

"Yeah, whatever," Jack mumbled. He grabbed his cymbals and his extra-large book bag and left.

"Maybe you were wrong, and the person was able to wash that stuff off, Osrick," Arielle whispered.

Osrick, looking quite sure of himself, shook his head.

Mrs. Sherman put down the black light and flexed her fingers. "Whew! My hands are cramping up on me. Peggy, would you finish up for me? Thanks." She handed the small black light to Miss Pringle, who seemed reluctant as she picked up the light's handle with her thumb and forefinger and nodded to Arielle to come forward. When Arielle came through clean, Miss Pringle motioned to Rosa Gonzalez. Arielle noticed that she did not go back to class as she was told, but lingered in the hall.

Osrick came up next, his small palms shining clean and bright under the light. Then he did something odd. He bumped the light with his left hand, and it slipped from Miss Pringle's grasp onto the table. As she reached to pick it up, her right hand slid under the luminosity of the UV light.

Glowing a blue-white bright, the iridescent imprint of the antitheft powder on Miss Pringle's fingers and palms screamed the accusation in the suddenly silent room.

ARIELLE GASPED. MISS PRINGLE DROPPED the black light onto the floor and the bulb shattered into tiny pieces. She looked at Officer Hammler and Mrs. Sherman, and then at her hands, which under daylight looked perfectly normal. She touched a key on the lanyard around her neck. Her eyes darted around rapidly, as if she were looking for an escape, or trying to figure out what to say.

"Peggy," Mrs. Sherman said gently, "let's go to my office and have a little chat, shall we?"

Miss Pringle nodded mutely. Officer Hammler put his hand on her shoulder as he walked out of the room with her. She did not pick up her coffee cup, so it sat there on the table, looking oddly out of place.

Arielle noticed Rosa still hovering in the hall, listening for any tidbit or detail.

"Osrick," said Mrs. Sherman, "thank you for your wonderful detective work. Until we get to the bottom of this,

I'm asking that you and Arielle keep what just happened to yourselves."

"Okay," Osrick said. Then he added, "If you check that storage room in the back of the chem lab, the one she keeps locked twenty-four/seven, I'll bet you'll find some of the stolen stuff."

Mrs. Sherman looked mildly surprised, then nodded sadly. "Go on to class now, kids."

"Okay, but we're in Miss Pringle's class second bell—there's no teacher up there!" Arielle protested.

"I'll send the building sub up in a few. You guys are seniors—I trust you to behave yourselves for five minutes. Understood?"

"Yes, ma'am."

Mrs. Sherman hurried toward her office. Rosa scurried a few paces behind the principal.

Arielle and Osrick headed in the opposite direction down the mostly deserted hall. "How did you know?" she asked him.

"I sit close to that storeroom door, you know. So I noticed that Miss Pringle was, like, *really* diligent about locking that door. Even if she went in there ten times during class, she'd lock it back up every single time, and double-check it by jiggling the lock to make sure."

"Well, she keeps chemicals and stuff in there. I guess she's required to keep it locked."

"No, there was something not normal—kinda like obsessive—about how she kept locking that door," Osrick said, shaking his head. "I made a kind of game of it—trying to peek into that storeroom before she could lock it back. Sometimes I'd catch glimpses of things."

"Like what?"

"I saw an iPhone on a shelf."

Arielle inhaled sharply. "You did? Why didn't you say something?"

"She *could* have brought her own iPhone."

"Yeah, I guess."

"I also saw a camera, a couple of cell phones, and a laptop—all neatly organized on a bookshelf."

"Lots of teachers have that stuff," Arielle reasoned.

"I know. I just had this funny feeling at first," Osrick explained. "But then I saw her take Paula Ingram's Game Boy."

"You did?"

"Yeah. She was real slick and quick about it. Remember when she was messing with Roscoe about copying off the Internet? While she was talking to him, I saw her slip her hands into Paula's book bag and drop the Game Boy into the pocket of those baggy pants she wears."

"Why didn't you say something?" Arielle asked.

"Be for real, Arielle. Who am I to accuse a teacher? You gotta have proof! That's when I started searching the Internet."

Arielle frowned. "I don't get it. Why would a teacher steal stuff? They make lots of money—at least more than any of us do."

"It's a sickness, I guess," he replied. "Like alcoholism or drug addiction."

"Freaky," she said, shaking her head. "Hey, I gotta make a bathroom stop. I'll see you upstairs. You all right?"

"Yeah, I'm fine." As she turned toward the girls' restroom, Osrick called out to her, "Hey, Arielle. Thanks for believing in me. This was the most fun I've had since I've been in high school."

"You're okay, Osrick. Really okay." She smiled, waved, and disappeared into the girls' bathroom.

UPSTAIRS, MISS PRINGLE'S ENTIRE CLASS stood by the windows watching the spectacle below. A police car had pulled up to the front of the school, red and blue lights flashing. Two officers had gone inside the building, but neither had come out yet. Kofi watched, trying to ignore his body screaming for a pain pill. *A couple more days,* he thought, *and I'll be past this. No more little Oxy babies for me. No more.* He felt like slapping himself on the back.

"Who they busting?" Cleveland asked.

"I don't know, man," Kofi replied with a shrug.

"What was all that blue light stuff about down in Room 123?" Brandon wondered.

"If your hands glowed under that light, that proved you were the school thief," Rudy explained.

"So who did they catch?"

"I don't know, man. After they checked each person, they made you leave. They obviously caught somebody, though. All I know is, it wasn't me!" said Jericho.

Eddie sat in the back of the room, his feet up on the desk in front of him. "And it wasn't *me*. Although I know lots of you hoped it was." He glanced at Dana.

Kofi tightened and released his fists. *I'm not gonna mess up the rest of my life by clocking this dude,* he thought. *But it sure would feel good.*

Kofi caught Dana's eye. *Not today,* she seemed to be saying. She took a deep breath as she watched him, and indicated he should do the same. He did, but it only helped a little.

Eric Bell said, "I notice they didn't call *me* down to be checked. I guess they were looking for somebody who could run real fast with the stolen loot!"

Jericho grabbed the handles of Eric's chair and gave him a twirl. "I've seen you get top speeds on that thing in an empty hallway, Eric. An electric wheelchair is an awesome motorcycle. Don't underestimate yourself!"

"And don't overestimate my chair. A kid on roller skates could beat me!"

"So where's Miss Pringle?" asked Kofi.

"The coffee queen? Probably downstairs in the cafeteria filling up," November replied.

"And where's Rosa?" Luis said, concern in his voice. "It's not like her to be late to class. The last I saw her was when we were in that room getting checked."

"Well, maybe she's the thief," Roscoe suggested. "Maybe that police car is for your girl."

"Don't you talk like that, man!" Luis rose out of his chair, his fist drawn back.

"Hey, chill, dude," Roscoe said apologetically. "I was just jokin'. Arielle's not back yet either. I can't help it if I notice beautiful women!"

"Crazy Jack is a no-show as well," Jericho commented, "but maybe he went home. He was actin' kinda whacked-out this morning."

Rosa bounded into the room, her eyes bright and her face full of excitement. "I know who the thief is!" she announced.

Almost everybody gathered around her. "Who is it?" they clamored, all speaking at once.

"Crazy Jack?"

"Ram?"

"Eddie?"

He glared at them from the back.

"Arielle?"

"Oh, be for real," Rosa said with a shake of her head.

"Rudy?"

"Weird Osrick?"

"No!" she said, bouncing up and down in anticipation. "It's not a student at all!" She paused for effect.

"Tell us!" they screamed.

"It's Miss Pringle!"

"Shut up!"

"That's crazy!"

"How do you know?" Luis asked.

"I work for Mrs. Sherman, you know, so I waited after I was checked. A little while later Officer Hammler took Miss Pringle back to the office, and I followed them."

"You mean *Miss Pringle*, our *teacher*, is the thief?" Jericho asked, incredulous.

"Yep. Hers were the only hands that turned blue."

"A teacher?" Roscoe echoed. "That's messed up!"

"How did they catch her?" asked Eric.

"Well, I listened on the little intercom that connects to Mrs. Sherman's office, and I heard everything!" Rosa seemed to bask in being the center of attention.

"Officer Hammler put some secret spy powder on some money and an iPod yesterday and hid it in Arielle's purse!"

"Arielle was in on it? No way!"

"No wonder she's not here."

"You know how Miss Pringle changes her clothes in the girls' locker room every day so she can go running on the track?"

"Yeah, I saw her yesterday," said November.

"Wasn't she supposed to be one of the locker room guardians?" Olivia asked. "They assigned certain teachers to look out for the thief."

"Well, that's really convenient," Dana commented wryly. "What a perfect setup."

Rosa could hardly wait to continue. "So Miss Pringle jacks the stuff out of Arielle's purse, goes on her run, and has no idea she's been caught!"

"You'd think she woulda washed her hands or taken a shower since yesterday," Cleveland mused.

"The stuff stays on for three days," Rosa said with newfound authority. "And if you rub it, it goes deeper into your skin."

"Wow."

"Remember when Mrs. Sherman got her wallet lifted in the cafeteria?" November asked the group. "Who supposedly found the wallet in the trash?"

"Miss Pringle!" Dana said, remembering.

"Nobody ever put two and two together!" Olivia smacked her head.

"They found the iPod and the money in her purse," Rosa announced. "And the rest of the stolen goods, I think, are locked in that storeroom." She pointed behind Osrick's desk.

"For real?" Roscoe ran to the door to check the knob, but it would not turn. "No wonder she kept that door tightened up all the time."

"You mean my Game Boy might be in there?" Paula asked.

"It's possible," said Rosa. "When Miss Pringle admitted to everything and told where she'd stashed the stuff, that's when Mrs. Sherman said she was forced to call the cops."

"Deep. A kleptomaniac!" Jericho said in amazement.

"Spoon would give you ten points for that word," Roscoe joked.

Rosa brought the conversation back to herself. "So I decided now was a good time to slip out of the office and tell people what I knew."

"Who else have you told?" Osrick asked from the back of the room. The whole class turned to look at him. His face was red with anger.

Rosa tossed her dark curls. "I told my two best friends,

Jennifer and Cecelia, and three other kids I didn't know, and then I came up here. Why?"

"That was private information, and not for you to tell," Osrick said furiously.

"Forget that! Juicy news like this has got to be told! How do you think reporters make a living?" She turned away from him as if she'd flicked away an insect.

"The woman deserved respect," Osrick insisted, "and privacy."

"She didn't respect *our* stuff!" said Luis, defending his girlfriend.

"And it looks like the cops aren't giving her much respect either," Cleveland reported, looking out the window. Kofi watched as well.

With hands cuffed and head bowed, Miss Pringle was being escorted out of the building by two uniformed police officers as the stunned students watched in silence.

THEN THE HUSH THAT FILLED THE ROOM was shattered. The fire alarm reverberated once again. *Clang-clong! Clang-clong! Clang-clong!*

"Not again!" Cleveland cried out in frustration. "I'm 'bout SICK of these alarms!"

"For real, now," Roscoe agreed.

Everyone in the room grumbled, moving away from the window to find their coats.

Jericho sighed. "Let's get Eric, dudes, and get on out of here."

"Hey, now they need to spread that blue stuff on the fire alarm, to get that crazy alarm ringer out of here," November said thoughtfully.

Kofi put both his hands to his head. The constant headache pounded, his stomach churned, and his shoulders itched. Everything seemed to throb like a purple cloud around him. And that clanging, clanging, clanging of the fire alarm wouldn't stop.

In the next moment, everything changed.

Kofi inhaled and almost forgot to breathe out. The classroom seemed to be suspended in time. Like a stop-motion movie scene, he stood by that window observing every detail, every person, every event separately, and at the same time.

The classroom windows—dull, yellowed, and streaked.

The stacks of chemistry books on the floor—covers curled at the edges.

The computers—humming and glowing with fuzzy printed text.

A wastebasket—overflowing with paper and chip wrappers and dirty tissues.

The sharp smell of orange peels and spilled chocolate milk—more trash.

Desks—scuffed, scratched, and bent, never quite balanced on all four legs.

The late winter sun—dull gold, trapped outside the locked windows.

The painted concrete floor—criss-crossed with the shadows of dusty footprints.

The periodic table of the elements—creased, ripped, and memorized.

A whiteboard—smeared with notes from colored markers.

Posters of several long-dead scientists on the wall—looking serious and cold.

Jericho—his face mirroring confidence, confusion, then disbelief.

Eric—intense, but helpless, his hand clutching the controller of his chair.

Rosa—screaming and screaming.

Luis—reaching out to pull her close to him, her screams turning to whimpers.

Olivia—her round face full of shock. She does not move.

November—frantically searching with her eyes.

Roscoe—silent for once. Hands trembling.

Cleveland—big and powerful, but unsure. Fear covers his face.

Brandon—pale, red-faced, one hand in his pocket.

Dana—his Dana—crawling on the floor.

Paula—stunned and silent.

Osrick—huddled almost unseen in the back.

Eddie—looking almost amused.

And Jack—red-eyed and crazed—standing at the door. Pointing an AK-47 assault rifle directly at them all.

"Everybody sit down!" Jack yelled. They sat. Dana stayed on the floor, curled into a ball. Rosa had curled herself into the arms of Luis.

This is unreal! Kofi thought. *Stuff like this only happens on the news.*

"What's up with this, Jack?" Jericho said, his voice steady.

"Shut up!" Jack screamed. He pointed the gun directly at Jericho. November gasped.

The fire alarm continued to ring shrilly in the background, a crazy accompaniment to Jack's appearance. *Clang-clong! Clang-clong! Clang-clong!*

"I will no longer be ignored!" Jack cried out. "It's time to *listen* to what I have to say!"

"We're here to listen, man," Jericho continued, looking

Jack in the eye, his voice quiet, soothing. "Just spit it out. We're here for you, Jack." He took one step away from Eric, whom he'd been shielding with his body, toward Jack.

Don't try to be a hero, Jericho! Kofi screamed in his head.

"Don't move!" Jack growled.

Jericho froze.

Jack looked around the room, taking in the scene, aiming the gun erratically—first at Roscoe, then Rosa, who cringed, and finally at Dana.

Kofi inhaled deeply. *Not my Dana. No way!*

Jack's eyes blinked rapidly. "Where's Pringle?" he asked.

"She's not coming back," Jericho explained.

"Why not?"

"She got arrested," said Eric quietly, using the same tones Jericho had.

"I don't get it." Jack looked confused.

"She was the thief."

"And see, they tried to blame *me*!" Jack raged. "Made me feel like dirt—checking my hands for poison." He rubbed his left hand on his jeans. His right hand held the rifle securely.

"They checked all of us, Jack," Jericho reminded him. "All of us." Somehow he seemed to have become the spokesperson for the class.

"That blue light!" Jack said. "They tried to burn me with the blue light!"

"The light is gone now, man," Jericho said softly.

Jack pointed the gun at Jericho once more. "Hey! Don't try to handle me, dude! I'm not crazy!"

Jericho put up a hand to show he was backing off.

"I know they call me Crazy Jack. But I'm NOT!" he screamed.

"You cool, Jack. Real cool." Kofi was amazed at how calm Jericho seemed to be.

"Blue poison. Blue light," Jack mumbled over and over. "Blue poison. Blue light."

Kofi glanced out the window. The school had emptied, and students and teachers stood in small groups, waiting for the all-clear bell. The police car that held Miss Pringle in the backseat had not yet left the driveway.

He also saw Mrs. Sherman with a clipboard, looking up in the direction of their room. She looked angry. She must have figured out that their class had not left the building.

I bet she thinks we ditched the fire drill because we don't have a teacher up here, Kofi reasoned. He wondered if there was a way to signal her. *If I can just jiggle these blinds a little . . .*

Jack brandished the rifle at Dana again. Kofi tensed, ready to spring forward to protect her.

"Get up!" Jack yelled at Dana. "Get off the floor."

Dana held her shoulders square, and her face was a mix of anger and fear. She started to ease into her desk chair, but Jack said, "No! Go stand over there." He pointed the gun toward the back wall.

She glided to the farthest corner of the back wall, whispering, "Stay cool, Jack. Stay cool."

Jack ignored her. To the rest of the class he said, "All

of you! Line up on that back wall. Everybody! Move it!" He waved the gun wildly, and kids scrambled to where he indicated. Kofi noticed that Jack's finger was on the trigger.

Jericho slowly navigated a path through the desk chairs and wheeled Eric to the back with the others. A couple of kids burst into tears, but everyone else was silent. Even Eddie got up and moved without comment. The fire alarm had stopped its clanging. All was silent.

I have to do something quick! Kofi thought. He continued to pull on the frayed cord of the window covering, hoping to give the people below some kind of indication they were in the room. *If only Sherman would get mad enough to march up here. We'd have help.*

He pulled the cord again. Nothing happened. He tugged harder. The shades had not been adjusted in months, and the sun had rotted the small wooden pegs that held the blinds in place. He gave one more yank on the cord, and with a *whoosh*, the entire window-shade assembly— shades, blinds, and cords—came thundering to the floor.

Jack pivoted to face Kofi, and as his irritation turned to rage, he pulled the trigger. The noise was overpowering, numbing, terrifying.

Throp-throp! Brat-brat-brat-brat! Thwuk-thwuk-thwuk! Rada-rada-rada-rada-rada! Rhacka-rhacka-rhacka! Throp-throp-throp! As the glass in the far window shattered, it sprinkled the screaming students with tiny diamonds of razor-sharp shards.

EVERYONE SEEMED TO LOOK UP TO THAT third-floor window at the same time, stunned by the *rat-a-tat-tat* of some kind of unidentified series of explosions, and the fracturing sights and sounds of fragmenting glass cascading to the ground.

Arielle didn't scream at first. It took her a moment to make sense of what she was seeing and hearing. Kids around her yelled and ran for cover, but she just stood there, stupidly staring at the gaping holes in the windows of what she knew was room 317.

Finally someone grabbed her and dragged her behind a tree. It was Mrs. Witherspoon. Several other students hovered there as well, peeking out to see what was happening.

"What's going on, Spoon?" Arielle asked fearfully.

"Sounds like gunshots," the teacher replied, her voice sounding as scared as Arielle felt.

"Gunshots? That's crazy!"

"Somebody from off the street, maybe?" Mrs. Wither-spoon trembled as her arms held Arielle.

"He took the time to go to the third floor to shoot up the place?"

"You want this to make sense?" asked Mrs. Wither-spoon, exasperated.

"But that's my chemistry class!" Arielle shouted. "I'm supposed to be up there."

"Well, thank God you're not."

"But my friends are in there! They might be hurt! They might be . . ." She started to cry. She couldn't bear to think that something might have happened to Dana or November or Jericho, or even Olivia. And Osrick. She'd almost forgotten him.

Mrs. Witherspoon patted her gently on the shoulder. "Stop talking like that! I'm sure they're all just fine." But she didn't sound confident.

Arielle looked back up at the shattered windows. No sounds or movement came from the room upstairs with the shattered windows. It was ominously silent above, but the area below had become a hurricane of activity.

The police who had been called for Miss Pringle were already in action. More police cruisers rushed to the scene, followed, seemingly instantaneously, by ambulances and EMT trucks.

Students were pushed back behind lines of yellow tape that appeared from nowhere, it seemed. Officers scurried around, barking orders and calling for backup.

"Shots fired! Shots fired at Douglass High School!"

the police radios reported to one another as officers surrounded the building and prepared the approach.

"We have a possible hostage situation."

"Bring in the SWAT team, George!"

"Take all possible precautions."

"Repeat—we have a possible hostage situation."

"Shots *have* been fired!"

"SWAT team at the ready, sir!"

Arielle shuddered next to Mrs. Witherspoon. All around her, other students were making frantic phone calls.

"Mommy! Come get me!" one girl cried. "Somebody is shooting people here at school!"

"Hey, Dad," a boy's shaky voice whispered. "Come to the school and pick me up. No, Dad—I'm not in trouble. But somebody has a gun. I heard the shots. Come quick!"

Another caller cried, "Grandma! Grandma! Turn down the TV so you can hear me! Tell Uncle Louie to come up to the school and get me! He's not answering his cell phone!"

Teachers called 911 on their cell phones. "Hello. We have an emergency here at Douglass High. We think somebody has been shot. Please—please hurry!"

Parents started to arrive in minutes. Cars screeched to a stop and parked sideways on the lawns of homes near the school. Mothers screamed their children's names. Students screamed out for parents. It was absolute chaos.

Arielle had no phone. She had no way to reach her mother.

Since nobody knew exactly what was happening, some of the calls she overheard were wild, fueled by terror instead of facts. And somehow, the information about Miss Pringle had leaked out and spread like a disease.

"Is this Channel Five? Connect me to Natasha Singletary. Tell her she'd better get down to Douglass High School. All hell is breaking loose! We got gunmen running up and down the halls! And a teacher has been arrested as a thief."

"Hey, Mom! Bombs exploded and blew up the whole third floor of the school!"

"It's the terrorists, Daddy! They've taken over the school building!"

"People are dead and dying! Hurry!"

"There's a teacher shooting at kids upstairs, Mom!"

"I heard screams and gunshots!"

"Somebody shot the teacher who stole everybody's stuff!"

"They wore hoods and vests and had bullets roped around their chests!"

"I heard ten students are dead—maybe more!"

Mrs. Witherspoon reached over to one of the callers and said, "Don't exaggerate, sweetie. We really don't know about any injuries yet. Let's just wait and pray, okay?"

The girl nodded but flipped her phone back open to make another call.

News trucks with huge antennas spiking to the sky arrived next, with perfectly coiffed reporters breathlessly repeating themselves and telling nothing at all. The only information they had was that shots had been fired, windows had been broken, and one class was unaccounted for.

Arielle thought it was a good example for a multiplication

lesson: Take a little info and multiply that by a lot of hype, add in a little speculation, and you've got a news story that can run for hours.

She recognized Natasha Singletary from Channel Five. Arielle thought she was a pretty good reporter. She'd seen the woman do interviews on TV, and she usually asked sensible questions and tried to be sensitive to the feelings of the people she talked to. She was taller and thinner than she looked on television. Her makeup was perfect, as if it had been painted on.

"This is Natasha Singletary, News Five Live," she began. "I'm standing outside Douglass High School, where just minutes ago shots were fired. We do not know yet of any injuries, but the entire window of a third-floor classroom has been just about disintegrated. Ominously, no students have shown themselves at that window, and we know that one class of seniors did not come out of the building during the fire drill. Rick, show our viewers a close-up of that area."

Ignoring the reporter, Mrs. Sherman, with her usually perfectly combed hair disheveled and unpinned, ran over to Mrs. Witherspoon. "Maggie, I need your help," she said.

"Of course," replied Mrs. Witherspoon. She moved from her hiding place to accompany the principal to an area where police had set up tables and communications devices. Arielle, fascinated with the news reports but not wanting to be alone, followed quietly.

"I was just about to go up to the third floor, give those seniors a piece of my mind, and drag them out of there by their ears," the principal told Mrs. Witherspoon. "But then the shooting started. The police wouldn't let me into the building!" She sounded distraught.

"You thought they were blowing off the fire drill?" the teacher asked.

"We've had so many false alarms, and you know how seniors can be this time of year. But now they're . . . they're . . ." She paused, seemingly overwhelmed. "I should have gone in to rescue my kids."

"Your job right now is to take care of the hundreds of students and families standing here outside," Mrs. Witherspoon said, her voice soothing. "They need you too."

Mrs. Sherman glanced up at the gaping hole above her. "You're right," she said quietly.

Arielle stood silently to one side.

"Thank you for letting me help," Miss Pringle told the principal. "They were just about to drive me away." Her hands uncuffed, her face a mask of confusion, she looked dazed.

"Well, it's *your* class up there." Mrs. Sherman looked angry, as if she needed someone to blame, Arielle thought.

"Tell us now, who are the students in that classroom?" a police officer who introduced himself as Officer Johnson asked Miss Pringle. "Is there anyone with a social or emotional problem who might be up there?"

"What makes you think it's a student?" Miss Pringle asked, a quiver in her voice.

"We don't know if it is, ma'am. But you know best who's up there and what the dynamics of that class should be. Am I right?"

"Yes, sir. You're right. But suppose someone off the street is up there shooting at my"—she choked back a sob—"my kids?"

"You didn't seem to have any problem taking their stuff," another police officer commented, but Officer Johnson—his superior, Arielle supposed—shot him a look and he said nothing more.

"We have another team working on that angle, ma'am," Johnson told her. "Just answer my questions, please. Who's up there that could maybe go bananas?"

"Well, there's Eddie Mahoney. He's just back from juvenile detention, and he's got a real mean streak. Lots of students are afraid of him, and I think there's bad blood between Eddie and a kid named Kofi Freeman." Arielle was amazed Miss Pringle knew so much about her students—she always seemed to be a little distant.

"Bad enough for a gunfight?" the second police officer asked. His nameplate read TORINO.

"I don't know. In my day, things like this were settled with a fistfight. Kids today shoot first and ask questions later."

Mrs. Witherspoon spoke up. "Kofi and Eddie had an altercation in my classroom a couple of weeks ago," she offered.

"Do you know what started it?" Officer Torino asked.

"Yes. It was over a girl. Dana Wolfe. She's Kofi's girlfriend."

Arielle held her breath. Hearing her friends' names being discussed like characters in a police television show was unsettling. Surely this couldn't be something Eddie had planned.

Officer Johnson jotted down the three names. "Anyone else?"

"Well," Miss Pringle continued, "there's little Osrick Wardley, but he's more of a computer geek than a fighter. He *is* a little odd, however. Kids pick on him—quite a bit." Miss Pringle bit her fingernails while the officer wrote down Osrick's name.

Arielle spoke up. "Excuse me, sir, but I'm enrolled in that class, and Osrick couldn't hurt a fly."

"Who are you, and how do you know?" Officer Johnson asked.

Arielle thought about it, and surprised herself by saying, "Because he's my friend."

That didn't seem to mean much to the officer. Instead he asked her pointedly, "So why aren't *you* in class, young lady? I need your name for my records." Arielle heard suspicion in his tone.

She shrugged. "My name is Arielle Gresham. I had to go to the bathroom. Then the fire alarm went off. So I never got to class."

When she said the words "fire alarm," Mrs. Sherman, Miss Pringle, and Mrs. Witherspoon all looked at one another and said at the same moment, "Jack Krasinski!"

"Who?" asked Johnson.

"The kids call him 'Crazy Jack,' but he's harmless. He plays the cymbals and the drums in the band, and he likes noise—lots of noise," Miss Pringle explained.

"And we've had a rash of false fire alarms lately," said Mrs. Witherspoon. "Nobody could prove it, but we all suspected Jack."

251

"I'd even planned to sprinkle the antitheft powder we used to catch you, Peggy," Mrs. Sherman said sadly, "on the fire alarms so we could catch that person as well."

Miss Pringle looked away, her pale face even more ashen.

"Well, the alarm *did* go off just before the shooting started. And Jack *is* in that class," Mrs. Witherspoon said, her voice trailing off as if she were thinking hard.

"The fire drill was a good thing, actually," Officer Johnson said. "It cleared the building of most of the students."

"We have standard emergency procedures in place that we practice once a month," Mrs. Sherman explained. "Each teacher has a kit that includes a clipboard of names and contacts, basic first aid supplies, and a flashlight. Every student, teacher, and administrator knows exactly what to do. My assistant principals tell me all students have been accounted for."

"Except for the kids in room 317," Arielle said, fear catching in her throat.

The principal frowned, thinking back. "Jack was acting unusually strange this morning, now that I think about it. I told him to get some food and see the nurse. Jack's one of our kids who is given his meds at school each day."

Torino and Johnson both scribbled furiously.

"But he's *never* shown any signs of aggression or violence," Mrs. Sherman added. "He's usually just fun-loving and noisy. We've learned to ignore him."

Officer Torino looked up. "Maybe he got tired of being overlooked."

IN THE CLASSROOM, SHOCKED SILENCE followed the gunshots and screams. Then a few whimpers. Some soft cries. No one moved.

Ducking just before Jack had unloaded the rifle on the windows, Kofi had dropped to the floor and crawled on his hands and knees to the far wall. Glass cut into his palms and knees.

He reached Dana, who grabbed him and pulled him to her. Her heart beat wildly against his, and he could tell from her forceful breathing that she was more angry than afraid. He knew she wanted to lash out somehow, but he held her tightly, sending her a mental message to be still and silent.

The class, suddenly cold with the rush of outside air, waited expectantly.

"How dare you try to destroy my kingdom?" Jack screamed at Kofi. "What were you trying to do—play the hero?"

"No, you the man," Kofi whispered evenly. He looked directly at Jack but didn't dare say more with the rifle pointing at him. The gun, about three feet long and made of polished brown wood and gleaming gray steel, was tucked securely in the curve of Jack's shoulder. The magazine protruded like a deadly appendage, ready to unleash more terror into the room. Kofi had never smelled gunpowder before, but he knew in an instant what that odd burnt smell had to be.

"This is *so* much better than a drum! So much louder!" Jack said, suddenly sounding almost gleeful. "SO MUCH BETTER!" He pointed the rifle wildly at the cowering students in front of him. "It's even better than the fire alarm. A gun blasts, and echoes, and destroys! And everyone hears it!" Jack was sweating profusely now, his eyes manic.

Kofi glanced over at Jericho and made eye contact. Jericho sat on the floor not far from him, blocking Olivia. The slightest tilt of Kofi's head sent a message: *Can we take him?*

Jericho blinked back with a tiny shake of his head. *Not yet.*

Jack then climbed up onto the front table of the classroom and aimed randomly at first one student, then another. "I'm the king of the world! I am power! I am light! I am better than fireworks! I am THUNDER!"

At that, he pulled the trigger once more. The room exploded with screams.

Pow-POW-POW-thwack! Rada-rada-rada-rada-rada! Rhacka-rhacka-rhacka! Throp-throp-throp! With a crunch and a crash, the first computer exploded in fiery blue and orange splinters.

"Blue light! More blue light! Did you *see* it?" Jack cried out as if to prove his theory. "They were hiding in the computers, spying on me! You saw them! You saw the blue poison come out of the monster! I have to make them stop!"

With that he shot three more computers. Sparks flashed out of one of them, so Jack shot it again.

When Jack eased his finger off the trigger, the screaming stopped, only to be replaced by the wail of what Kofi imagined had to be dozens of sirens. Although he couldn't see outside, he knew the authorities would rescue them soon. At least he hoped so. He didn't know how much longer Jack would be content shooting computers instead of people.

LIKE A DELAYED ECHO, AS SOON AS THOSE outside the school heard the round of shots and shrieks, they started screaming as well. Officer Johnson pushed Arielle and Mrs. Witherspoon under the table and pulled out his own weapon. The mood seemed to shift from shock and horror to hysteria.

"It's the terrorists!" someone cried out.

"They're killing our children! DO something!" a parent screamed, tugging frantically at Officer Torino's arms.

Arielle squatted under the table, terrified, as the police scurried like ants in response to the new gunfire. They seemed to be mobilizing to go in and take out the shooter or shooters.

"My daughter is in that room!" a familiar voice yelled from the crowd.

"Parents are to meet at the recreation center across the street, ma'am," a police officer said back.

"Why don't YOU go across the street?" And Arielle knew who *that* was. She scrambled out from under the table as her mother gave Officer Torino a piece of her mind. "I am not leaving this block of concrete I'm standing on until somebody gets my daughter out of there safely! Now get out of my way and get back to rescuing those children!" The officer retreated, and Arielle flung herself into her mother's arms.

The two hugged for a very long time. "I'm okay, Mommy," Arielle said, wiping away the tears that streamed down her mother's face.

"How did you get out?" asked her mother, touching her daughter's face.

"I was never in there. I was late to class," Arielle explained.

"Thank God. I thought . . . oh God . . . I thought I'd lost you," her mother cried, pulling Arielle in tight again.

"How'd you get here?" Arielle thought to ask.

"I took a cab. Nice guy. I told him my daughter was at the school where the shooting was going on, and he didn't even charge me for the ride."

"My friends are up there," Arielle told her. "I'm scared, Mom."

"We've got to pray they'll be okay," her mother said softly, taking Arielle's hand in hers.

Natasha Singletary and the other reporters babbled continuously, frantically trying to keep up with each new development. Since none of the police or administrators would talk to them, they interviewed students and parents instead.

"Do you know any of the students trapped upstairs?" Natasha asked Susan Richards.

"I know all of them," she told her. "I'm a senior, and I'm terrified for them."

"Do you have any idea who might be shooting?" the reporter asked her.

"No, ma'am," Susan replied. "It's got to be somebody who's really, really sick."

Just then a third set of explosions rocked the air above. The cries and wild speculations from the parents and students below continued.

"Oh God! Have they all been killed?"

"Who's the shooter?"

"A student, I heard."

"I bet it's one of those strange kids who wear black coats and make death threats on their MySpace page."

"Quit stereotyping!"

"All teenagers are a little strange, if you ask me!"

"Where would a kid get a gun?"

"It's easy. The Internet, eBay, Gunstupid.com. Who knows?"

"I buy guns off the Internet all the time. But I'm a hunter," a parent commented.

"Well, somebody is hunting our kids up there because of idiots like you!" the man standing next to him replied angrily.

"Don't blame me for the crazies in the world!"

The two men, about to come to blows, were silenced by the forceful voice of a diminutive girl from the crowd. "I just got a text message from room 317!"

The crowd hushed as Susan Richards raced to Mrs. Sherman, who gratefully took the girl's cell phone.

Mrs. Sherman read the message, then passed the phone to Officer Johnson, who nodded. The news reporters pushed their way forward. The principal held up the phone, then announced, "We have information to share. A text message has been received from Osrick Wardley, one of the students in the room!"

"What does it say?" a father yelled out.

"I'll read it," Mrs. Sherman replied breathlessly. "'JACK KRASINSKI IS THE SHOOTER. NOBODY HURT. EVERYBODY SCARED. HELP US!'"

KOFI, WHO HAD MOVED HIS BODY SO THAT Dana was behind him, surveyed his trembling classmates. Some held their ears; most curled themselves into the smallest possible target. Eric sat in his chair, higher than the others, gripping the wheels of his chair. He was exposed to the greatest risk. Osrick, almost hidden in the corner, seemed to be fiddling with something in front of him. Kofi hoped it was a cell phone and that the kid wasn't so scared that he'd forget to turn off the sound. He also prayed Jack wouldn't notice Osrick's furtive movements.

The girls in the room, even though they were teary-eyed, also looked angry and ready to fight back. Kofi knew that November would fight to make sure that her baby saw her again, and that Dana was as fierce as the wolf of her name when she had to be. Olivia's physical strength and power could overwhelm a small combat force. Rosa's one-inch fingernails could be useful.

Of the boys in the room, in addition to himself and Jericho, he guessed Cleveland, Luis, Roscoe, Brandon, and Eddie were big enough and tough enough to take a skinny kid like Jack. Make that a skinny kid with a loaded rifle—big difference.

Jack still stood on the front table, swaying crazily and talking even crazier.

"Let there be light! Sunlight only!" Jack screamed. *Pow-POW-POW!* He shot out first one of the fluorescent lights in the ceiling, then the other. More sharp-edged glass particles rained down on the screaming students.

Somebody's gotta do something, Kofi thought. But what?

Jack glanced up at the closed-circuit television in the corner. "They're watching me," he said, ducking down. "Spies are everywhere, but I know their secrets. They hide in the television and try to steal my thoughts."

From a squat, without warning, he shot the television. It burst into thousands of fragments. The noise was tremendous, but the students did not cry out this time—they only huddled closer to one another.

Where are the cops? Kofi wondered. *What's taking them so long?*

Then Eddie stood up.

Dana and a couple of the others gasped.

"Hey, Jack," Eddie said in a voice that sounded so lazy, so mellow that Kofi could hardly believe it. Eddie carried a freshly sharpened yellow pencil in each hand. He didn't look scared. He took two steps forward.

"Don't move!" Jack warned, aiming at Eddie.

"You *are* the king of everything, Jack," said Eddie. He took two more steps. His voice was quiet, yet still had that gravelly quality. "I like your noise."

Jack cocked his head. "Yeah," he said. "Noise."

Eddie took one more slow, deliberate step. "Drums are my favorite," he drawled.

"Drums," Jack repeated. He seemed mesmerized.

Eddie took the two pencils and began to play a rhythm on the back of the desk closest to him. "Flamadiddle, paradiddle, double-stroke, roll," Eddie chanted as he bopped the pencils. "Ratamacooey, ratamacooey, rimshot, bop!"

"You're good," said Jack. He blinked rapidly. "Where'd you learn percussion?"

"I used to be in a band," Eddie said, his voice even and slow. He never stopped his rhythmic tapping with the pencils.

"It's not *loud* enough!" Jack complained. He lowered the rifle a few inches, but his finger stayed on the trigger.

"So make it louder. You got your sticks with you?" Eddie never took his eyes off Jack. He kept drumming.

"Yeah, I do."

"Get 'em out. Play with me. Let's make it loud! Flamadiddle, paradiddle, double-stroke, roll," Eddie said once more.

"I need my drum," Jack said hesitantly, looking confused.

"No, you don't, man. Just your sticks."

"My sticks are in my bag!" He glanced quickly to the floor, his eyes lingering on his book bag. His finger, however, was still firmly curled on the trigger of the gun.

"We can play on the table," Eddie's voice could have melted concrete.

"I'll dominate, man."

"Show me," Eddie said, still tapping, still tapping. He took two more steps forward.

"I gotta get my sticks."

"You and me—we'll rock the house!" Eddie nodded gently, encouragingly.

Jack eased himself slowly off the table and carefully reached behind him for his book bag.

Kofi looked to Jericho and Cleveland and mouthed the words, "Get ready."

Jack began to dig down in his bag for his drumsticks with his left hand.

Eddie kept tapping.

Jericho moved slightly.

Jack kept searching.

Kofi shifted his weight forward. Jack didn't seem to notice.

Eddie kept tapping.

Jack turned his head slightly to look in his bag.

That was all they needed.

It all happened at once.

Jericho lunged forward, all his football training exploding as he tackled Jack to the floor.

As Jack fell, the rifle went off and disintegrated the glass cabinet. Beakers and flasks and tubes and cylinders exploded.

Screams blended with the sounds of shattering glass.

Cleveland and Roscoe landed on Jack as well, pinning

him down so he couldn't move. Then Olivia leaped on top of the pile as well, hollering, "No more shooting!"

The gun, however, was still firmly in Jack's hand.

Kofi saw what he had to do. He darted around the pile of kids on Jack, slid to the floor, uncurled Jack's forefinger from around the trigger, and carefully but forcefully pulled the gun from Jack's hand. Jack had no struggle left in him.

Kofi stood up and gazed at the rifle like it was a specimen from an alien museum. He held it firmly in both hands, awed by its sleekness and power. He breathed a deep sigh of relief.

Instead of silence, however, suddenly Kofi was surrounded with even more screaming, because the classroom door burst open. What seemed like hundreds of police officers with helmets and shields and guns drawn stormed into the room. "Don't move! Police!" one of them bellowed at Kofi.

Another officer yelled, "Put down the weapon! I repeat. Put down the weapon NOW!"

Are they yelling at me? Kofi thought in confusion. He opened his mouth to explain, but before he could say a word, two massive cops slammed into him, ripping the gun from his hands, dragging him roughly to the floor.

Kofi cried out in pain. His face was being pushed into the broken debris on the floor. Like a close-up on television, he could see the sharp edges of the glass shards. They looked like tiny jewels, but he could feel the glass cutting into his face.

They're gonna kill me! They think I'm the shooter! He tried to speak up, but he could barely catch his breath because of the weight of a heavy boot on his back. Kofi felt cuffs being laced around his wrists. He knew his nose was bleeding.

"Hey!" he heard Dana shout. "You got the wrong guy! Get up offa Kofi!"

"Is anyone hurt?" a policeman's voice called out, ignoring Dana.

"We're all fine," Dana insisted. "But *you're* hurting Kofi!"

"The perpetrator is not injured," another officer's voice replied. "We have secured him for your safety. Now everyone out of here. Now!"

"You don't get it!" November cried out.

"Kofi is no perp!" Dana screamed.

"He's not the shooter!" said Rosa, her voice sounding exasperated.

"So who is this Kofi?" an officer said, sounding perplexed, but finally listening.

Finally! Kofi thought.

Brandon's voice followed. "You want the dude under there!" he shouted, pointing to the pile of kids on the floor.

"Jack Krasinski is the shooter!" Dana tried to explain. "Kofi took the gun from *him*!"

Kofi could imagine the looks on the faces of the officers who were gradually figuring out what was going on. He hoped they looked real stupid—and sorry.

He could hear the other kids in the class. It seemed to take the cops a million years to admit they were wrong and let up on him.

"Kofi wrestled the gun from Jack."

"He ripped it from the hands of Crazy Jack! Then you stomp on him like that."

"He did *your* job, man."

"We all did. What took you all so long?"

"Let him *up*!" Dana's voice shouted again.

Kofi then felt himself being lifted from the floor. The cuffs were removed. He rubbed his wrists.

"Sorry, kid," an officer said as he brushed off Kofi's shirt. It was covered with tiny pieces of broken glass.

"We thought you were the shooter," another one explained. "You *did* have the gun in your hands."

"Protocol," said a policeman with a deep, officious voice. "Disarm the suspect first."

Kofi, trying to maintain a bit of his dignity in front of the rest of the class, replied, "I'm just glad you didn't come in here and start shooting! I'd be dead, and all the 'sorries' in the world wouldn't make a bit of difference."

The cops looked away without responding. Finally the first officer asked him, "Are you hurt?" He peered at Kofi's face.

"Nah, but you guys sure don't operate like the cops on television!"

Kofi looked around. There must have been twenty-five heavily armed police officers in the classroom. They all wore helmets and thick protective vests. Some were talking with students, asking questions and jotting down notes.

"I'm Officer Garfield," another officer said, addressing the whole group. "Let me ask once again: Is anyone injured? Anybody need medical attention?" He had put away his gun and replaced it with a pad of paper and a pen.

"I don't think so," Olivia replied, looking around the group.

Glass crunched under the heavy boots of the officers as they helped Jericho and the other boys up. Finally Jack was lifted from the floor.

Roscoe, Cleveland, and Jericho looked stunned, and pleased with themselves. "That was awesome, man," Jericho said, brushing dirt and debris off his shirt.

"It was like a slow-motion movie," said Cleveland.

"Best tackle I ever made," Jericho whispered. "And my girl Olivia is the bomb!"

"Coach would be proud of her," Roscoe added. For once he didn't joke or grin.

They all watched Jack, who had gone completely limp, mumble incoherently. He looked pale and dazed as the officers cuffed him roughly.

Kofi said, "He's sick, man. He didn't hurt anybody."

"Where're my drumsticks?" Jack asked. His voice sounded thick and syrupy.

"We heard so much shooting," one of the officers said.

"He only killed computers," Dana explained.

Once Jack was cuffed, the police officers appeared to relax. They almost seemed a little disappointed, Kofi thought, that they really had nothing to do but take Jack into custody. Two of them walked Jack toward the hallway.

Eddie, who leaned against the door of the classroom

watching the drama unfold, told Jack, "We still gonna play together one day, my man."

Jack nodded in confusion as two officers led him out.

Kofi caught Eddie's eye. "You saved us, man," he said in amazement.

Eddie just shrugged. "It was no big deal." Then, like a shadow, he quietly slipped out of the room.

Making their way through the unbelievable mess of glass and broken electronics, the police took photographs and continued to question the still-shaken students.

One by one everyone stood up shakily, dusted themselves off, and hugged one another in relief.

Jericho grabbed Olivia and enveloped her in a bear hug.

Kofi ran to Dana and kissed her passionately. He didn't care who saw them.

Luis wiped Rosa's tears and brushed away bits of glass from her face.

"We're going to need statements from each of you," Officer Garfield told them all.

"I wanna see my mother first!" Rosa cried out.

"And my baby," November added quietly.

"I gotta get out of here!" shouted Olivia. "You can talk to us downstairs!"

Garfield replied with understanding. "I have everyone's name and address. After you have found your parents, please come with them to the communications area we have established outside so that you can be properly interviewed."

Everyone nodded in agreement, and they filed out of the room slowly. Roscoe pushed Eric and headed toward the elevator. Brandon, looking pale and shaken, followed behind with Cleveland. Olivia held Jericho's hand tightly. Rosa and Luis stood so close together they looked like one person. Osrick walked alone.

Kofi whispered to Dana, "I'll be right down." He kissed her lightly, and she hurried out with the others.

Kofi looked back at the shattered room as they left. The police, who worked quietly and effectively, collecting data for their reports, ignored him. Kofi inhaled and realized that he felt great—no itching, no chills, no yearning for the pills. *Dana will be proud of me.* Then standing taller, he said to himself, *Heck, I'm proud of me!* He knew he'd never go back. A small fragment of the tattered window shade flapped noisily as the wind blew through the gaping hole where ordinary used to be.

AS THE HOSTAGE STUDENTS EMERGED from the doors, the throngs of people outside cheered. Everyone, from news reporters to parents, teachers, and other students, crowded in on them, clamoring for interviews and information. Cameras flashed, microphones were extended, and videotape was streamed back live to TV studios in town and across the airwaves to national news services. Arielle figured Natasha Singletary finally had enough information to televise for days.

November's mother pushed her way to the front of the crowd with tears in her eyes and the baby in her arms. November collapsed with relief right there on the ground, clutching Sunshine to her chest. Arielle watched as a camera operator zoomed in for a close-up.

Arielle had never been so glad to see a group of people in her life. She surprised herself by running to Olivia first and hugging her tightly. "I'm *so* glad you're okay," she said, her voice breaking. Then she started to pull back, worried that she'd gone too far. "Uh, I'm so sorry, Olivia, for everything." And then she burst into tears.

But Olivia hugged her just as hard in return. Then she released Arielle, dug in her pocket for a tissue, and handed it to her. "Chill, girlfriend. We're straight. But thanks."

Arielle nodded numbly.

"I gotta admit—I came pretty close to wettin' my pants," Olivia said, "but I knew Jericho wouldn't let anything happen to us."

Jericho smirked. "Hey, I'm big, but I don't think I'm bulletproof!"

Arielle didn't hug Jericho, but she poked him in the arm and told him, "I heard the NFL is looking for players. They tell me your tackle was world class!"

"Aw, it was me and a bunch of other dudes," Jericho said with a shrug. "I'm no hero."

Arielle then ran to embrace Dana and Kofi, as well as Rosa and Luis. When she got to Roscoe, he said, "Hey, pretty girl-face! Why don't you kiss me and erase the trauma of my ordeal? I think I may need to be kissed all day long." He made a silly pucker face of his lips.

"Get a goldfish," she told him, but she said it with a smile.

Everyone seemed to be talking at once. Arielle inhaled it all, glad to be included in the hugs and well-wishing.

"When the windows exploded, I thought I was gonna die!" Rosa exclaimed.

"How did he get a gun into the school?" Miss Singletary asked.

"I think he hid it under his coat," Brandon replied. He waved at Arielle as more reporters surrounded the group.

"What made him start shooting?" Natasha Singletary continued.

"We don't know."

"Did he say anything that could give us any indication of what was going on in his mind?"

"Jack's mind was parked in a no-parking zone. He was talkin' off the wall," Luis said.

"He kept talking about noise and light and power and more stuff that didn't make any sense," added Rosa.

"So what exactly was he shooting at?"

"Windows. Lights. Computers. Televisions. He killed them all," Roscoe told them dramatically.

The cameras moved in for a close-up as Roscoe spoke. Arielle knew he loved the attention.

"Where's my mother?" Dana pleaded. When she saw her mom push her way through the crowd, she sprinted over to her, picked her mother up, and spun her around. The cameras captured that as well.

"Is anyone hurt?" a medic asked.

"I have a headache from all the noise," Cleveland replied, "but I'm okay."

"I got, like, a million tiny cuts on my face," Rosa told the medic. "I'm not gonna need plastic surgery, am I?" She sounded half-serious.

The medic replied, "Not likely, but let me take a look."

"I have some small cuts on my arms and face from the flying glass," Paula told him. "It's nothing."

Each student was treated with Band-Aids or alcohol

swabs or antiseptic cream, but no one seemed to be seriously injured.

Finally Eric spoke up. "I think I broke my back," he said to the medic. "I don't think I can walk!"

The EMT, who at first looked concerned, finally laughed. "Don't do me like that, kid!"

"Well, if I can't joke about it, who can?" Eric replied sheepishly.

"Are all my puppies okay?" Mrs. Witherspoon called out as she ran over to the group. It was clear she had been crying.

"I can't think of a word big enough to describe how I feel, Spoon," Jericho admitted.

"How about 'thankful'?" said the teacher.

"That's not a big word."

"Oh, yes it is." She gave Jericho and every student standing there, including Eric, a big hug.

"So Jericho, Cleveland, and Roscoe tackled him? I knew my football players were heroes," Coach Barnes declared as he joined the group. He patted his men on the back.

"Olivia, too, Coach," Roscoe added. "She was awesome!"

"Then I'm proud of you, too," the coach told her.

"You know what blew everybody away?" Roscoe told the coach and the assembled crowd. "It was Eddie Mahoney who actually saved us!"

"Eddie?" Mrs. Witherspoon said, disbelief in her voice.

"Yeah, man. He talked that dude down from a way high place," Roscoe explained. "He was like a lion tamer in the cage—it was awesome, man."

"It was unbelievable," added Kofi, shaking his head. "But it was Eddie who made it possible for us to tackle Jack."

"So where is this Eddie Mahoney?" one of the reporters asked.

"I have him down as a classroom troublemaker," another reporter said, checking her notes.

"Where *is* he?" the first reporter asked again.

Kofi just shrugged and pointed vaguely toward the other side of the school yard. Several reporters raced to find Eddie, but he seemed to have disappeared into the crowd.

Mrs. Sherman, the stress of the day showing on her face, touched Kofi on the shoulder. "You and your friends risked your lives in there today, son. I can't tell you how proud I am and how thankful that you're not hurt."

"We didn't even think about it," Kofi replied. "It was no big deal." Arielle thought he looked a little embarrassed at all the attention.

"Yes, it was, son," the principal insisted. "And in all the confusion of the past couple of days, I have not had the opportunity to congratulate you on being selected by the Freedom Achievers Association for their scholarship!" She shook his hand firmly. "I am doubly proud of you. Your parents must be thrilled to know what a fine young man they have raised."

Arielle looked around but did not spot Kofi's parents in the crowd. He simply thanked Mrs. Sherman and walked away with his arm around Dana.

Brandon sauntered over to Arielle then. *Man, he looks good! I wonder if my hair is messed up.* "Hey, Lollipop," he said with a smile. *Mmm—he smells good too!*

"You okay?" she asked.

"Yeah, I'm fine. A little embarrassed that I was so scared."

"It's okay to be frightened. It shows you're human."

"That's something about Pringle, huh?" Brandon looked serious.

"Yeah. Who woulda thought?"

"You think your phone is in that back room?" he asked.

"I sure hope so. Mrs. Sherman said they had to wait until the police investigations of both crimes are finished before we can get anything back."

"By that time the iPhone will be obsolete!"

"For real!"

"I'm glad all of you got out safe, Brandon. Really."

"Me too. So, Miss Lollipop, you want to, uh, go to a movie this weekend—or, like, when my heart rate goes back to normal?" he asked.

"Well, me and my mom are kinda between places right now," she told him.

"Oh yeah? Where?"

She took a deep breath and decided to tell him the truth. "We're staying in the women's shelter downtown. Long story, but we got away from my crazy stepfather."

"I don't care where you live," he told her. "I just want to hang out with you sometimes. And you know you've got a date for the prom if you'll have me."

Can this be happening? Take it slow. Don't screw this up and chase him away, she warned herself.

She gave him a genuine smile—nothing phony, nothing

put on. "You're sweet. If I ever get my cell phone back, I'll call you," she promised. "And if the shelter can help me with a prom dress, I might take you up on that offer!"

He pretended to tip his hat to her and headed to his car. He waved before he drove off.

Yes!

The fire trucks and many of the police cars began to leave, although the police presence was still quite thick as final reports were made. Arielle noticed that the car carrying Miss Pringle finally left as well. News trucks remained, however, with reporters standing in front of each one, telling the story over and over again. It seemed they needed the outside of the school for background shots. The police would not let them inside the building.

Mrs. Sherman dismissed school for the rest of the day and Friday as well. "Today we have witnessed a tragedy and a miracle," she told reporters and parents. "Let us go home and give thanks that our children are safe. This incident will receive, of course, intense scrutiny. The safety of our children is of utmost importance. Security procedures will be reviewed and changes will be made." She paused. "The young man at the center of this incident today has been taken to a medical facility for evaluation and treatment. Whether he will face criminal charges is yet to be determined."

As the crowd began to thin and parents and students who had been reunited headed for their homes, Arielle noticed Osrick sitting alone on a bench by the flagpole. She asked her mom to wait a minute and walked over to the bench.

"Hey, Osrick." She sat down next to him.

"Hey."

"I see you took your hood off. The sunshine feels great."

He sat up a little straighter and inhaled deeply of the crisp air. "Yeah, feels good. I'm tossing the hoodie."

"Good move," she said encouragingly. She paused. "Was it bad up there?"

"I was pretty scared," he admitted.

"I guess there won't be any more fire alarms for a while," Arielle said.

"Or thefts." It was Osrick's turn to pause. "Or YouTube videos. Never again," he finally said firmly.

"You told Mrs. Sherman who the boys were?"

"Yeah. When you left me in her office to go to the gym and set up the blue-covered stuff in the locker room, I told her everything."

"I'm so glad you did, Osrick."

"She's already started the paperwork. I guess when we have school again, they'll get suspended—maybe even expelled."

"Great!" she cheered.

"I'm sick of being at the bottom of everybody's boot. Enough already!" He stole a glance at Arielle. "Uh, and thanks for letting me do this when I was ready. I know you wanted to go and tell, but it was something I had to do for myself." He stood up and stretched.

"I understand."

Osrick picked up a stick and tossed it onto the lawn. The newscasters in front of the building still talked into their microphones, repeating themselves. "Amazing how the newspeople come out of the woodwork when there's trouble—kinda like roaches," he said.

"Yeah, you got that right. So, did any of the reporters interview you?" asked Arielle.

"Me? Why would anybody want to talk to me? I just survived the chaos of the day."

"You've been a hero all day, you know."

"I didn't tackle anybody. I didn't have enough nerve to talk to Jack. I just sat there praying that I wouldn't die."

"But Osrick! Your plan found the thief."

"Dumb luck. I actually feel bad for Miss Pringle."

"They never would have found her without you, Osrick."

"Aw, she would have slipped up and been discovered eventually," he said with a shrug.

"And you were the one who sent the text message that let the police know where you were, and more importantly, you let the parents know that nobody had been killed."

"That was no big deal."

"Oh, yeah, it was. You should have seen it down here. Parents were having heart attacks and planning funerals!"

He smiled a little and sat back down. "I was glad you weren't in there when it happened."

"Why?"

"I kept thinking if you had been there, what I could possibly have done to save you." He shook his head and chuckled. "I gotta admit—I didn't have a lot of options!"

"No chain saw in your book bag, huh?"

"Just notebooks and homework. Maybe a paper clip and a pencil."

"It would have been enough." She knew that neither of them believed that.

"You're like a flower, Arielle, and pretty things like that don't need to get shot."

"That's the sweetest thing anybody has ever told me," Arielle admitted. She leaned over to kiss him on the cheek, but he gently pushed her away.

"You know what I was thinking while I was sitting in that room?"

"What?"

"That if Jack had decided to do target practice on students and he'd killed me, nobody would *really* know who I was. Nobody but you, maybe."

She wasn't sure what to say. "Go on," she told him, trying to sound encouraging.

"So I'm done with being stomped on. I'm trying out for the school play this month. And you know what? I've decided to go to the prom!" he said triumphantly.

"All right!" she said gleefully. She jumped up from the bench, did a silly little dance, then stopped. "But I think I already have a date," she added carefully.

"Oh, I wasn't going to ask you," Osrick told her, looking away. "You know Susan Richards in Spoon's class? I've had my eye on her since school started. And I think she's been checking me out as well. I've just never had the nerve to call her. But all this stuff today made everything come together."

Arielle laughed inwardly, mildly embarrassed at her assumption that Osrick would even ask her to go out. She hoped, she really, truly hoped, Susan would say yes.

"So that's why Susan got the text message! Do you talk to her often?"

"I've had her number forever. I've never used it until today," he admitted.

"I think that's wonderful, Osrick," she told him. "Seriously awesome."

"Hey, there's my dad," Osrick said then as he saw a car pull up into the lot. "I gotta go, Arielle. I'll see you next week. This has been an amazing day." He strode away toward the car, seeming somehow bigger and stronger than he had that morning.

Arielle stood alone by the flagpole. He was right. It had been an unbelievable day. She hoped Jack could find peace, Eric would find smooth roads to travel, and Osrick could find the power he needed. She thought of Dana and Kofi, Jericho and Olivia, and November and even Roscoe—thankful that they were alive, and so very grateful that they were her friends. Chad, like a fleeting storm cloud, crossed her mind only briefly.

Arielle could hear Miss Singletary still speaking excitedly about the day's incidents. Arielle caught the names of Jack, Eddie, Kofi, and Jericho as she slowed to listen to the woman. "So what makes a hero, and who is the hero of the day?" the woman was asking the audience on the other side of the camera she faced. After pausing for effect, the reporter said, "We'll bring you updates on the school shootings in an hour. This is Natasha Singletary, News Five Live."

Arielle breathed deeply of the spring air that promised flowers as well as rain. She ducked under a ribbon of crime scene tape, sprinted toward the parking lot, then whispered the answer to the reporter's question into the soft breeze.

Turn the page for a peek at the first book in the Hazelwood High Trilogy, *Tears of a Tiger.*

CRASH, FIRE, PAIN

Newspaper Article

NOVEMBER 8

TEEN BASKETBALL STAR KILLED IN FIERY CRASH

Nov. 8 — Robert Washington, age 17, captain of the Hazelwood High School basketball team, was killed last night in a fiery automobile accident on I-75. Witnesses say the car, driven by Andrew Jackson, 17, also of the Hazelwood team, had been noticeably weaving across the lanes of the expressway just before it hit a retaining wall and burst into flames.

Jackson, who police said had been drinking, was taken to Good Samaritan Hospital, where he is being treated for burns and bruises. He is listed in good condition. Two other Hazelwood students, B. J. Carson, 16, and Tyrone Mills, 17, who were also in the car, were treated and released.

The three students who escaped serious injury were able to jump from the four-door Chevy immediately after the accident, say witnesses. Washington, however, who was sitting in the front seat next to the driver, had his feet on the dashboard. The force of the crash sent his feet through the windshield, pinning him inside the automobile. The car's gas tank then exploded. Although Jackson tried frantically to rescue Washington, he and his friends watched helplessly as Robert Washington burned to death.

HIT THE SHOWERS!
HIT THE STREETS!
Locker-Room Conversation
after the Game
NOVEMBER 7
9:30 P.M.

—Hey, Rob! Live game, man. You be flyin' with the hoops, man! Swoosh! Ain't nobody better, 'cept maybe me.

—Yo, Andy, my main man! I see you been eatin' bull crap for dinner again! You only *wish* you was as good as me! I, Robert Orlando Washington, will be makin' *billions* of dollars playin' for the N.B.A.! Want me to save you a ticket to one of my games?

—Man, you be trippin'! You better be lookin' out for *me*—here's my card—Andy Jackson—superstar shooter and lover to the ladies—'cause I'm gonna be the high-point man on the opposin' team—the team that wipes the floor with you and your billion dollars!

—Dream on, superstar! Just for that, I'm gonna make you *buy* your ticket!

—Let's get outta here, man, before I feel the need to dust you off. This locker-room smell really funky tonight.

—I'm with you, my man Andy. You the one with the raggedy ride. Hey, and when you take them funky basketball shoes and your underarms outta here, I bet this locker room be smellin' like roses.

—You fulla mess, Rob. See, one minute, you makin' plans to keep me outta your N.B.A. games, and the next minute you beggin' a ride in my raggedy wheels. You think the brew is cold, man?

—Yeah, man. It oughta be. We put it in the trunk of your car hours ago—Ain't nothin' like some cool bottled sunshine in the moonlight after a hot game!

—Talk about hot! Didja see my Keisha up in the stands? She had on this short, butt-huggin' skirt, and she kept jumpin' and shakin' every time we scored and . . .

—Well, she did a whole lotta shakin' then! I was in there! No wonder you only scored six tonight. You too busy scopin' the women in the stands. Keisha got your nose wide open. She say "jump" and you say "how high."

—Hey, jumpin' with Keisha is like touchin' the sky. I'd say I had an honorable excuse, my man. Yo, I betcha I score more than six with Keisha tonight!

—That girl got you wrapped and slapped, my man.

—Oooo! Well, slap me some more! Let's raise.

—Hey Gerald, what's up, man?

—Nothin' much—cold-blooded game, Rob. Twenty-seven points—you be dealin' out there!

—What can I say? College scouts from all over the world are knockin' on my door, beggin' me to drive six new Cadillacs to their school, to instruct the women in the dorms on the finer points of—shall we say—"scorin'"— and to teach skinny little farm boys what it is, what it is!!

—Andy, I don't see why you hang with this big-head

fool, except maybe to learn some basketball. What you score tonight—four?

—Hey, Gerald, I thought you was my man. You sound like the coach—and it was six points, thank you. I got more important things on my mind tonight.

—Yeah, maybe Keisha can teach him some basketball! You wanna go with us tonight, Gerald? We got some brew and we just gonna be chillin'.

—Naw, Rob. I got to be gettin' home. And my old man . . . you know how he is. . . . Besides, who would wanna be seen with two dudes named after a couple of dead presidents anyway?

—Forget you, man. You seen B. J. and Tyrone?

—Yeah, man. They waitin' for you out by Andy's car. Tyrone went out early to see if he could catch up with Rhonda. He said he wanted to see if she was leavin' with anybody. He ain't called her yet, but he's got that puppy-dog look—kinda like the look on Andy's face when Keisha walks into study hall.

—Naw, man. Ain't no girl got me hooked up. I got her well trained.

—You better not let Keisha hear you say that!

—You got that right!

— Hey Andy, when you gonna get that raggedy red car of yours painted?

—When my old man gets tired of lookin' at it, I guess. He said something about a reward if my grades get better, but you know how that is.

—Yeah, man. Parents be trippin'. But don't get me talkin' 'bout fathers. He's the reason why I gotta raise outta here now. Where y'all goin'?

—No particular place. We just gonna chill. We might try to find a party, or we might just finish off them beers and let the party find us. Then I'm headin' over to Keisha's house, after I take these turkeys home.

—Don't let Keisha find out you been drinkin'. I swear, sometimes a girlfriend is worse than a mother!

—Not to worry, Gerald, my man. Besides, we got B. J. with us. He keeps us straight—or at least gives us breath mints. —Ooowee! Them shoes need some breath mints! I'm outta here! Peace.

—Let's raise, Roberto. Tyrone and B. J. gonna freeze to death!

—I'm with you, Andini. Let's heat up the night!

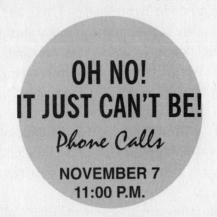

OH NO!
IT JUST CAN'T BE!
Phone Calls
NOVEMBER 7
11:00 P.M.

—Hello, may I speak to Keisha, please.

—Keisha, this is Rhonda. Sit down, girl. There's been an accident. Some lady who works at Good Sam with my mother called her a few minutes ago and told her that they had just brought in some kids from Hazelwood—basketball players, she thinks.

—Oh, Rhonda, I just called Andy to find out what was taking him so long. He was supposed to be here an hour ago. There's no answer at his house. I was gonna kill him! You don't think it was Andy, do you?

—I don't know, Keisha. I called Robert's house and all I got was that stupid recording. But then that's all you ever get when you call Rob.

—What about Gerald? He usually hangs with them after the game. I'll call him and then I'll call you right back, okay?

—Gerald, this is Keisha. Have you seen Andy?

—Naw, I went home right after the game, but Andy

and Rob, and I think Tyrone and B. J. too, left together in Andy's car. Andy said he was comin' by your house after he took those clowns home. He ain't there yet?

—Uh-uh. Well, if he calls you, tell him to get in touch with me right away, okay? Hey, you haven't heard anything about an accident, have you?

—Why is it the first thing a girl thinks about if her boyfriend is late is that he been in an accident? I bet he's in the backseat of his car, kissin' all over some real sexy mama!!

—All you fellas are alike—worthless. Call me if you hear anything, okay?

—Sure. Later.

—Hello, may I speak to Rhonda? Rhonda, is that you? This is Keisha. I hardly recognized your voice. Have you heard anything? . . . Rhonda? What's wrong?

—Oh, Keisha, it's terrible. There was a crash, and the car exploded, and my mother's friend said she thinks at least one of the boys was killed, maybe more. She said the police officer who came in with the ambulance told her that the car involved in the accident was a red Chevette. Isn't that what Andy drives?

—Oh my God. Rhonda, I've got to go. I'll get my mom to drive me to the hospital. Oh, please let them all be okay. I'll call you from the hospital.

—Rhonda, me again. I'm here at the hospital. . . . It's Robbie Washington. He's . . . He's . . . He's dead! Oh, Rhonda, he died in the accident. No, Andy, B. J., and Tyrone are okay. Tyrone and B. J. have already been sent home. Andy has been admitted, but he's not seriously hurt. Rhonda, what are we going to do? I've never known anybody who died before, except my grandmother, and she was old.

—Oh, Keisha, this is so scary. I don't know how to deal with it. Have you talked to Andy?

—No, they wouldn't let me in there. But I saw him through the door. He looked bad—not injured, but his eyes looked funny—I guess he was in shock. I've got to go now. My mom is taking me home. I'll call you tomorrow.

MEMORIES OF FIRE
Tyrone's Statement to Police
NOVEMBER 8

—Tyrone Mills? My name is Officer Casey, and I'd like
to ask you a few questions. I understand you were in the
car involved in the accident last night. I know you are
upset, but it is necessary that we complete this report
while the facts are still fresh in your mind. I'd like for
you to tell me, in as much detail as possible, what happened last night.

—Well, the game was over 'bout nine-thirty and we was
all in a good mood 'cause we won big—by something like
forty points, so we was gonna celebrate. Me and B. J. and
Andy and . . . and . . . Rob—we left after we all got
changed. Gerald was gonna come with us . . . yeah, Gerald
Nickelby, but he had to go home. His stepfather beats . . .
uh, I mean, his old man is real strict. So it was just the
four of us. . . . Naw, B. J. don't play on the team—he's too
short, but the four of us hang together. We been tight
since seventh grade.

So, we get in the car . . . yeah, Andy's car, and we start
drivin' around, you know, just foolin' around, havin' a

good time, yellin' out the window at old white ladies—it always freaks 'em out. . . . Yeah, we was drinkin'—all 'cept B. J.—he don't drink. We had put about four six-packs in the trunk of Andy's car before the game. Since the weather's been so cold, puttin' 'em in the trunk was as good as a cooler, so they was nice and frosty by the time we got to 'em. . . . Yeah, all of us was drinkin', 'cept B. J., like I said, but Andy probably had the most. He was in a *real* good mood 'cause this girl named Keisha had started goin' with him and he was goin' over to her house after he took us home.

After a while the car started to sway, but I wasn't sure if it was me gettin' dizzy or if the car really was weaving across the expressway. At the time it seemed really funny. We was laughin' so hard—especially when people started honkin' at us. The more they tried to signal us, and I guess, warn us, the more we was crackin' up and laughin'. Rob had his feet up on the dashboard, partly actin' silly, and partly 'cause his legs was so long that they got cramped in that little car of Andy's. Me and B. J. was in the backseat. I was sittin' right behind Andy, and B. J. was sitting next to me, behind Rob, 'cause he had the shortest legs, and Rob could push the seat all the way back.

Then, all of a sudden, like outta nowhere, this wall was in front of us, like it just jumped out in front of the car, and Andy was trying to find the brakes with his foot, and then there was glass everywhere and this crunchin', grindin' sound. My door flew open, and I rolled out. I remember I was cryin' and crawlin' around on my hands and knees—that's the only thing that got hurt on me—I got glass in my hands and in my knees.

I got to my feet, and I helped Andy outta the front seat.

His head was bleedin' pretty bad, and he was holdin' his chest like he couldn't breathe so good—I think he hit the steerin' wheel pretty hard. We could smell gas real strong—it made me dizzy—like the gas station smells when some lady don't know when to stop and she spills gas all down the side of her car.

By that time, B. J. had gotten out, and we was lookin' for Rob. He musta passed out at first, 'cause all of a sudden we hear this screamin'. We ran around to that side but the door was bent shut and we couldn't get it open. All of us was screamin' by that time, 'cause we could see his feet stickin' through the windshield. His legs was cut and bleedin' really bad. All we could see was these brand-new Nikes stickin' out the window, with the rest of Rob screamin' and hollerin', stuck inside.

So then Andy and B. J. climb on top of the car and start to knock the pieces of the windshield out of the way, so we can try to get Rob out that way. But then . . . then . . . we hear this heavy, thick sound, like an explosion in a closed room, and Andy and B. J. is knocked off the hood. Me and B. J. grab Andy then, and we have to hold him back, 'cause the whole car is in flames, and Rob is still stuck inside, and we can hear him screamin', "Andy! Andy! Help me—Help me—Oh God, please don't let me die like this! Andy! . . ."

He screamed what seemed like a long time. Then it was real quiet. All we could hear was the sound of the flames, and little pieces of the car sizzlin' and burnin', and then the sirens of the police cars. I think I passed out then. That's what I remember—and that's what I'll never be able to forget.

"DEAR LORD"

B. J.'s Prayer

NOVEMBER 15

—*Dear Lord, this is me, B. J. Carson. You know, the one You made too short. But that's okay; I know You had Your reasons. I know I don't pray very often, and I know You haven't seen me in church lately, but I feel like I need to pray or something. There's some stuff I don't understand about this accident—like why it happened and why Robbie had to die and why I didn't die. Mama keeps huggin' me, sayin', "Praise the Lord" and stuff like that. But what about Robbie's mama? What is she saying?*

Is it my fault that Robbie is dead? I wasn't drivin'. I wasn't even drinkin'. Andy and Rob and Tyrone all knew that I didn't drink—they never bothered me much about it. I think they even respected me a little because of it. I told them that drinking at an early age had stunted my growth, so I had given it up in favor of other vices. (Actually I think beer tastes like boiled sweat socks.) So they knew not to push me. Maybe that's all I have left over from those days when I used to go to church every Sunday with Mama. So why do I feel so guilty?

I don't sleep so good at night. I keep seein' the fire and hearin' his screams and feelin' so helpless. He was too young to die like that. It's not fair. He never had a chance. Was all this done to teach us kids a lesson? Will it stop us from drinkin' and drivin'? Maybe—a few. But the rest will keep on doing it, no matter what. So I still don't understand why.

Mama says the Lord knows all, and that He in His infinite wisdom knows the reason for all things. But Mama is gettin' old, and she's known a lot of people who've died, so she probably understands all this death stuff a whole lot better than I do.

Maybe I shoulda tried to stop them that night. Maybe I shoulda been drivin'. But I'm always so glad that they include me in their group, I hardly ever try to change their plans. I'm just glad to go along. Actually, I never really understood why they like me. They're all tall, popular with the girls, and basically outrageous. Me, I'm short—never once made the basketball team—kinda quiet, and still unsure of myself when it comes to girls. But somehow, I was always "one of the boys"—and the four of us did everything together, ever since seventh grade. And I've just been glad that I had such good friends. Now one of them is gone and I feel responsible.

I think I'll go to church with Mama this Sunday. I know people will say that it's because of the accident that I came back to church—well, they're right. I'm not too proud to know when a problem is bigger than I am. Of course most things in life are bigger than I am, but I'm learnin' to live with it.

Please, Lord, help me to learn to live with this too. Thanks for listenin'. See you Sunday.